Also by Jane Lythell

THE LIE OF YOU

AFTER THE THE STORM

JANE LYTHELL

To my courageous brother Michael Hilborne Clarke

Caribbean Sea, off Honduras

Some nights Owen Adams tried to sleep next to his wife Kim in the saloon of his boat. He rarely lasted a whole night there. The slightest sound would wake him and, in an instant, he would be hyper-alert and watchful. Kim had suggested he use ear plugs. He'd tried them a few times but had given them up because he did not like the sensation of not hearing what was going on around him. It was better to be aware of the slightest noise in the boat or a disturbance on the water, even if it meant that his sleep was disrupted. Most nights he went up on deck and lay there with his blanket around him, looking up at the sky.

When he did fall asleep the nightmare would come. It was not every night but it was always the same one. When he first started having sleepless nights he worried, knowing that lack of sleep could send a man mad. He devised a way of dealing with it: he would imagine that he was floating above his body looking down on himself. Tonight, as he lay stretched out on the deck, he visualised looking on his prone figure and seeing the outline of his boat, the *El Tiempo Pasa* with its tall wooden mast. Then he imagined himself moving higher up into the sky so that he could see how his boat was floating in the sea edged by the distant lights of the mainland. As he rose ever higher, he shrunk to nothingness, the boat becoming a speck and the horizon a dark curve. This exercise always calmed him even if he did not sleep.

Occasionally, if they had no guests on board, Kim would come up on deck and lie with him through these nights. He didn't like her to lose her sleep and would tell her to go back down to the comfort of the saloon. She would say, always making the best of things, that when they were back in Florida they would remember these nights as special ones, lying on deck and looking at the stars and the moon while the *El Tiempo Pasa* rocked them back and forth. There were places he went to in his mind where Kim could never follow. He didn't understand why she loved him but he was glad that she did. Kim was his anchor, holding him to earth.

Anna helped the old man down from the coach. His hands were rough and dry and stained a deep purple. As they got off the air-conditioned bus a blast of hot air hit them. Rob had gone ahead and was standing with the other passengers waiting to retrieve their rucksacks from the undercarriage of the bus. She watched as the old man crossed the square slowly and lowered himself onto a bench. He settled himself carefully as if he was in for a long wait. He looked frail and she hoped someone was coming to meet him. Rob lifted her heavy rucksack onto her back and they walked away from the coach station. Stagnant, mud-filled, mosquito-clouded waterways criss-crossed the city.

'We'll find a hotel, dump our stuff and get down to the water for a cold beer,' Rob said.

He was in front of her and she kept close to him. It was always difficult arriving in a new place. You had no bearings and had to make sense of the sights and sounds that flooded your senses. This part of the city looked poor. He stopped at a shabby hotel that had a sign saying rooms were available.

'Shall we look inside?'

She nodded. They were taken to a room on the first floor. It was high ceilinged and might have been an elegant room once. Now there was crumbling plaster, a double bed in an iron bedstead, rickety drawers and a cubicle shower in the corner. They were tired and decided to take the room for one night only. They could find something better the next day. It was not the kind of hotel where you would leave your money or your passports. Rob peeled off his clammy T-shirt. He put all their dollars into a small fabric bag that hung low around his neck and then put a clean T-shirt on top. He zipped their passports into the leg pocket of his long khaki shorts and they left the room.

They headed towards the water. Large wooden colonial buildings faded on the quay. They saw a pub on a corner called O'Brien's with the name written in a green Celtic font.

'You'll find an Irish pub wherever you go in the world,' he said. 'We won't go in there.'

Further along there was a small bar that looked local.

'Let's try in here.'

They took their bottles of beer out to the pitted metal tables and plastic chairs that stood at the water's edge and looked at the gaggle of boats tied up in front of them. The beer fizzed in Rob's glass as he poured it.

'It's not very cold,' he said, disappointed after his first sip. He held the glass up to the light and assessed its colour then picked up the bottle.

'Belikin, the beer of Belize...'

'Did you see how his hands were stained purple?' Anna asked.

He looked at her, not understanding.

'The old man on the coach; his hands were dark purple.'

At the table next to them a couple were drinking beer. The man was tall and thin with long limbs. He looked over at them now and said:

'That would have been the vegetable dye. He'd have been making and dyeing hammocks. They use a vegetable dye out here.'

4

'Oh I see,' said Anna.

'You see the hammocks all over, purple and turquoise, drying between the trees.'

He had an American accent and the longest legs. His face was thin with high cheekbones and his dark hair curled under his jaw. In spite of his thinness his shoulders were broad and strong-looking and he would have been strikingly handsome, Anna thought, if it wasn't for the deep shadows under his eyes which gave his face a haggard look. He was dressed in a grey T-shirt and washed-out jeans and was wearing boat shoes on his long bony feet. Sitting next to him was a petite tanned woman with a mass of curly dark blonde hair that she'd tied up with a rainbow-coloured bandanna.

'Yes I saw some hanging in the trees, from the coach. And they were selling the hammocks too at the roadside,' Anna said.

Rob raised his glass to them.

'We just got in.'

'We did too,' said the man. 'Sailing for three days from Honduras.'

'You have a boat?'

The American man got up and pointed to a yacht moored a few yards away from them.

'That's ours – the *El Tiempo Pasa*. I'm Owen.'

'Rob, and this is Anna.'

The blonde woman said:

'Hey, I'm Kimberly, pleased to meet you.'

She had a fluty voice with a southern lilt to it. The two women smiled at each other uncertainly, as you do when you're thinking: shall I continue overtures with this stranger?

Rob asked Owen:

'Does that mean: Time Passes?'

'Time Marches On; do you wanna take a look at her?'

'I'd love to.'

The women stayed sitting at the tables to finish their drinks and watched as the men headed for the boat. Owen walked with a long easy stride and he jumped onto the boat and helped Rob aboard. It was an old wooden sloop, thirty-seven feet in length that looked as if it had sailed through many rough seas. They stood on the deck and Rob touched the tall wooden mast and looked up at the night sky. Then the two men disappeared down into the cabin. Kim put her glass down.

'So how did you guys get down here?'

'We came on the coach. We've been in Mexico for a week and decided to come down and look around Belize,' Anna said.

'You may be disappointed. Belize City is the pits. But you can get everything you need here and we gotta get provisions for the boat.'

'I don't think we'll stay here long, more a stopping-off point while we decide where to go next.'

Kim nodded thinking that Anna was a pretty woman but with a noticeable defect. She had large grey eyes and there was a mole right between her eyebrows and while this did not quite turn her eyebrows into a mono-brow it did give her eyes a kind of weird intensity. If it was Kim she would have paid to have that mole taken off as soon as she hit her teens. It was the first thing you noticed about Anna. She also had one of those classy English voices and there was a reserve about her that Kim associated with English folk.

The men were now up on deck again and beckoned to them to come on board. Owen helped Anna get into the cockpit. This had seats around the sides and was roomy with a canvas roof over the top. Kim went below and came back with a half-full bottle of rum, some limes and four plastic glasses on a tray. She poured a generous amount of rum into each glass. She had cut the limes already and she squeezed them and the smell lingered on the air.

'Sorry I can't offer you any ice,' she said handing a glass to Anna first.

'Thanks so much, lovely smell of lime...'

They touched glasses.

'Cheers.'

'This morning some kid stole one of the oars from our dinghy. I'd forgotten to tuck it away. Brought it back this evening and said he'd sell it to me for three US dollars. No way was he gonna take Belize dollars,' Owen said.

They all laughed. Owen explained that they were from Clearwater in Florida and had been sailing around the area for three years, chartering their boat to travellers who didn't mind that it was an old wooden boat and fairly basic. It was certainly no fibreglass gin palace he said. Rob said he much preferred handsome old boats like this.

'Where are you headed?' Owen asked.

'We want to see as much of Central America as we can. We're thinking we'll maybe go to Guatemala next. We've got three weeks left.'

'There are some special islands off Honduras, the Bay Islands. Do you dive?'

'I do.'

'It's sensational there.'

Anna sipped her rum and looked on as Owen described the islands. Roatán was the largest of the Bay Islands he said and it was ringed by a coral reef, the third largest reef in the world. Too many tourist ships came into Roatán now, but if you knew where to go you could still find pristine reefs and the clearest waters in the Caribbean. And he knew where to go. There was Mary's Place which had this narrow cleft in the reef. You swam through the cleft and there in front of your eyes were huge sponges and seahorses and shoals of brilliantly coloured fish. Anna recognised the expression that was growing on Rob's face; he was being well and truly seduced by Owen's descriptions. She looked over at Kimberly who hadn't said much since they sat down.

'And all the different types of coral you can see,' Owen was saying. 'Elkhorn and staghorn, flower coral, smooth starlet, grooved brain, pillar coral...'

'Such great names...' Rob said.

'We could take you there. Show you the unspoiled places. Kimmie and I wanna do a last run out there before we sell the boat and head back to Florida for good.'

Rob looked over at Anna, his face lit up. She half smiled back and didn't say anything. She was trying to convey wordlessly her reaction which was 'be careful'. Kimberly had said nothing in support of the plan either. Her head was bent over her glass and she looked ill at ease.

'We don't have a lot of money,' Rob said when he could see that Anna was not going to commit to any such plan.

'I don't know how much you charge to charter the boat? We've got enough for the two of us to get around for the next three weeks...'

'Well you'd be doing us a favour. We wanna say goodbye to our friends on the island. If you were willing to share what money you've got we could provision the boat and take you to Roatán. Show you the reefs and the hidden places. Think about it and let us know tomorrow.'

'We will; thanks,' Rob said.

8

It was dark and the rum bottle was empty when Anna and Rob left the boat and headed back along the quay and into the streets of Belize City. Owen and Kim sat on in the cockpit. He moved closer to her and started to play with her hair.

'Do you think they'll do it?' he said.

'Owen for Chrissakes, why are we even thinking of going out again?'

'You can't wanna leave all this, Kimbo?'

He gestured at his boat and at the sea. She tried to think of the words to use. They had just completed what she thought was their last sail and it had been a tough one. The plan had been to sell the boat in Belize City. She knew he hated the idea of returning to Florida, but she felt they had reached the end of the line. It seemed he did not.

'I'm not sure how safe it is any more.'

The sails were worn, the sail stitches were rotted and the lines were chafed. They both knew this. The engine had failed them on their entry into Belize City. He was a fine sailor but even fine sailors need their boats to be seaworthy.

'You know I hate to say goodbye to her, but we only just made it here this time. It's best we bite the bullet and sell her now.'

She said it gently. She knew how much he loved his boat.

Owen had worked in boat repair and maintenance in Clearwater for fifteen years. He had often had to patch up their boat over the last three years. He had sewn ripped sails and nailed planks back in when they had sprung. That was what happened with an old wooden boat. It needed a lot of upkeep. You expected that. But the engine was a worry to him because it was corroded inside and he couldn't afford to buy a new one.

'I can replace the lines that are bad and I'll work on the engine tomorrow.'

He stroked her earlobes knowing she liked that.

'One last run out... Come on Kimmie.'

'I think they'll say no. He wants to do it but she's gonna put a stop to it.'

'You think?'

'She seems a buttoned-up English type to me with those big serious eyes of hers, looking and reckoning and not saying much.'

They sat in silence for a while, listening to the slap of the water against the boat. She didn't say it but she hoped fervently that the English couple would say no. It was time to sell the boat and go home to Florida.

'I can pawn my wedding ring if they say no,' she said.

'I don't want you to do that.'

She looked at her ring. It was a thick gold ring. She had wanted a big wedding ring. She wanted the world to know that she was married to Owen Adams.

'It would give us enough till we made the sale.'

Anna and Rob said little as they walked back to their hotel on Orange Street. Rob seemed to know the direction. Anna gripped his arm tightly as they passed through the poorly lit and unfamiliar streets. Rob was moving purposefully but was watchful as they were far downtown and in a poor neighbourhood. Then he noticed a man standing in a dark doorway. There was something about the way the man was standing that alarmed him. The man was poised on his feet, like a cat when it's ready to pounce on its prey. Rob could see a lighted road ahead, some way in front of them. He took Anna by the hand and said quietly:

'When I say go, run as fast as you can to that lighted street, and *don't* let go of my hand...'

'Oh Rob.'

She gripped his hand and they took a few more steps, their hearts knocking. Then Rob shouted 'Go!'

The man had sprung out of the doorway and was chasing them. The road was rough and uneven and Anna was gasping, finding she couldn't get enough air into her lungs as she ran. Her fear was making her breathing so shallow. She looked back over her shoulder in terror and the man was closing the gap between them and his face had a look of focused aggression. She was nearly tripping in her panic and Rob was yanking her along the road. They reached the lighted street. There was no-one about and still the man pursued them, close behind them now, almost at reaching distance. Rob noticed a house on the street with its door slightly ajar and light pouring out from it. He pushed the door open, hauled Anna in and shut the door behind them with a bang.

They had stumbled into someone's house. A large family were sitting around a TV set. Some of the small children were asleep on the sofa and the crashing door woke them up. The older children and their father turned as one as the door was slammed shut.

'Sorry. Sorry,' gasped Rob. '*Lo siento. Perdon.*'

He spread his hands in a gesture of helplessness while he tried to get his breath back. Anna stood there unable to speak, her chest heaving from the chase. She felt she might throw up as Rob nodded towards the street.

'A bad man...' he took a deep shuddering breath. '*Un hombre malo...*'

The man of the house had stood up and he came over to them.

'*Ingles...?*'

'*Si. Perdon, perdon...*'

'OK. OK,' the householder said to them making soothing gestures with his hands.

His young children had all got up now and were gathered around their father and staring up at Anna and Rob. A woman had come into the room from another door and she was staring at them too.

'You are *desviados*... er... lost, no?' said the man.

'Yes, *si*, we are looking for our hotel on Orange Street,' Rob said.

The man nodded.

'I show to you.'

Anna looked at the children, such large dark eyes gazing up at her. One little girl had her hair in cornrow plaits from her forehead to her nape. Anna wished she had something she could give them. The man spoke to his wife briefly and then indicated that they should follow him. He opened his front door and there was no sign of the man who had chased them. Their guide kept to lighted streets and delivered them to the door of their hotel a few minutes later.

'*Gracias, gracias...*'

Rob shook his hand warmly and insisted the man take the ten-dollar note and the coins which were all he had in his pocket. Most of his money was swinging in the bag around his neck and he wasn't going to reach for that in this street.

Anna and Rob entered the dimly lit foyer of the hotel and hurried up the stairs to their room. Rob closed the door, locked it with its big old fashioned key and hugged Anna. They were both clammy with sweat.

'He had a knife, didn't he?' Anna was trembling.

'I think so. I think I saw something flash.'

He hugged her more tightly to him knowing how scared she got.

'It's OK now.'

'We were lucky we found that man,' she said.

'Yes.'

'And all those lovely children…'

She kissed him and pulled away.

'I need a shower.'

She stripped and stepped into the plastic cabinet shower in the corner of the room. It was a useless shower that trickled tepid water. She soaped and rinsed herself as best she could and wrapped the thin towel around herself. As she got out she saw a huge brown cockroach on the wall below the window.

'Oh God, it's huge. It must be four inches long.'

Rob looked at where she was pointing in horror and he put on a thoughtful face.

'Three and a half inches I would say.'

'Rob…'

He flattened it with one of her shoes that was lying on the floor. Even after he had battered it hard several times she noticed that its antennae still seemed to be moving slowly. Plaster dust had fallen where he had swatted the wall. Anna sat watching the cockroach lying in the dust as if mesmerised. She remembered a vivid moment from her childhood. Her granny hated wasps and to get rid of them she would smear raspberry jam on a jar, and half fill it with water. She would leave the baited jar at a forty-five degree angle on the steps near the back door of their cottage. Anna was five years old and living with her grandparents. She had come out into the garden and had seen the jar and its contents. In the bottom of the jar were the accumulated bodies of many drowned wasps.

Above these more doomed and drowning wasps were trying to crawl out of the jar over the bodies of the dead. To the little Anna it was a jar of horrors and she started to wail in terror. Her granddad came out and saw her distress. He picked the jar up, took it to the top of the garden and poured its contents onto the compost heap. A few of the half-drowned wasps had crawled away. Anna had had a horror of wasps and insects ever since. Rob kissed her wet shoulder now and she jumped. He nuzzled her neck.

'So how about it sweet face? Our chance to charter a boat…'

She picked up a comb and started to pull it through her long dark brown hair.

'No way Rob, it's far too risky. We know nothing about them.'

'They seem like a good couple.'

'They talked to us because they want our money.'

'They talked to us because they want us to charter their boat. We both get something out of it.'

'They could slit our throats on the first night.'

He laughed.

'My darling Anna; frightened of everything…'

'Why can't we go on like we've done so far?'

'Another three weeks on a coach? Looking out of windows? No thank you.'

'We've seen lots of great things. Those villages…'

'This is a chance to see places we could never get to,' he said.

They both had a bad night. They covered themselves with insect repellent and pulled the sheet over their heads. They lay in a sticky fug of chemical smells and as they hugged each other Anna whispered that she couldn't get that huge cockroach out of her mind. And did he think there were bed bugs in the mattress? She kept imagining bed bugs burrowing into her flesh. He lay in the sticky bed and thought about how to persuade her that they should go on the boat. It had taken a lot of persuasion to get her to fly to Mexico. Anna was always calibrating risk. Would he be able to convince her that they would be safe on the boat with the American couple?

Owen and Kim were up early the next morning giving the boat a thorough cleaning. They worked for two hours and then Kim brought four over-ripe bananas up onto the deck where Owen was sitting.

'Breakfast time and it's all we've got left.'

Owen groaned theatrically.

'There's a coconut somewhere too. Can you face that?'

'I'm so sick of coconut and bananas. But you still look real beautiful on them,' he said seeing that Kimmie looked troubled. She managed the food side of things and prided herself on making meals for them with whatever was to hand. But the cupboard was bare and they were down to their last few dollars. She sat next to him, peeled a banana and took a bite.

'I'm out of butter to fry them in, and rum.'

'I'm dreaming of fried chicken,' he said.

'Lobster with melted butter, or baked with a butter and honey sauce. I can never decide which is better.'

'Keep it simple I say.'

Anna sat up in bed.

'Horrible night,' she said.

There was a slick of sweat under her breasts and between her thighs, wherever skin touched skin. She looked over to where the dead cockroach had been lying under the window and it had disappeared.

'Where's it gone?'

Rob sat up.

'The cockroach, where's it gone?'

He put on a serious face.

'Its relatives took it off for a funeral.'

'Ha ha… Where's it gone?'

'I didn't want to worry you last night. You were freaked out enough. As I turned the lights off the room came alive with bugs. They've eaten it of course.'

She shuddered.

'I want to get out of here now.'

'There wouldn't be any cockroaches on the boat,' he said.

They showered, dressed and packed their rucksacks quickly, paid for the room and went in search of a café. There were several to choose from along the main street. Rob favoured the third one they passed and they went in and ordered coffee and fried eggs with tomatoes. When they arrived the eggs were runny. Rob tucked into his hungrily while Anna gave them a dubious look, but the tomatoes had lots of flavour and she ate these with the bread. Rob went back on the charge making the arguments for chartering the boat. Since childhood he had dreamed of having an adventure like this; he had an urge to seek out his own wilderness. He wanted to be on that boat and he wanted to see those islands very much.

'You're suggesting we hand over most of our money to them. That seems risky to me,' she said.

Rob resisted a flash of irritation. Many of his discussions with Anna entailed the subject of risk.

'That's the deal Anna. They give us accommodation and

food, so yes it will be most of our money. But see what we get for it, we get to see those islands and we learn to sail too.'

'I'm worried about the lack of privacy. It didn't look that big to me.'

He could see however that her resistance was weakening. Last night's chase through the streets and the huge cockroach had helped persuade her in a way that none of his arguments could. Finally, and reluctantly, she agreed that they should charter the boat.

'Let me do the negotiations,' he said.

'Fine, but please keep some money back Rob, in case we need to escape.'

He pulled a face at her.

'You know sometimes I think you've missed your vocation: drama queen needed here.'

She punched him playfully.

'At least we get to leave here today. Now *that* makes me glad.'

They found their way back to the quay. Owen, who had been scanning the quay for the last hour, saw them in the distance walking towards the boat.

'They're gonna say yes,' he said to Kim. 'They've got their rucksacks with them.'

Rob waved to Owen and made a thumbs-up signal. Kim watched the couple approach the boat and felt a sharp pang of regret, another delay to their return home. Owen couldn't keep putting it off.

Owen and Rob sat in the cockpit to talk money while Kim showed Anna around the boat. They entered a saloon which you stepped down into from the cockpit through a narrow door. It had settee berths on either side of a rectangular wooden table that was screwed to the cabin floor. This table could be folded down and the settees doubled as beds at night. The cooking was done in a tiny galley which had a two ring hob with a small oven below and a porthole above. There was a sink next to the stove with cupboards above, lockers Kim called them, and drawers below.

'Everything has its place see. You can't leave anything lying around when you're sailing.'

'It's a clever use of space,' Anna said.

But she was wondering with rising anxiety whether this was the main living space. If they all tried to be in the saloon together it would be a case of having to move around each other in formation. She noticed that the interior of the boat was shabby but spotless. The table was scratched but the glass in front of the shelves had a high shine. Kim showed her the small cabin that could sleep one person at the back of the boat.

'We use that for storage,' she said. 'You two can have the forecabin, it's larger.'

She showed Anna the forecabin at the front of the boat. It was triangular in shape and a double bed could be made up on its platform, and that was about it. There were drawers beneath the bed space and two portholes that had curtains you could pull across.

'You stow your stuff in the lockers here,' Kim said. Then she pulled open a narrow door on the right between the fore-cabin and the saloon.

'This is the heads.'

She pointed to a small toilet which had a metal lever by its side.

'Now this is real important, Anna. You must flush out the heads after you've used it. You can't leave any waste in there. It gets blocked if you do and believe me you don't want a blockage on a boat. You pull that lever up and down and that brings seawater in. You need to pull it a lot, ten to twenty times to make sure you've flushed it right through and left nothing but seawater in the system.

'There's a pull out washbasin, see,' Kim carried on, unbolting and pulling out a small basin that rolled out above and over the toilet.

'You get the water for the basin from this foot pump. And make sure you bolt the basin back after you've used it. Do you wanna try it out?'

Anna squeezed herself into the compact cubicle. She tried out the foot pump tentatively and water came into the basin. She pulled out the plug and bolted the basin back. She gave the toilet lever a couple of pulls and it thundered and slurped as seawater was sucked up into the system.

'No room for a shower so we use buckets of water on deck as our shower. It's OK; it does the job. Oh and the guys usually pee over the side of the boat,' Kim said with a grin.

Opposite the heads was a wet locker where some oilskins and lifejackets were hanging. Back in the saloon Anna noticed the only picture on display. It was a framed photo of a cat that was tucked in with the books and maps behind the table. She picked it up.

'Is that your cat?'

'Yep, that's Moses, our cat in Florida. We had to leave him with Owen's aunt when we came away.'

'And that was three years ago?'

'Yep, longer than we ever intended.'

In the cockpit, after some negotiation, Owen and Rob had agreed an amount for the chartering. Rob counted out the dollars and gave them to Owen. That was the bulk of their holiday funds gone so the die was cast.

'Thanks. If you wanna make some cash back I'm gonna buy five cases of liquor, to sell to some bars I know on Roatán. If you buy some you can make a profit too,' Owen said.

'Maybe I'll do that.'

'Come to the warehouse with me and you can decide then.'

Kim and Anna joined them in the cockpit.

'Tomorrow I'll teach you both to sail,' Owen said. 'You'll find we're not very technological on this boat. We rely on the wind and the sails. Today we need to provision up.'

It was agreed that Kim and Anna would get the food in. The men would get the fuel and go to the warehouse. As they got off the boat a young Belizean man was standing on the quay and he had been waiting for them.

'Do you need any help today?' he asked Owen, recognising him as the owner of the boat.

'Yep, we could do with help carrying some loads.'

The Belizean man was called Elbert and Owen hired him for the day. Elbert said he had a trolley for transporting things and Owen asked him to fetch it and to meet Kim and Anna at the big supermarket in a couple of hours to help them carry the groceries back. Later he would need him to come out to the warehouse.

As they walked towards the outskirts of the city Owen told Rob that he would be offered a knock-down price by Raul, the man who ran the liquor warehouse.

'Did him a big favour once and he's never forgotten it.'

'What did you do?'

'A member of his family needed to get out of Belize fast and I got him out.'

'On the boat?'

'Yep, so if you want in on the deal let me do the buying. I'll say all the cases are for me.'

'And there'll be no problem selling the booze on?'

'None at all, I've done it before and made a good profit.'

Rob was thinking he could use their escape money to buy the booze. He wouldn't tell Anna though. He made up his mind about people quickly, always had, and he sensed that Owen was a man who had seen some troubles in his life. He looked like he was in his late thirties; maybe even forties and that was surely beyond the age when you would expect to be living in this hand-to-mouth way in Central America. In a way it was Owen's very disregard of a conventional life that Rob admired. And he did not think that he was scamming him now.

'OK. I'll come in for five cases,' he said. 'I probably won't tell Anna though.'

'OK. Understood.'

They reached a stretch of wasteland whose perimeter was edged by a wrecked wall colourful with graffiti. The ware-house stood at the far corner and was a large, high building. Inside it was dirty and echoey and smelled of dust and wood.

There were bays with cases of liquor stacked high and two men shouting instructions to each other. A third man, Raul, came up to Owen and thumped him on the back. He indicated they should follow him into his small partitioned office between two bays. They sat down and he poured three whiskies for them into smeared glasses. He had a flat head, a pitted nose and a striking scar that ran from the corner of his left eye to his jaw. Rob wondered what Anna would have made of that face. Owen introduced Rob and tasted the whisky.

'This is good stuff Raul,' he said.

'The best we have.'

Raul spoke English with a heavy Spanish accent.

'How is the beautiful Kimberly?'

'Still beautiful...'

'You're a lucky man.'

On their second drink Rob explained that he too was in the booze business. He ran a small brewery with two friends and they made specialist beers for real ale enthusiasts.

'There's a market for it at home, a growing market,' he said.

'What do you think of our Belikin beer?' Raul asked.

'Very refreshing,' Rob answered diplomatically.

They spent some time looking at what was on offer in the bays and Owen selected ten cases of spirits, twelve bottles a case, mainly rum, some gin and a few bottles of whisky. He did not go for the cheapest brands. He went for the middle priced ones.

'I've got a fella turning up with a trolley in a while,' he said.

'Time for another drink,' Raul said.

'Where can I take a slash?' Rob asked.

Raul pointed to the back of the warehouse. Rob walked

the length of the building and noticed the motes of dust lit up in a shaft of light from one of the few high barred windows. He was slightly pissed. The toilet was a filthy stinking cubicle inhabited by a cloud of flies. He thought better of going in, so he wandered out of the warehouse and took a slash against the wall. Two boys were kicking a football around the wasteland and he stood and watched them for a while. The ball landed at his feet. He kicked it back to them. They kicked it at him and he joined in a few passes. Then he asked the lads what teams they followed. They wanted to know about English football clubs. They had heard of Manchester United and Chelsea. He told them about Tottenham Hotspur, the team he supported.

As Rob came back into the warehouse and approached Raul's office he caught a glimpse of Raul handing Owen a large package that was wrapped in plastic and secured with a lot of gaffer tape. Owen put it into his rucksack and zipped it closed.

Kim and Anna were walking towards the centre of Belize City. It was a steamy sultry day and as they reached the large open air fruit and vegetable market they were assailed by a stink of rotting fish near the entrance and something even nastier under that, Anna thought. As they moved into the market other less noxious smells took over. There were dozens of stalls and loud-voiced vendors shouting out to anyone who was walking by. Some stalls sold a single item spread on the ground, a mound of watermelons or bright red peppers, much larger than the ones you could get in England. There were stalls where you could buy liquidised fruit drinks: mango, papaya or melon. There were stalls selling spices and others with mountains of neon-coloured candies. Anna felt overwhelmed by the heat and the smells, the colour and the noise; somehow the holiday she had dreamed about, and saved up for, was slipping away from her. It was moving in a new direction where she was not in control. She did not want to be here now in this hot, noisy, frenetic market, following Kimberly through the crowd.

Kim dived into the throng and scanned the vegetable stalls with an expert eye. She bought onions, potatoes, red and green peppers, some chillies, lots of garlic. Anna trailed behind her as Kim examined the fruit stalls and stopped in front of one.

'Fruit goes off fast. I'm thinking one watermelon and maybe pineapples, oranges and limes.'

She got the seller's eye and pointed at two large green pineapples and he put them in a bag.

'What on earth are those?'

Anna pointed at some pale looking potato-type fruits which were pitted with pale green circles.

'Noni fruit. They taste like vomit and even the crabs won't eat them when they fall on the beach.'

'He's selling them though,' Anna said.

'They're disgusting but real good for you. Let's have a coffee now,' Kim said, stopping in front of a stall. She ordered a coffee and a large sweet pastry, powdered with icing sugar.

'Do you want one of these?'

'Just a coffee please.'

Kim ate the pastry with relish and licked the sugar off her fingers.

'Sometimes a sweet pastry is just what you need,' she said cheerfully.

'Jam doughnuts, fresh out of the oven, are my favourite,' Anna said.

They drank their bitter coffees from small paper cups and dropped them into an overflowing bin.

'Is there anything you and Rob don't eat?'

'We eat most things. I don't eat kidneys though. I hate the smell and taste of them.'

'I won't get kidneys, I can promise you that.'

They came out of the market carrying two full bags each and headed for the large supermarket in the centre of town. On their way they passed a barber shop which had its windows and door wide open. It looked like it was a popular hangout for the local men. A large speaker was balanced on the windowsill and it was playing reggae music at full volume. The barber was bobbing up and down to the beat of the music as he worked.

'Not sure I'd want him to shave me,' Kim said.

When they reached the supermarket Kim found a trolley and took charge again.

'OK. We need a big tin of cooking oil, rice and pasta.'

Anna helped her collect these items still feeling disconnected from the activity around her.

'We get fish as we go along. Buy it from the fishermen. I'm gonna get some chicken though, for tonight,' Kim said.

They reached the canned goods section and Kim stacked a pile of canned tomatoes, kidney beans, chick peas, sardines and tuna into the trolley. Anna looked up and saw three people who stood out from everyone else in the store. The woman was dressed in a green gingham dress that reached mid-calf, and sensible lace-up shoes. Her fair hair was scraped back tightly into a single plait and she wore small glasses on her nose. Beside her were two smaller versions of herself, presumably her daughters. They too were wearing the long gingham dresses, the tight plaits and the sensible shoes of their mother. They even had the same glasses. She was striding along the aisles pushing her trolley while her two ugly ducklings followed behind her. Among the laid back Belizeans and the travellers all clad in shorts and T-shirts with logos, they proclaimed their difference.

'Who are they?' Anna asked Kimberly.

She parked the trolley and looked over.

'They'll be Mennonites. There are several Mennonite communities here in Belize. They don't believe in technology.'

'Like the Amish?'

'Yeah, German descendants I think. Now could you bear to wear gingham every day of your life?'

Kim noticed that Anna had a serious look on her face and thought, Jeez here I go again. Maybe Anna was religious; maybe Anna would take offence at her flippant remark. She had been influenced by Owen and shared his distrust of all religions. Of all their friends in Clearwater they were the only couple who did not belong to a church.

'Now don't mind my nonsense. Are you religious, Anna?'

Anna pulled her gaze away from the Mennonite family.

'No, I'm not. I was thinking how strange it is to see them here. They look so different to everyone else and it's kind of brave not to mind that, isn't it? What do they do here?'

'They're farming people. I was told a lot of them came out here after Hurricane Hattie, to do relief work. Good people I guess.'

Kim steered them to the soaps and shampoos.

'I'll get us shampoo and conditioner, not that it works for me. My hair is so wild.'

Kim's dark blonde hair was a mass of springy curls that bounced around her face and shoulders.

'You're lucky Kimberly. My hair is so straight.'

Anna pulled her band out and her dark brown hair dropped to just above her breasts. She had no fringe and her hair parted naturally in the centre. The two women looked at each other.

'We always want what we haven't got,' Anna said.

They smiled at each other and it was a moment of connection, the first moment of connection all day.

'Tea bags,' Anna said.

'What?'

'Can we get some tea bags? I can't survive without my tea.'

'Sure.'

Anna fetched a big box of tea bags. Kim spotted a stand of magazines and newspapers against the wall. She pushed the loaded trolley over and reached for a copy of US *Vogue*. She started to thumb through the pages.

'Oh these clothes... look at these clothes. I used to dress up once. You wouldn't think so now, would you?'

Anna looked over her shoulder as Kim flicked through the photos of New York Fashion Week, the tall angular models striding along the catwalk and the celebrity audience watching from the front row.

'Rob's sister Savannah is a model. She does some of the big shows. She's quite a big deal really.'

'That's so cool. Are you close?'

'She's a lovely girl, but quite a lot younger than Rob, and we don't see her that often.'

'I *love* clothes. But you have to give up out here.'

Kim was wearing black shorts and a fitted turquoise tank top with a thick yellow-and-green woven money belt clinched around her trim waist. To Anna's eyes she looked perfectly fashionable. She was a jeans and T-shirt woman herself and had never got the whole fashion thing. Kim turned the pages, closed the magazine and looked at the cover price. She wrinkled her nose:

'Stupid price for a magazine...'

She put it back on the rack but still she looked at the magazines laid out in front of her. She turned to Anna:

'I forgot to get any tomato puree. Can you go get two tubes Anna?'

'Sure.'

Anna moved away. At the end of the aisle she glanced back and saw Kimberly slipping two of the magazines into her bag.

Kim paid for the groceries with Rob's dollars and they walked out of the supermarket.

'Elbert should be over with his trolley soon. There's no way we can shift this lot on our own.'

They watched as the Mennonite woman and her two daughters came out of the store and stacked their groceries into a horse-drawn cart. A young boy was holding the horse's bridle. He was dressed in denim overalls and a straw hat and looked about twelve years old. The family got up into the buggy and the mother drove them down the road. Anna saw how the woman was expert at controlling the horse and the buggy. And she also seemed driven by her own firm sense of purpose that had nothing to do with the norms of the present day. How strange an accident of birth and fate it was that this group of German descendants should be living and farming in Belize in Central America.

They waited outside the store with their many bags grouped around them and there was no sign of Elbert. A sudden violent rainstorm broke overhead and they had to move everything back under the canopy of the store. The rain hurled down with such force that it made the windows of the store rattle.

28

'We'll have to wait till it stops,' Kim shouted.

The summer storm continued for ten minutes. There was an awkwardness between them now. Anna stood looking out at the sheet of rain.

'These rainstorms come from nowhere. Nothing we can do,' Kim said finally. She was finding Anna hard work. Her first impression the night before was right, Anna was reserved and not an easy person to talk to.

And then as fast as it had come it stopped. The streets were covered in puddles and water gushed along the gutters. A few minutes later Elbert showed up with a flat wooden trolley on four wheels. The three of them loaded all the bags onto his trolley and he steered it back to the quay. It was low water and the boat was no longer swinging, its keel had dug into the mud. They unloaded the shopping and carried it below. Then Elbert went off with his trolley to meet Owen at the warehouse as instructed.

'Where exactly did Rob and Owen go?' Anna asked.

It had now been hours since they had set off together.

'To this liquor warehouse on the edge of town and I'll bet Raul's been giving them drinks. He's the owner and he's always generous with the whisky bottle.'

Kim was sorting through the provisions, putting some foodstuffs in the cool box and others in the food locker, singing under her breath.

'I think I'll unpack our stuff and lie down for a bit. I had a bad night last night,' Anna said.

'Sure, I'll help you make up the bed.'

Kim got a clean double sheet out of one of the lockers and spread this over the two mattresses to make it into a double. She gave Anna another sheet for the top. There was a yellowing quilt which was rolled in the corner.

'Usually the sheet is enough. You've got that quilt for colder nights.'

'Great, thanks.'

Once she was alone in the forecabin and the door was shut Anna allowed herself a few tears. There was so little space on this boat and nowhere to escape to if you felt the need to be alone, except for this one small cabin. And they would be living in such close quarters with two strangers they knew nothing about. Kimberly had sent her off to get the tomato puree so that she could take those magazines. It was the sneakiness of the act rather than the actual taking of the magazines that had jarred with her. She did not want to give in to these negative feelings. She was tired out by the events of the last twenty-four hours and hoped that once they were sailing, her spirits would lift. She stretched out on the thin mattress and closed her eyes.

Two hours later Owen, Rob and Elbert appeared with the trolley stacked high with the ten cases of liquor.

'I see we won't run out of rum,' Kim said.

Owen supervised the stowing of the cases in the small berth at the back of the boat. When this was done and the others had left the saloon he pushed Raul's package right down the side and lashed this and the cases in with a rope. He knew what Kim's reaction would be if she got wind of Raul's package. They had fought about it before. He paid Elbert his fee for the day and then went to work on the engine.

Rob went through to the front cabin and found Anna stretched out on the mattress. She was half asleep and was very pleased to see him. She put her arms around his neck and he kissed her fondly and started to nuzzle her.

'I smell whisky,' she said sleepily.

It was too late to sail far that evening. Owen had got the diesel engine working again. It was corroded inside, that was the problem. He rarely used the engine, except for getting in and out of moorings. Truth be told he was suspicious of sailors who over-relied on their engines. The wind and the sails were what you should rely on. The tide had risen slowly so that the *El Tiempo Pasa* was now afloat. He said they would motor a little way out and anchor some distance from Belize City. As they moved away from the Quay Rob noticed how the water changed colour from a sludgy brown to dark turquoise. The dinghy was attached to the boat by a rope and it moved smoothly through the water behind them. Rob liked being on this old wooden boat, it was his kind of vessel. Anna came up and sat with them in the cockpit. There was now an easy banter between Owen and Rob.

Kim was down in the galley and she could hear the three of them talking up above. She opened the cool box and took out some chicken thighs and breasts and put them on the chopping board. She unzipped her belt and got out her knife. Then she heard someone coming into the saloon and she quickly threw a tea towel over the chopping board and the knife. It was Anna.

'Can I help?' she asked.

'That's real kind of you, but there's so little room down here,' Kim said.

It was true. The saloon felt crowded if there were more than two of them down there. And the galley space was particularly restricted.

'If you're sure?'

'I am, thanks. I like cooking. It's what I want to do one day.'

'Be a chef?'

'Have my own café. You know, paninis at lunchtime and dishes in the evening. I'd do a Menu of the Day and offer a few good dishes.'

'Sounds a good plan, hard work though,' Anna said.

She went back up the steps into the cockpit thinking that just as Owen looked at ease moving around the boat above so Kim looked completely at home in her tiny kitchen.

Kim lifted the tea towel and picked up her knife. She made incisions in the skin of the chicken breasts and thighs and rubbed salt, black pepper and cayenne powder into the meat, then spooned brown sugar and squeezed the juice of an orange over it all. The orange was full of pits, not like the ones at home. Florida oranges were the best. She had worked as a waitress in Clearwater at one of the upscale restaurants and Manny, the chef there, had taught her this dish. He had been the kindest man and she would never have lasted at the restaurant without his friendship. Unfortunately he had fallen for her in a big way and wanted more. She was already in love with Owen, had been for years, although she was not dating him. She told Manny that, when he asked her out. They became good friends anyway. At the end of her shifts she would stay behind at the restaurant and Manny would teach her how to make sauces and how to cook fish and steak the right way.

Kim brought up the spicy fried chicken with rice, the food already served up in four plastic bowls, and forks to eat it with.

'This is so good,' Rob said.

'Yes it's delicious, thanks Kimberly.'

'Kimmie can cook,' Owen said.

'I worked in this restaurant back home and the chef taught me a lot.'

Later she handed them glasses of rum and lime and they sat looking out at the distant lights of Belize City as the boat rocked gently.

'It looks a lot nicer from here,' Rob said.

'I don't want to go back there ever,' Anna said.

'It's not that bad is it?' Owen said.

'Last night we were chased through the streets by this man with a knife!' she said.

Kim looked startled and darted a glance at Owen.

'You were unlucky there,' he said.

Anna and Rob decided to turn in for their first night on board. They negotiated the cramped washing facilities and then discovered there was no room if they both stood up in their cabin at the same time to undress. Rob stripped off first and climbed onto the bed. Finally they were lying next to each other with the porthole curtains drawn, the sheet pulled over them and the cabin door closed. She whispered to him:

'We won't get much chance to have private conversations.'

'We won't get much chance to have sex either.'

She dropped her voice:

'Kimberly stole two magazines from the big store we went to.'

'Oh well, you two spent a fortune in there.'

'I know we did. I didn't like the sneaky way she did it. She asked me to go get some stuff and took them then.'

'Don't brood on it. It's not important,' he said.

He considered telling her about the package he had seen Owen slipping into his rucksack but he knew this would worry her. He had his suspicions about what it contained. He kissed her and rolled over and she snuggled into him and the boat rocked gently from side to side and they fell asleep.

33

Kim washed the dishes and put them away, folded the table and made her bed up in the saloon. She stretched out and closed her eyes. She could see that Owen and Rob were already comfortable with each other but she wondered why Anna had agreed to come on the boat because she had looked ill at ease all day.

Owen was up on deck lying with a blanket around him. He was thinking about how to organise the next day's sailing. Living on a boat took some careful planning, and he knew Rob and Anna would need some time to adjust. They would do the short sail to Home's Cay tomorrow so that he could teach them the basics of sailing the boat. He wanted to make sure they were up for the longer sail to Roatán. The island was 138 miles away and he intended to take the sail slowly.

Anna woke up in the middle of the night. Her stomach was cramping badly and she needed to go to the toilet. She didn't know if it was the spicy chicken or that bitter coffee she'd had at the market that had upset her stomach; probably the coffee, which had been a mistake. Rob was asleep. She wriggled out from under the sheet and opened their cabin door as quietly as she could. The door to the heads was on her right and the door to the saloon where the others slept was closed. In the dark she fiddled with the door and got it open. She went into the cubicle and sat down on the toilet, just in time. There was a small porthole in the wall behind her and faint moonlight came in. She wiped herself thoroughly. She knew she had to use the lever and flush the system through as Kimberly had said. In the silence of the night it was going to make the most awful racket and wake the others. Well, she had no choice.

34

With a grimace she started to work the lever, pumping it up and down. It was even noisier than she remembered and made a horribly suggestive sucking sound. She was cringing inside as she worked the lever up and down again and again. This was what she had feared, the lack of privacy on a boat. Rob often teased her about how fastidious she was. For good measure she pumped the lever two more times. The noise seemed to go on for ages and then it gurgled to a stop. She peered into the toilet bowl and it was clear.

She wanted to wash her hands so her next task was to unbolt the small washbasin. She inched it out as gently as she could. Then she had to use the foot pump to get the water to wash her hands. This wasn't so noisy thankfully. She remembered to push the basin back and to secure it. She felt her way back into their cabin and got up onto the platform. She had woken Rob up.

'You OK?' he asked.

'What a palaver to go to the loo,' she whispered back as she wriggled under the sheet. 'My stomach was cramping badly. I hope I'm not getting the runs. That would be desperate.'

It was still dark when Owen woke from the hateful dream he often suffered. A brutal crime was taking place in his home, in his kitchen, right in front of his eyes. Two people were being battered to death with a shovel by a man with the whitest skin you ever saw; a bloodless man. He didn't know who the two people were and he was a helpless onlooker as he saw and heard the killings in hideous and graphic detail: the crunch of their bones as the edge of the shovel was used as a blade to sever their limbs, and the blood, so much blood, how could there be so much blood? He couldn't look at the pooling dark liquid on the kitchen floor which was running into the cracks between the floorboards. Now the killer was burying the bodies under the floor, grunting with the exertion of jemmying up the floorboards. The white-faced killer turned. He walked towards him holding his bloodied shovel. Owen crouched in the corner trying to make himself smaller by hiding his head on his knees and holding his hands over his bowed head, paralysed with terror.

He woke with a dry mouth and the familiar feeling of sick dread. It always took him a few minutes to shake off the terror. His blanket was twisted around him as he had thrashed around while he dreamed. He sat up and unwound the blanket from him. Everyone else was asleep below. He stood up and steadied himself by holding onto the mast of his boat and he waited for the sun to rise.

Rob pulled the curtain open and their porthole became a brilliant rectangle which filled their small cabin with light. He felt joyful and full of energy.

'Wake up sleepy head,' he said.

He kissed Anna, sat up and rummaged for his shorts in the tight space of their cabin.

'How's your tummy?'

'Feels OK at the moment thanks.'

She stretched fully, pointing her toes. Her outstretched arms touched the walls of the cabin on either side.

It was their first full day on board and Owen spent the morning teaching them about the boat. He had checked the barometer; it was a calm day and would present few challenges. He explained the function of the two sails, the mainsail and the smaller foresail. The foresail was clipped onto the forestay at the front of the boat. The main sail had to be winched up a track in the mast and he got them both to do this. He showed them how you steered the boat with the tiller. He moved nimbly across the boat hardly needing to hold onto anything whereas Anna was clinging to the lines, worried she might pitch into the water at any moment. She transmitted her nervousness and Owen was patient with her. Rob looked altogether more comfortable and had taken to the sailing at once.

Kim left them to it for most of the day, only joining them at lunchtime when she brought up plates of tuna salad for them.

'This tastes great, again,' Rob said.

'I make this special dressing for the tuna, the zest of a lime and one teaspoon of wasabi powder in soy sauce. Kinda zings it up, doesn't it?' she said.

'I'll say.'

After lunch their task was to make the sail to Home's Cay. It was a short distance to cover and a place where Owen and Kim had moored before. Owen kept an eye on them but let Rob and Anna do the sailing. As the El Tiempo Pasa approached the Cay he explained that the length of the anchor chain needed to be four times the depth of water where you were anchoring. Rob fed the chain out. They headed into the wind and dropped anchor as the boat backed up and the anchor bit. Owen watched them drop the sails.

'You both did fine. Now rest and relaxation for what's left of the day,' he said.

Home's Cay was a tiny island with a few yards of sand, thirty palm trees, a lone wooden shack and a dozen mangrove plots that had rooted in the mud at the perimeter.

'I'm intrigued by that little shack. Who does it belong to?' Anna asked.

'One of the fishermen will have built it. May still use it from time to time,' Owen said.

Kim came up from the saloon.

'Why don't you guys take the dinghy and explore the island. Owen and I did that once.'

'Great idea, we'll do that,' Rob said.

He and Anna got into the dinghy and rowed over to the island. As they moved out of earshot Anna said:

'You do realise we've left all our money and all our possessions on the boat and they could just sail away.'

'They could but they won't. They need their dinghy right?'

'I suppose so.'

'And they probably want some time on their own. Maybe they want sex. Come on give me a hand.'

They pulled the dinghy onto the sand.

'Owen was patient with me today. He didn't say much though. Did you notice that?'

'No, not really...'

Rob was tying the rope from the dinghy to one of the palm trees.

'He was so talkative that first night, when he was doing his sales pitch.'

'You've got to stop being so suspicious Anna. You won't enjoy this if you're suspicious all the time.'

'I'm not sure about Kimberly.'

'Because she took a couple of magazines?'

'No that's not the reason, but I'm not sure about her. And he seems a troubled man to me.'

Rob loved the fact that Anna was straight as an arrow and had bags of integrity. It was one of the things that had attracted him so strongly to her. It did mean though that she held everyone to impossibly high standards. He remembered the recent incident with her smart phone. She had just received her new state-of-the-art phone and five days after getting it had dropped it and cracked the screen badly. She'd been upset at the damage particularly because she hadn't had a chance to insure the phone. He told her to take out insurance and then, in a month, claim for a new phone. She had been insistent that she could not possibly do that. No, she said, the cracked phone face would be a reminder to her that she should be more careful with her things. It was her fault and she would live with it. He was reminded that Anna's moral compass was calibrated more exactingly than his. Her high-mindedness could be off-putting if you didn't also know that Anna had generous reserves of patience and compassion when she was dealing with vulnerable people in her job.

39

'Come on, I'll race you to the shack,' he said running ahead. She ran after him and they peered into the meagre hut. There was nothing in it except a pile of driftwood that had been stacked in there for future use. There was a hole in the roof and some bird shit on the floor. They chased each other around the tiny plot of the island until they were breathless and dropped down onto the warm sand. Rob found a ripe coconut on the ground.

'We can take this back with us.'

He spotted a procession of tiny hermit crabs walking away from a coconut they had been eating.

'Come look at this.'

She rolled over and watched as the tiny crabs moved quickly and in unison over the sand. Then they both sat up back to back supporting each other, a way they often sat so that each had a different view in front of them. They sometimes played a game where they had to describe what they saw in front of them with each trying to outdo the other in their descriptions.

'I can see a tall palm tree and its trunk is like the hide of a very old and very wise elephant,' Anna said.

The first time Rob saw Anna she was sitting on a London tube heading north and she was totally absorbed in a text book on speech development. He was sitting opposite her. As she sat there reading he noticed that a thin trickle of blood was coming from the side of her mouth. She seemed oblivious to this. He sat and watched fascinated as the blood moved down her chin. Then he leaned forward and offered her a clean tissue from his pocket. As he touched her arm gently she jumped.

'I'm sorry. I didn't mean to startle you.'

She had large grey eyes and a mole on her forehead just above the space between her eyebrows. This defect was strangely beautiful as it had the effect of drawing even more attention to her eyes. He explained that she had blood on her chin. She touched her chin in the middle.

'To the side…' he said indicating the right side of her face.

She touched that side and looked at her fingers which had blood on them.

'Oh…'

She took his tissue then and dabbed at her mouth and chin.

'Been to the dentist, wisdom tooth out, my face is frozen,' she said thickly, her tongue was having difficulty forming the words.

He nodded.

'Has the blood gone? I haven't got a mirror.'

The people sitting next to them on the tube were watching them now.

'Yes, all gone.'

The tube drew into Tufnell Park. This was his stop but he didn't intend getting off. He wanted to see where she would get off. The tube moved off towards Archway.

'Just the one wisdom tooth out?' he asked.

'Yes, that was bad enough.'

'I remember. I had to go to the dental hospital and have all four out at the same time.'

'How awful…'

She looked at him sympathetically and he thought she had the most wonderful eyes.

'I'm Rob…'

'Anna. Thanks for the tissue. And for telling me,' she said thickly.

'You did look like a rather beautiful vampire,' he said.

She gave a lopsided smile. They had passed through Archway and Highgate and were approaching East Finchley.

'This is my stop,' she said, putting her text book into her bag.

'Mine too,' he said.

They got off the tube together. As they came out onto the street she said:

'I go this way, thanks again.'

She was turning left and he was thinking quickly. He didn't want her to go.

'I'm going that way too.'

He had remembered that the Phoenix Cinema was a little further up the road.

'I'm going to the Phoenix,' he said.

'That's a great cinema. I go there a lot.'

As they reached the Phoenix he looked up at the board that ran along the façade of the cinema. It was the Easter holidays and there were a lot of animation films listed, clearly aimed at children. He saw Anna look up at the list of films too and he wondered if she had seen through his subterfuge.

'I'm early. Do you have time for a coffee or a drink?'

She nodded shyly and he felt absurdly pleased. They sat over several cups of coffee for over two hours and he said that he was happy to miss the film. He would come back another day. He learned that she was completing her training to be a speech therapist. She was not a Londoner and it had taken her a while to like London. He did most of the talking, encouraged by her large grey eyes and sympathetic way of listening, and he found himself telling her that his father was an American musician he had never met. His mum had got involved with another musician when he was eight. He had left home young and shared a flat with two mates and they were setting up a company to brew specialist beers. She was

42

not musical at all, she said. Her father was the musical direc-
tor at a church school in Canterbury. Her two younger
brothers were the star turn in her father's choir. Not her, she
was a croaker. When they parted she agreed to see him again.
It was clear to him that they had had very different upbring-
ings and that she was what he needed.

The sun was low in the sky when they rowed the dinghy
back to the *El Tiempo Pasa*. Kim was sitting on the deck on
her own.

'Owen's catching up on his sleep down below,' she said
keeping her voice low.

She helped them tie up the dinghy and get on board.

'We swam round the island,' Rob said keeping his voice
soft.

'Good job. A fisherman went by and I bought some
grouper. We'll have it tonight.'

Six fish lay on the deck next to her. She unzipped her
woven money belt and took out a small case. Inside the case
was a small sharp knife. She cut the heads off the fish and
gutted their insides working fast and expertly and threw the
heads and bones over the side of the boat. Then she placed the
gutted fish into a pan she had put near her.

'Looks like you've done that a few times,' Rob said with
admiration.

'I surely have.'

She used a wet cloth to clean her knife thoroughly before
she wiped it dry, put it back into the case and zipped it away
in her belt. Rob was intrigued. How clever of her to carry the
knife like that in her belt so that she always had it to hand.
She struck him as a capable woman who understood and
managed the challenges of life on board.

The plan was to anchor at Home's Cay for the night. Later,

Owen joined Anna in the cockpit. She was watching three pelicans sitting on the mangroves of the Cay. Kim had gone below to cook the fish and Rob had gone down to make a coffee.

'They don't look at all comfortable, do they,' Anna said. 'Those great big beaks look too heavy for their bodies and the mangroves look flimsy to me.'

'You should see a pelican land on a mangrove. That's quite a sight,' he said.

The sea was turning that particular shade of palest, silvery blue that only happens at sunset. They sat in companionable silence watching the still scene in front of them.

'I could sit and watch all evening,' she said finally.

'Me too, nature doesn't let you down, does it,' he said.

She glanced over at him.

'That's what I always say,' she replied.

A large pelican flew into sight and approached the Cay. It landed on the squat mangrove which bounced deeply under the weight of the bird. The pelican sat on unperturbed and stately as a judge as the branches rocked up and down. Anna laughed out loud.

'Oh that's priceless.'

Owen grinned over at her.

'See what I mean? And you should see them crash dive too.'

The sun set quickly and it was dark but still hot. Rob and Kim came into the cockpit carrying four bowls with the fried grouper and potatoes and some salsa Kim had made. The four of them ate in silence relishing the taste of the fresh fish and the tanginess of Kim's salsa.

'Food tastes so good on a boat,' Rob said when he had cleared his bowl. 'And I guess meals become more important too, a real highlight of the day.'

44

'Watermelon for dessert,' Kim said. 'I'll go slice it.'

She came back with a piled plate and they passed it around. The only sound was them sucking on the red watery flesh of the fruit and spitting out the black pips.

When the moon was high and bright in the sky Owen rolled a joint and he passed it first to Anna.

'No thanks.'

'Don't you smoke weed?'

'No, it does nothing for me.'

'Helps me to sleep,' he said, 'Sometimes...'

Anna handed the joint to Rob who took two deep draws on it and then handed it to Kim.

'Rob told me he's a brewer. What's your work Anna?' Owen asked.

'I'm a speech therapist.'

'Yeah?'

'Yes, I work in a health centre in London, mainly with old men who've had strokes and can't talk very well, or sometimes not at all.'

'Sounds kinda tough.'

She nodded.

'It can be, especially when the stroke is severe. It's a very frightening experience for them and a long journey back into speech.'

'Anna loves her old men,' Rob said affectionately.

'I do. It's such a triumph when they start to be understood again.'

They got to talking about whether it would be a good thing or a bad thing to have loads of money, so much money that you would never need to work again.

'A bad thing, I think,' Anna said.

'Why do you say that?' Kim asked.

'Because having to work gives you a purpose and it's good to have a purpose in life isn't it?'

'Well yeah, but being short of cash is no joke,' Kim said.

'Poverty's no fun at all,' Rob agreed.

'But waiting for things, saving for things, it makes them more special doesn't it?' Anna persisted.

'It does,' Owen said. 'I had to save for years to buy my boat. And I sure have met some fucked up Trust kids over the years, with more money than sense. A bunch of them chartered the boat once. They were slumming it of course.'

'Would you like a lot of money?' Rob asked turning to Kim.

'Oh yeah, then I could open my restaurant in style. I'd love having the cash to splash and I'd make it the best place in town.'

After a second joint Rob and Kim got a fit of giggles over a blocked heads situation that had happened with some folks who'd stayed on the boat the year before. They were both crying with laughter as Kim described the lengths the guests had to gone to disguise the blockage and the difficulties Owen had had unblocking it. Owen grinned at the tale but didn't join in the telling. Anna sat there feeling awkward because she wasn't stoned and it didn't seem that funny, and anyway all she could think of was that come what may she must not block the heads.

Later, lying in their cabin, Rob and Anna had another whispered conversation.

'Kim told me tonight that Owen had a falling out with his family and doesn't like to talk about them,' Rob said.

'When did she tell you that?'

'When she was cooking the fish and I was down there.'

'Must have been a big falling out if he won't talk about them?'

'I think so. She was kind of awkward about it.'

'I'm glad you told me. I was going to ask him about his family. I nearly did tonight.'

'Don't Anna. It's best not to enquire too deeply into people's lives.'

'What do you mean?'

'We're living in such close quarters with them. It's better to keep things a bit impersonal. Mum taught me that when we were living in the commune.'

Rob had spent his early childhood in a large commune in North London with his mum and a group of environmental activists. He had learned the hard way that sharing intimate information nearly always got you into trouble. He knew that Anna was interested in people and liked to know their life stories. He hoped she would follow his advice as he loved being on this old wooden boat and he wanted it to work. He could sense already that Owen was a man who needed people to respect his privacy.

Kim was lying awake on the settee berth in the saloon. She could hear Owen up on deck moving around, another sleepless night. Was his insomnia getting worse? He rarely had an undisturbed night and he hardly ever slept by her side any more. She longed for more physical contact with him. At the beginning, when they were living in that duplex in Clearwater, they had taken such pleasure in sex. He loved that she was a small woman and he would lift her onto him several times during the night. Sometimes during the day he'd carry her around their sitting room and they'd make love against a wall, her legs wrapped around his long torso. It was wonderful. Now their couplings were infrequent and it made her sad.

It went quiet on deck and she listened intently. She was often gripped by a dread that Owen had rolled himself over the side of the boat and into the ocean. She knew how much he loved being in the sea. He had told her it was the only place he felt completely safe. That would be the way he would choose to die. To slip into the water at night while everyone slept. On many nights she had made herself get up, even though she was so tired and sleepy, to check on him. She was checking on him the way a mother checks that her baby is still breathing. Tonight she lay and listened and after a long time she heard some reassuring creaks from above, Owen turning over, wrapped in his blanket, trying to get comfortable. She fell asleep then.

DAY THREE

Because he slept on deck Owen would usually wake at sunrise. He would fetch his hat from the cockpit and sit and watch the track of light stretching over the ocean. The sea was never still. This morning he saw a crowd of tiny fish leap in a perfect arc out of the sea into the dangerous air and back into the water.

Kim joined him soon after and they got the boat ready for the long sail ahead. They had brought the dinghy onto deck and lashed it down on the foredeck. Owen sat at the chart table and tracked their course while Kim made them a big breakfast of omelette stuffed with onions and red peppers.

For the first ten hours the weather was fine and the sailing was good. They reached Glover Reef at the time Owen had estimated. The high point of their day was after lunch when six porpoises followed them as they sailed along. The porpoises seemed to be surfing in the bow wave created by the forward motion of the *El Tiempo Pasa*. Owen said the bow wave gave the porpoises something of a boost. They watched them leap playfully into the air and swim around the boat for nearly an hour.

Owen had been checking the barometer regularly and had noticed that over the last three hours it had dropped. That generally heralded the onset of bad weather. He discussed this with Kim but said nothing to Rob and Anna. Around five in the afternoon from a clear sky Anna saw what looked like black fingers of smoke on the horizon. The black fingers grew and spread and within a relatively short time the sky was a sulphury yellow criss-crossed with thick black streaks. The sea was getting rougher too. It was all so sudden and she found it rather alarming. She went down to the saloon to use the heads. Then she put the kettle on to make tea. As she waited for it to boil she noticed there were a lot of books tucked behind the glass locker in the saloon. She looked at the authors: Ernest Hemingway, Saul Bellow, James Baldwin and Annie Proulx. Someone was clearly a reader, a serious reader. Owen? She saw there were a couple of Stephen King novels too including his epic *The Stand* which she had read. Next to the books was the framed photo of Moses. She took it out. He wasn't a particularly handsome cat. He had chewed ears, small eyes and looked a bit of a bruiser. Her parent's cat, Plum, was a dark grey Burmese beauty with golden eyes. She put the picture down on the table and poured boiling water onto a teabag. She had remembered to put the mug in the sink as Kim had shown her. The boat pitched forward strongly and the picture of Moses flew off the table, hit the floor and the glass in the frame shattered.

'Oh no!'

She felt stupid and guilty. Kimberly had told her everything had to be stowed away when sailing. She tried to remember where they stored their brush and pan. She opened the locker nearest the sink. No brush and pan. She pulled open the bottom drawer under the sink and saw the two stolen magazines lying in there. The boat lurched again and the shards of glass moved across the floor, with some going right under the stove. Shit! Anna lifted the washboard and called out for Kimberly.

Kim heard Anna calling her in an anxious voice and she skipped nimbly across the deck and down into the saloon. Anna was breathless with her apologies.

'I'm so sorry. I was looking at Moses and the boat moved fast. I couldn't find the brush.'

Kim reacted quickly. She grabbed a brush and pan from one of the other lockers.

'Let me...' said Anna. 'I caused the damage.'

Kim said nothing. She seemed to be terrified of the shards of glass. She picked the larger pieces up gingerly and wrapped them again and again in sheets of kitchen roll. Then she started to sweep up the smaller pieces, her face set.

'Some went under the stove,' Anna said in a small voice. 'I'm so sorry. I'll buy you another frame.'

Kim got onto her knees and swept under the stove and searched for any fragments of glass on the higher surfaces. Then she wrapped the glass sweepings in kitchen roll too.

'I'm an idiot for not putting the picture away securely,' Anna said.

It was as if it was only then that Kim became aware of her.

'It's OK. You just have to be so careful of broken glass in a boat.'

The boat lurched again and Kim picked up the ruined frame and tucked it away in a locker.

'It's getting rough and I'm needed up above.'

'I'll come too.'

Anna poured her tea down the sink with a heavy heart. She was so clumsy and inept in this setting. Kim picked up the bundled glass and as Anna followed her up the steps to the cockpit she saw her look over to where Owen was on the foredeck. He was checking the lashings on the dinghy and had left Rob on the tiller. Kim dropped the kitchen roll bundles of broken glass over the side of the boat. She said nothing to the others about the accident, for which Anna was grateful.

The waves were getting bigger and visibility was becoming worse. Owen now warned Rob and Anna that a storm was on its way and he gave each of them an oilskin to wear. They put their lifejackets back on over the top of the oilskins as large waves started to smash against the boat.

'Go below if you want to, but I reckon you'll be more comfortable up here,' Owen said above the rising roar of the wind.

He and Kim reefed the mainsail, moving it down the mast and securing the bottom to make a smaller sail area against the driving wind. For the next hour they sailed into the headwind, trying to keep to their course. The bow was rising then crashing down into the waves and sea spray was hitting them all in the face again and again, making their eyes sting from the salt. The boat was taking a pounding and they were making no headway at all.

'We best drop the sails and run off downwind don't you think?' Owen said.

'As long as there's enough open water,' Kim said.

'Plenty of water, we're miles from land.'

They took the sails down.

Owen went below and came up with a bottle of rum and sat with Anna and Rob in the cockpit. He offered them the bottle.

'We've hit a rough patch and it looks to me like this will go on all evening, maybe all night. This is what we're gonna do. We'll work in three-hour watches: Kimmie with Rob and Anna with me.'

'You took the sails down?' Rob said.

'Yep, we're running bare poles, going with the wind. Means we'll be blown off course. Not much choice really...'

'But we're safe?' Anna asked, her fear getting the better of her need to appear brave.

'We're fine. Just need to sit this storm out. Kimmie and Rob you rest now and I'll do the first watch with Anna.'

They did as he said. As they lifted the washboard to go down into the saloon a big wave washed into the cockpit and flooded into the cabin.

'Aww hell,' Kim said as she pushed the washboard back into place.

'Wet below already.'

She folded the table down and made up the two berths on either side of the saloon and secured the hammock-like lee-cloths that would stop them from falling out of the berths as the boat pitched and rolled.

'Lie down with your eyes closed Rob. It should help against any seasickness.'

She stretched out on her berth and shut her eyes. He followed her example.

Up above Owen clipped a lifeline to the harness of Anna's lifejacket and clipped this to a ring in the cockpit. She felt that was ominous. The boat was now being driven through the water by the wind. She looked out and all she could see were heaving masses of water. The waves were fifteen, maybe twenty feet high, she couldn't tell but it looked like a wall of water. The boat rode the waves down and then up the other side. The riding down was terrifying as the sea opened up before her like a valley. The boat rode up and a great wave washed over the foredeck.

'The waves seem awfully big.'

Her voice came out all squeaky and childish.

'The boat can take them. She's been through much worse storms than this,' he said.

She took another swig of rum from his bottle, which he was keeping in the pocket of his oilskin. He had his hand on the tiller and his face was impassive as they were battered by the waves. He had a striking profile, she thought, because of his high cheekbones and long straight nose. He looked composed as the boat rode another big wave. No, he looked more than composed; he looked unconcerned as if he had no fear about what might happen to them, as if he was strangely detached from any sense of danger.

Then the rain started. It was a torrential downpour that reduced their visibility to nothing. She heard what sounded like a deep thump, right out in the middle of the ocean. Why was the sea thumping like that? What did it mean? She was wet through to her skin. She could put up with that. And she didn't feel sick, which was a blessing; but what plagued her were her fears.

'I heard a deep thump out at sea Owen. What was that?'

'Probably thunder,' he said.

'No, it was right out in the ocean, maybe even under the ocean.'

'It might have been turbulence caused by the impact of water on something below. There's a landscape under the sea, mountains and cliffs and valleys. People think the land ends where it rises above the sea but of course it doesn't, there's a whole world down there.'

The boat rode down another deep wave and Anna clung to the side of the cockpit, her face pale and her knuckles white. He could see that he was frightening her even more with his explanation. He was not good at comforting people. He could never find the right words.

'We'll be OK. It seems scary when you're not used to being on a boat, but it would take a bigger storm than this to give us any real trouble.'

She wished she could believe him. She knew they were completely alone, no-one would find them here. In their safety drill Owen had shown them the rocket flares that you let off when in trouble. It was like those stupid whistles on an aeroplane, to draw attention to yourself if the plane ever came down in the sea. What nonsense it was. Who would ever see their flares above this black boiling sea?

'I'm a terrible coward, Owen. Rob always says I'm a "great girl's blouse" and he's right.'

He laughed out loud.

'What a great saying.'

Her eyes were large and fearful and the mole between her eyebrows was somehow touching to him, it made her look vulnerable. It was unfortunate the storm had happened so early into their trip. This was not the initiation he had hoped for them.

'I promise you it's gonna be all right.'

She asked him for the rum bottle again and took another long swig. Why had she ever agreed to get on this bloody boat? It was entirely possible that the boat would capsize and they would all drown.

When their three hours were up Anna went below with Owen and they lay down on the berths in the saloon. He stretched out with his eyes open. She felt slightly drunk from the rum and closed her eyes to stop the sensation of the saloon pulsating around her.

Kim and Rob took over the watch. Rob was looking pale. Lying below while the boat was rolling and pitching so violently had made him feel queasy and he was glad to get out into the air even though the relentless battering of the waves had not let up. His eyes were sore from the constant spray and all he could see ahead were more implacable rolling waves. He spat over the side of the boat a couple of times and kept swallowing down his feeling of nausea.

'Anna told me your sister's a model?' Kim said.

'She is. Weird isn't it, my kid sister earning a fortune for having her picture taken and for walking up and down a catwalk.'

'How did she get into that?'

'She was scouted when she was fifteen.'

'Scouted?'

'Yes, she was at Glastonbury Festival with my mum and a model scout took some Polaroids of her and told her to ring the agency. When they got back to London my mum followed up. And now you see her everywhere.'

'What's her name?'

'Savannah Hunt...'

'I'll look out for her. So you're Rob Hunt?'

'No, I kept my mum's name; Sherburn. Savannah's my half-sister.'

'And you're close?'

'We're very close, but she'll always be a daft kid to me.'

The boat lurched down a big wave and he shivered. The feeling of nausea that had been building in him threatened to overwhelm him.

'Are you cold?' Kim asked.

She offered the rum bottle to him. He shook his head.

'No ta, I'm feeling too queasy for rum.'

'Bummer... I should have picked up some Dramamine when we were in Belize City.'

He started to feel very sick and crouched miserably in the

cockpit as Kim managed the tiller. He felt useless as waves of nausea assaulted him. Around midnight he was sick over the side of the boat. He kept throwing up for the next hour until his stomach was empty and still he retched.

Kim was having a bad night too. She had sailed through many storms with Owen. Tonight felt different. Why had they put themselves through this again with the boat in such poor shape? And to make matters worse Owen had forgotten to replace the batteries in his GPS, so they couldn't work out their position. That was unforgiveable. Was Owen getting more reckless?

Three hours later Owen and Anna returned for their watch and Kim helped a weakened Rob down to the saloon and back onto the berth. She gave him some water which he sipped, his face a greenish white.

'You may be able to sleep now you've been sick,' she said.

She left a bucket by the side of his berth which she tied to the legs of the table.

'You're kind Kim and I appreciate it,' he said closing his eyes.

Anna went down to see how Rob was doing. He was lying on sea-soaked bedding with his eyes shut. The canvas lee-cloth kept him from falling off the berth but the boat was rolling so much that he kept being pushed up against it, and his face was getting chafed. He looked so ill and so uncomfortable and there was little she could do to help him. She found a small towel in their cabin that was still dry. She rolled this up and put it next to his face to stop the chafing. She put her hand on his forehead and stroked the wet hair away from his closed eyes. It was nearly as wet down there as it was above. Kim appeared to be asleep. Anna struggled back up into the cockpit and crouched close to Owen. It was deep into the night now and the storm was still raging around them. She had got used to the constant spray in her face, the salt on her lips. It was simply a case of endurance she told herself. This misery would come to an end sometime.

'Go and lie down in the forecabin Anna. I can manage here alone,' he said.

She knew she was doing nothing to help but she didn't want to leave his side.

'I feel safer being up here with you.'

And she did feel safer sitting with him. She watched his hands on the tiller. He had wonderful hands, long graceful fingers that gripped the wood. He wore a good diver's watch on his right wrist. She made herself focus on his hands as she tried to shut out her importunate fears.

Rob was having a dreadful night as he was tossed on the wet bedding below. The lee-cloth kept rubbing against him and disturbing his fitful sleep. He thought he might feel better if he could only get out into the air again. The saloon seemed enclosed and fetid and he could smell his sick. He tried to sit up. He had no strength to do anything. He couldn't even raise his head. He drifted in and out of a disturbed sleep and had vivid dreams that made his body jerk. Later, he didn't know if he was dreaming or remembering, but a song kept going through his head, 'Heaven is a Place on Earth', and he lived again every detail of being at a music festival with his mum when he was eight years old.

They had camped. He saw again the dark night as he and his mum picked their way through a field of tents of all shapes and sizes. His mum used her small torch to see where to unzip the flap into their tent. Then it was morning and he was lying awake in his sleeping bag and noticing how the light coming through their red tent made everything pink. He had sat up and reached for his mum's backpack to look for the custard creams he knew were in there. He was opening the packet when she said sleepily:

'Eat outside sweetheart and I'll get you an egg roll later.'

He poked his head out of the tent. There were a lot of people about. He sat at the door of their tent and ate custard creams and watched the people queuing for the cubicle showers with their wash bags and their towels over their shoulders. The toilets were always smelly at these festivals. He told his mum he didn't like to use them. He liked the festivals though, even when he got tired because his mum stayed up late to listen to the bands. She would roll out a small mat and he'd fall asleep on the mat while she sat cross-legged listening or stood up and danced along to the music. She never left him to go to the front of the stage. People would come and talk to her, usually men. She was so beautiful.

When his mum got up he felt proud to be walking through the field with her. She would often say to him 'it's just the two of us darling, Robin and her Robbie, her little man.' She didn't look anything like his friends' mums. Her hair fell in long curls down her back. The field was muddy and they had tucked their jeans into wellington boots. The sun was trying to burn though the clouds as they waked to a stall selling bacon, eggs and sausages and joined the queue.

'I'd like a bacon roll today please, Mum,' he said.

'You sure about that? Bacon is very salty you know.'

They shared a commune in London with vegetarians and his mother was a half-hearted vegetarian.

'I want to try it.'

She ordered a bacon roll for him and he put a lot of tomato sauce on it. She got a tea for herself. She always brought her own mug to these festivals and she took this from her backpack and poured the tea from the paper cup into her mug. This year there was a funfair and she'd promised to take him on the dodgems.

'We need to get to the dodgems at two Robbie. I met such a nice man last night. He said he'd go on them with you.'

'But I want to go on them with *you*.'

'You know I don't like them. They're so jerky. It'll be much more fun with him. He's a musician.'

She got out her festival programme and showed him the listing.

'He plays lead guitar. They're playing the second stage at seven so we must make sure we go see them.'

At 2 p.m. they were standing by the dodgems and she waved to a tall man in jeans wearing a full length embroidered Afghan coat. He came over to them and Rob saw that he had a strange mouth, full pouty red lips that looked odd on a man. The man was staring at his mum in a way he didn't like.

'Robbie, this is Elliot.'

'Hey Robbie, I hear you're a fan of the dodgems,' the man said.

Rob nodded doubtfully. The man was holding a long cotton scarf which had small blue roses all over it.

'I got this for you Robin,' he said holding the scarf out to his mum.

His mum held the scarf up looking pleased. She wound it round her long pale hair. It was his first meeting with his future stepfather and he had wanted very much to punch him in the stomach.

Rob was fully awake now. Thinking about his stepfather always made him feel bad.

Up on deck Owen gripped the tiller and looked into the

darkness. He was remembering an incident from long ago when he was little, maybe seven because his mom was pregnant with Megan. Dad had taken them out on a family outing, a picnic on the beach. As they walked back to their car his mom spotted a bird of prey circling overhead and she pointed her arm up at the sky and cried out in excitement.

'Jim, Owen, look, over there.'

They all stopped in the road and watched the bird with its wings fully spread as it swept in a wide arc as though it owned the sky. It was surveying the ground below for any signs of life among the dunes.

'Great bird. So proud, so majestic...' his dad said.

They got into the car. It was very hot inside because the windows had been shut for several hours. Owen liked the hotness of the car but it made him sleepy. As his mom opened her window she let out a cry of distress. She was looking at the third finger on her right hand.

'My ring, oh my ring. It's gone!'

Dad had bought Mom an eternity ring with a red stone and it was gone.

Her eyes filled with tears.

'I shouldn't have worn it to the beach.'

'When did you last see it?'

'I think I had it when I was packing up the picnic.'

'So it's somewhere between the beach and here. We'll retrace our steps.'

They all got out of the car and Owen followed them up the hill dragging his feet because he had wanted to sleep. Mom and Dad were looking in the banks on either side of the road. He thought about the moment when his mom had pointed up at the bird in the sky. He'd seen something move in the air as she swung her arm down. He got down on his knees and started to scrabble among the verges, pushing the grasses aside.

'This is hopeless,' Mom wailed. 'Best we go home, Jim.'

But Owen didn't want to give up now because his mom loved that ring. So he kept looking in the grasses, inching up the road and running his hands through the plants. And then he saw it. Lying in the dust and the dead leaves he saw his mom's ring. He picked it up and held it above his head and the sun struck it and it gleamed so brightly. And Mom and Dad were hugging him tight. Finding something precious that was lost felt so good.

A large wave washed over the boat and hit Owen in the face so that his eyes stung. He grimaced and shook his head vigorously thinking how much his dad had changed only a few years later. No. He wasn't going to let himself think about that.

It was an achingly long night for them all.

DAY FOUR

At last tentative signs of morning came. The sky lightened slowly to dark purple and then to grey. The rain had stopped and they could see that the sun was obscured behind thick clouds. The sea became gradually less turbulent and the wind lessened in force. They were all tired and shaky. Kim went below to fire up the stove and make them coffee. Owen had hauled the mainsail up again and was trying to sail them back onto their original course but they were making little headway.

The day passed slowly as they sailed for hour after hour and scanned the horizon and saw no other boats or ships or any sign of a coastline. Owen could not understand why they hadn't spotted land, which he had expected to see from about three o'clock that afternoon. He looked at his chart again and regretted that his GPS was dead.

'I know we were blown badly off course, but where are we?'

Kim shrugged and said nothing. It was as if they had all been battered into a kind of torpid submission by the rough night, the empty sea and their own unspoken anxieties.

Rob however started to feel better. He washed his face and cleaned his teeth, changed his T-shirt and came up and sat in the cockpit. He was ashamed that he had been so sick the night before. He wanted very much to be a good sailor and Anna had managed to get through the storm without throwing up. She sat next to him now saying little. She didn't have to, her face said it all. She looked as if she was enduring a particularly painful ordeal.

About an hour later Rob spotted a group of large purple-blue jellyfish floating by the boat.

'Come look at these,' he shouted.

They gathered round him and looked to where he was pointing.

'Those are Portuguese man-of-wars,' Owen said. 'You have to be careful around those. They have these long tentacles that float below them; can be thirty feet long sometimes. And even dead man-of-wars can give a sting.'

'Yep, we had a buddy who brushed by a dead one and he got a nasty sting from it,' Kim said.

They all gazed fascinated, almost mesmerised, as the purple-blue colony moved rhythmically across the surface of the sea and they watched until they were out of sight.

'Now I understand "The Rime of the Ancient Mariner",' Anna said. 'You are so glad to see any sign of life in this huge vastness.'

'The sea can be a lonely place,' Owen said.

'We need food. I'll get cooking,' Kim said.

She cooked them spicy vegetable stew with rice. She sliced onions and red peppers and fried them with garlic and spices, then added a can of tomatoes and a can of kidney beans to the pan. It was quite a thing to watch her cooking under those conditions. She used a canvas strap to clip herself to the crash-bar in front of the stove. This allowed her to keep on her feet as the boat rolled. She unlocked the gimbal on the stove so that it pivoted and remained level as the boat moved up and down.

'I couldn't cook without my bumstrap,' she said.

They sat in the cockpit and ate her stew.

'This is making me feel better. You're a miracle worker,' Rob said.

'My pleasure, and it should be an easier night for us all tonight.'

'I'll stay on watch with Kim. You two try to get some sleep,' Owen said.

Anna and Rob went to their cabin and undressed in silence. They lay side by side while the boat pitched, though less violently than the night before. They were both awake and Rob was brooding. All she had said to him in the last hour was that she had a chapped bum. Usually they would have laughed about this. They hadn't this time. He was learning how tensions were intensified when you lived in such a small space. There was nowhere to go and reactions that needed to come out had to be pushed down and contained. He was still feeling rough and her silence was weighing on him like a judgement.

'Sometimes I find your negativity so oppressive you know. It's like a burden I have to carry,' he said.

'That's not fair.'

'You've been making it clear from the beginning that you think this is all a big mistake. So when things go wrong, like last night, you make me feel guilty.'

She knew there was some truth to his complaint. She *was* feeling resentful that he'd persuaded her to board the boat. The problem was that she didn't know how to shake herself out of that feeling because her fears would not be stilled.

'I'm scared, OK? I don't feel safe with them.'

'So you give me the silent treatment.'

'They said they knew these waters but we're completely lost. They haven't got a bloody clue where we are.'

'We've been blown off course,' he said.

'Yes but he should still know roughly where we are.'

'His GPS is down.'

'Well we'd be a bloody sight safer if his GPS wasn't down,' she hissed.

'You always make such a big thing about everything Anna. Grow up!'

She sat up quickly and banged her head against the roof of the cabin. She rubbed her head crossly.

'We're in the middle of nowhere with two people we hardly know in a boat without the proper equipment – that's not a small thing.'

'That's life Anna, trying out new things. I want to do this and I don't want you to make me feel bad about it.'

'I'm not trying to make you feel bad—'

'Oh no? Giving me the silent treatment? It's a good thing to be out of our comfort zone, to be tested.'

'I'm on my holiday. I don't want to be tested.'

He was about to retort when they heard a cry of joy from Kim up on deck. They both leaped up and rushed out of the cabin and into the cockpit.

Owen and Kim were standing on the foredeck looking out. For the last half hour Owen had been watching an intermittent glow on the horizon. He had said nothing until the light had become clearly visible over the horizon, the flash of a lighthouse.

'Thank heavens,' Anna said with far greater emphasis than she intended. Did Owen realise that she'd been sure they were done for? They joined them on the foredeck and watched as Owen used his watch to time the flashes of the lighthouse.

'That's a group of four flashes every thirty seconds. I'll check it on the chart.'

He went down to the saloon and came back with his chart.

'Every lighthouse has its own characteristic flash and that lighthouse is at Punta Sal. That explains it. We've been blown along the Honduran mainland. Land is about twenty miles away I reckon, best not to approach till morning.'

'Should we heave to?' Kim said.

'Let's do that. We can see more in daylight.'

They adjusted the sails so that the boat was side on to the wind and Owen lashed the tiller. This caused the boat to shift and stop its forward motion. The four of them sat in the cockpit and celebrated the sighting of the lighthouse with mugs of rum.

'It's been a tough two days for you both, a baptism of fire,' Owen said.

'And you did OK.'

'I didn't,' Rob grimaced.

It was to be another night of rolling and pitching although the boat didn't move very far as the storm had spent itself. Owen stayed on watch up above while the others tried to sleep below.

At sunrise they knew it was going to be a glorious day. They sailed towards the lighthouse through a calm sea and followed the line of the shore. Now they could see land rising in front of them: steep and rocky mountains that were thick with green trees, palms and shrubs.

'That looks like the Garden of Eden,' Rob said with feeling and it did look marvellous to his land-hungry eyes.

They all laughed as they stood and drank the hot sweet black coffee Kim had made them. Owen spotted a fisherman in his cayuka rowing fast through the water and he signalled him over. The fisherman rowed up alongside their boat and they spoke in Spanish for a few minutes, the fisherman pointing back towards the lighthouse nodding his head and gesticulating. He rowed away.

'We've been blown sixty miles off course and we're headed towards Tela. I reckon we all need a day on land before setting off for Roatán again,' Owen said.

'Yes please,' Anna said.

He looked at his chart.

'We'll head for Triunfo de la Cruz. We've been there before Kimmie.'

They sailed close to Triunfo and anchored. From the boat they could see a long beach fringed by palm trees that shone bright green in the brilliant sunshine. There were modest houses along the beach and small boats and canoes at the water's edge. Kim stripped the damp sheets off the beds and hung the sheets and quilts out to dry and Anna helped her. Two men rowed over to the *El Tiempo Pasa*. They were in a pongo, a shallow canoe, a smaller frailer version of the cayuka and they had fruit and fish with them which they offered for sale. Kim bought some small yellow mangoes and Owen asked the men to come back in an hour and he'd pay them to clean the boat.

It was going to be their hottest day yet. Anna put on her bikini and had a shower on deck using buckets of cold water. Rob watched her as she shampooed her long hair and lathered it, her eyes shut tight. Her bikini was made up of two small triangles of bright blue that just covered her breasts, and tiny panties that stretched over her bottom. She was tall and slim and he loved the way her belly stuck out a bit over her hipbones. He sometimes wondered why meeting Anna on the tube with the blood trickling down her chin had made such an impact on him. He thought it was because he was drawn to her intensity, both the intense way she was reading her book and the intense way she looked at him when their eyes met for the first time. Maybe it was the mole between her eyebrows that gave her eyes their extraordinary power. Of course some people might consider that mole a defect. His classically beautiful mum probably did, though she'd never said anything about it. He remembered the first time he introduced Anna to her. They had been invited round to lunch and Anna was dressed simply in jeans, a white shirt and ankle boots. She had put her little silver earrings in but wore no other jewellery. She wasn't a woman for bangles or necklaces. As he rang the bell on the house in Crouch End, which his mum shared with Elliot and

Savannah, Rob had looked over at Anna to give her an encouraging smile and at that moment he thought her the most beautiful woman on earth.

His mother opened the door to them. She was wearing one of her flowing white linen outfits and a turquoise necklace with heavy uneven stones which complimented her brilliant blue eyes. She was scanning Anna over his shoulder as she leaned forward and embraced him and then she took Anna's hand. Anna held out a bunch of Sweet Peas to her. She had insisted on getting those particular flowers and they'd had to go to two flower shops to find the blooms. Later his mum had told him that she approved of Anna as his girlfriend. She thought she was a young woman of substance and that if anyone could straighten Rob out then Anna could.

Kim came up onto the deck and this stopped his reverie. She was also in her bikini which was acid yellow. She looked good too he thought.

The men from the village came back to clean the boat and Owen told the others to go ahead and he would join them in a while. They got into the dinghy and made the short journey to the beach.

'We'll eat here today. There should be places where we can get some good fish,' Kim said.

She tried not to show it to Rob and Anna but she was feeling miserable and out of sorts with Owen. She watched as they strolled in front of her through the village of Triunfo de la Cruz. It was a clean, well-kept village with traditional wooden houses that had thatched roofs of palm and one or two modern concrete bungalows too. She remembered the time she and Owen had come here before, about a year into their adventure. It was a happier time then and they had been more united.

Triunfo de la Cruz was a Garifuna community and Rob was telling Anna about how the Garifuna were descendants of Caribbean and West African people. Rob was pleased at everything he saw: the chickens scratching at the grit, a pile of coconut husks outside a bar, the smoky bonfire smell of the village. The streets were sandy and children were playing outside their houses and calling out 'Hola, hola' to them as they walked along. Rob called back to them and there was the inevitable 'Ingles?' from the children and his reply 'Si, Ingles'.

At the end of the main street he spotted a bar and suggested they go in. He bought them cold beers and they carried them outside and sat on a wooden bench by the side of the bar. The wall was hot against their backs.

'It was a tough two nights, wasn't it?' Rob said as he sampled the local brew.

Anna stretched her arms above her head.

'The night of the storm seemed to go on for ever.'

'I can't wait to get to Roatán though. It will all be worth it when we get there,' Rob said.

Kim nodded her agreement but said nothing.

A while later Owen found them seated outside the bar. He put his arm around Kim and she said at once:

'You *must* buy batteries for the GPS today.'

'Sure,' Owen said dropping his arm.

Rob had noticed that she'd been quiet all day, had said very little as they drank their beers and her voice sounded tense now. They set off back to the shoreline to find a place to eat.

'Let's see if I can find one of my favourite dishes,' Owen said.

'What is it?' Anna asked.

'Raw conch with lime juice and hot pepper sauce...'

'You can eat conch?'

'It's delicious. You must try it.'

They found a restaurant not far from the beach which had a large verandah covered with a thatched roof. They sat at a table outside and Owen ordered his raw conch dish and the others chose the conch stew. They drank rum with fresh pineapple juice and looked out from the verandah to the beach below. The sea was as calm as a millpond.

'You see how quickly things can change at sea,' Owen said.

'It was *so* sudden,' Anna said.

'It was, but we were never in any real danger. We'll moor here tonight and set off at sunrise. We have at least two full days of sailing before we get to Roatán.'

After they had eaten Kim and Owen headed for the general store in the village and Anna and Rob ambled along the beach until they found a secluded spot near the edge of the sea. They swam lazily in the warm clear water. Later they stretched out on the sand side by side with their legs in the sun and their faces shaded by a mature palm tree.

'This is more like it,' Rob said.

'I'll teach you a relaxation exercise I know,' Anna said.

She started to speak slowly and sonorously as her teacher had done:

'Close your eyes and feel your body sinking into the sand. Your legs are getting heavy and are sinking into the ground. Your back is heavy and...'

He chuckled at her affected voice.

'Where did you learn this?'

'Shh, no talking... at my yoga class...'

'Your arms are getting heavy, your shoulders and neck are getting heavy, your head is getting heavy. You are letting go completely. The ground is supporting you completely. Now listen to the sounds around you. Just lie and listen.'

Rob lay and listened. He could hear the whisper of the sea as it spread itself onto the sand. The palm trees were making all kinds of noises. He could hear them crackle, rustle, creak and sigh. And there was a clicking noise as a single dry palm frond hit the trunk of their tree. There was the faintest sound of scurrying as some insect or crab scuttled over the hot sand. There was the sound of their breathing. Anna could feel herself relaxing into the moment. Her fears had melted away. They both fell into a delicious, much-needed sleep.

Owen rowed Kim back to the boat and she carried the fresh vegetables and fish down to the galley. He followed her down there and put the new batteries into the GPS. He turned it on and it worked.

'GPS is back up,' he said.

She said nothing in response.

'Are you OK, Kimbo?'

'That storm got to me,' she said in a tight voice.

'It would take a bigger storm than that to knock us down.'

'I'm not sure I agree.'

'You're on edge, I can see that.'

'Anna thought we were done for. She looked out of her mind with fear.'

'She's not a natural sailor.'

'She was scared, Owen. I'm sure she's regretting coming on the boat and that's creating an atmosphere about the place.'

'It was a rough night. She'll get used to it.'

'She's kinda straight and I find her difficult to talk to.'

'She's what my aunt Cally would call a still-waters-run-deep kinda person.'

'You think?'

'Yeah, I think she means well,' he said.

'Maybe it's me, but I'm finding all this tougher than I used to, sharing our lives with strangers.'

'What are you worried about? You didn't say anything about my father did you?'

'No. You know I wouldn't. I did say to Rob that you had a falling out with your family and don't like to talk about it.'

He put his arms around her and hugged her tight. She was a little woman and only came up to the middle of his chest. She pulled away from him and looked up at him.

'But it's not about that Owen. I'm missing having our own home; just you and me and nobody else.'

'You're my best Kimbo,' he said.

He took off her clothes and stroked her pretty little bottom and they lay naked on the double berth in the saloon. He knew that his insomnia and his inability to spend his nights next to her were impacting badly on their sex life. They used to have sex a lot. He regretted how seldom they did these days and he wanted sex now, to make them close again.

When the sun was low in the sky Owen rowed over in the dinghy to pick up Rob and Anna. He had managed to sleep for a couple of hours after the sex. As he moved through the water he found himself thinking about his aunt Cally, his father's older sister. She was a brisk efficient woman who worked as a secretary at the Marina in Clearwater. She had a flat in the Marina and it was her pride and joy, a light white flat always spotlessly clean. He reckoned she washed the drapes every three months. You didn't need to do it that often. His mother hadn't. She had given him the back bedroom, her guest bedroom, when he moved in with her. It was a single room and the furniture was all new and modern. The single bed had never been long enough for him and his feet stuck out at the end if he stretched out fully. He had never said anything to his aunt about this. He would have days when he felt completely numb and had to remind himself that when his aunt spoke to him she would expect a response.

He remembered the night of his fifteenth birthday. Aunt Cally was making him fried chicken because she knew it was his favourite meal. She was going on about how his teachers had told her that he was real clever and could get into college no trouble. He told her he didn't plan to go to college. He was gonna leave high school at sixteen and work in the boatyards. She said there was plenty of time for him to be working when he was older. He said nothing to that. She had no idea what it was like for him at high school. He was the boy they pointed at. He was the boy they whispered about.

He saw Rob and Anna entwined beneath a palm tree and rowed over to them.

'I'd like to go for a last swim if that's OK?' Rob said as he sat up and stretched.

He felt refreshed by his sleep and his body was vital again, fully recovered from the seasickness. He waded out into the warm sea.

Owen had brought some of the small yellow mangoes with him, which Kim had bought that morning. He offered one to Anna and showed her the best way to eat it. You pressed the mango hard, you rolled it between your palms and squeezed and squeezed it without breaking the skin until the fruit had been turned into a pulp under the skin. Then you bit off the top and sucked out the sweet mango pulp like a drink.

'Oh that's heavenly,' Anna said after following his instructions. Her mouth was filled with the honey sweetness of the mango.

'Have another one.'

'I will; thanks.'

She repeated the process and bit off the top of the mango and sucked happily at it.

'I think Owen is a Welsh name isn't it?' she said.

'Yeah, my granny was Welsh, on my mother's side, from Pontypridd.'

'Have you ever been there?'

She knew she was starting to probe, as Rob had told her she must not.

'No, never.'

He reached for another mango which he pressed between his palms.

'I hate America,' he said.

It was a strong statement and it had come out of the blue.

'Why do you say that?'

'It's a country that looks after its businesses but doesn't look after its people.'

She pondered this for a moment. It was the sort of thing her granddad would say to her, that society cared more for its corporations than its citizens.

'But you're going back there?'

'Yeah we are. Kimmie wants to open her café and it's her turn now. We won't go back to Clearwater though. We'll find ourselves another place.'

'It'll be a big change for you both after living on the boat for three years.'

'A big change...' He looked out at the sea.

'We'll find a place on the coast and I'll get work in a

76

boatyard. I need to be around boats. I'm not equipped for anything else.'

'I'm sure that's not true,' she said.

'It is. Boats are the only things I know anything about.'

'Are they your books I saw in the saloon?'

He nodded.

'I read a lot in down time,' he said.

'I saw you had some by Stephen King.'

'Do you like him?'

'I do, he's a brilliant story-teller. I saw you had *The Stand*. That book terrified me. Rob was away and I remember being so spooked... the sound of those worn-down cowboy boots tramping along the road telling you the dark man was coming. I had to keep the lights on all night.'

'But that wouldn't have helped. The dark man came to those folks in their dreams.'

'Yes he did.'

'King understands the dark stuff,' Owen said.

'For most of the book you think evil is going to triumph. You think how can they ever beat him? It seems like he's got all the power and all the weapons.'

'But it's not enough, not in the end.'

'No, because all he can offer ultimately is fear and dread,' Anna said.

'And because evil is inherently unstable,' Owen said.

As he came out of the sea Rob saw a lone fisherman pulling his boat onto the beach. He went over to take a look. The man had caught some grouper, a few grunt and he had some oysters too. On an impulse Rob decided to buy a dozen oysters.

'Please wait and I'll get some money,' he said to the fisherman who looked up at him not understanding what he said but guessing that a sale was in the offing. Rob walked up the beach to where Owen and Anna were sitting and took a few dollars out.

'I'm getting us some oysters for tonight, my treat,' he said. 'What should I pay for twelve?'

Owen told him the price that locals would pay and said he should offer a bit more. Rob went back and the fisherman counted twelve oysters into an old plastic bag. They got into the dinghy and Owen rowed them back to the *El Tiempo Pasa*.

Rob went down to the saloon to prepare the oysters. Kim was down there going through the lockers, tidying the books and maps. She was always tidying up he had noticed, keeping the boat neat and clean. He squeezed past her and peered in the drawers beneath the sink. He could find no knives anywhere. There were just forks and spoons lying in the drawer. He asked to borrow Kim's knife so he could open the oysters. She seemed reluctant at first. Then she unzipped her belt, took out the case and handed over her small knife.

'Be careful though Rob. It's very sharp.'

He started to prise open the oysters. He opened five successfully and placed them on a large plate. He was pleased. They looked succulent. The sixth one would not open. He pressed the knife hard into the tiny opening of the hard shell and the knife skidded and he cut his hand.

'Shit...!'

Kim spun round and saw blood spurting out of his palm. She reacted quickly, grabbing the first aid box from an overhead locker. There was quite a lot of blood and she held his hand over the sink. She cleaned his wound efficiently, stemmed the flow and tied a bandage tightly around his hand. She washed the blood off the sink and the surfaces and rinsed the cloth repeatedly until the water ran clear. He noticed that she was trembling slightly.

'You'll be OK. It looked worse than it is,' she said as she wrung out the dishcloth for the last time.

'Are you scared of blood?'

She looked up at him.

'No...'

'You seemed scared just now.'

'I'm not scared of blood but you have to be super careful in a boat, that's all.'

'Sorry, I'm a clumsy idiot.'

'Don't worry. The oysters were a great idea. Let me open the rest.'

Kim opened the rest of the oysters with her knife and laid them on the plate. She was thinking it was strange how when you feared something on behalf of another person it made you even more frightened. She had never been scared of blood. Rob's question had made her realise how much of Owen's terrible fears she was carrying within her. She sliced two lemons in half, wiped her knife carefully and put it back into its case and into her belt. She called to the others as she carried the plate of oysters up into the cockpit. Rob held up his bandaged hand.

'I'm in the wars,' he said.

'Oh no...' Anna said.

'I cut myself.' He said it ruefully.

'Does it hurt a lot?' she asked.

'It's throbbing a bit. I'll live.'

They sat in the cockpit and ate the twelve juicy oysters with lemon juice and black pepper and watched as the sun set and the sky darkened.

That night lying curled up with Anna in their cabin Rob said:

'There are no knives on this boat, except for Kim's knife.'

'I noticed that. She always gives us forks and spoons. It's odd isn't it?'

'Yes, it's strange...'

'Why would that be?'

'I don't know. Unless...'

'What?'

'Well maybe they've had some odd types on the boat and they're playing it safe,' Rob said.

'Do you think?'

He fell asleep. Anna lay and thought about it. Kimberly carried that knife around with her, always zipped up in its case in her belt. Why did she carry it with her all the time? Was she frightened she might get attacked? Central America certainly wasn't the safest place to be living and she was a small woman. Perhaps carrying the knife on her person made her feel safer. Then she remembered Kimberly's panicked reaction when she broke the glass on that picture frame of Moses. It had almost been as if she were in a trance.

Anna was in the habit of thinking long and hard about things that happened to her and trying to understand them, even the small details that might seem unimportant to other people. It was why she kept her journals and it was what she did in her job, piecing together what her old men were trying to tell her. Rob said she spent too much time looking inwards; that she needed to look outwards at the magnificence and variety of the world. Something was not quite right though. No knives on the boat and Kimberly's reaction had been strange.

DAY SIX

It dawned calm and bright. There was no wind at all and the sea was flat. It made for a day of frustrating sailing and they made little progress towards Roatán. Owen and Rob were in charge of the sailing. Anna lay on the hot deck in her bikini reading Dickens' *Bleak House*.

'I don't get how you can read about foggy Victorian London when we're here,' Rob said opening his arms wide and gesturing at the brilliant blue sky and sea.

'But it's perfect holiday reading. The plot is so engrossing.'

She had read him the first page of the novel when they were on the plane coming over:

'Smoke lowering down from chimney-pots, making a soft black drizzle, with flakes of soot in it as big as full-grown snowflakes – gone into mourning, one might imagine, for the death of the sun.'

He left her to it. There had been no recurrence of his sea-sickness and he and Owen were now sailing partners. In the afternoon the sky clouded over and it was one of those still pale uneventful days at sea.

They were about twelve hours out of Triunfo and Owen and Rob were looking for an anchorage for the night. The light was fading and they spotted a tiny Cay ahead. It was not much more than a cluster of mangroves that had taken root on a small circular atoll. It afforded some shelter so they decided to approach it. The atoll was so small it was not shown on Owen's chart and sailing in was a challenge. They entered a complicated reef system and had to feel their way in to an anchorage. Owen sent Rob forward to peer over the bow and make sure there were no rocks below. There was no beach to speak of, just a small plot of mud that had been colonised by the ubiquitous mangroves.

Anna had gone below and was sitting in the forecabin in her bra and knickers writing in her notebook. She always kept a notebook on her holidays. It was her way of trying to crystallise experiences that mattered to her. She was trying to find the words to describe the storm they had endured and then the blissful day that followed in Triunfo. What a contrast that had been. The day after the storm had been an almost perfect day, except for Rob cutting his hand.

Kim was in the galley making a fish stew in her large stock pot. Rob had christened this her magic pot because he said she could make the most ordinary ingredients taste wonderful. She liked that: her magic pot. She sliced the large beaten up grunt she had bought in Triunfo with strong rapid stokes. It was an ugly brute all right. It would be tasty though. Anna had irritated her today. There was something about the way she talked to Owen as if he was so interesting and then talked to her as if she was not that was starting to rankle with her. Anna would hang on Owen's words as if he was the fount of all wisdom and she wondered if Rob had noticed it. And Anna was still calling her Kimberly for Chrissakes. She'd said to her a few days into the trip: 'You can call me Kim you know, most folks do.' What had Anna's response been? 'Oh I think of you as Kimberly now and I'm more comfortable sticking with that.' A typical buttoned-up response.

While they were in the village Kim had paid the man in the restaurant for the use of his phone to make a call to her parents in Clearwater. Jared, her older brother, had picked up. He'd been cold with her and said their parents were out. So she'd kept the call short saying she'd call again when they reached Roatán and to be sure to send her love to Mom and Dad. She tried to keep in touch as often as she could as her mom worried if too much time went by without a call. Jared was seven years older than her and had moved back home recently when his marriage broke up. He had been Owen's best friend since childhood and for years they'd been inseparable, like brothers. Owen had always been the more dominant one in the friendship, he had led and Jared had followed. That had all been fractured years ago and her relationship with Owen had been the cause of it.

'He's not right for you, sis,' Jared had said when he found out they'd started dating.

'Why not? I've been in love with him for years.'

'He's borderline crazy you know.'

'That's not true.'

'I know him better then you do and I'm telling you he goes to some pretty dark places in his head.'

'What dark places?'

'He took crazy risks a few times when we were out in his car. One time I thought he was trying to kill us. And then there was all that trouble with Mr Peterson.'

'Mr Peterson was a jerk.'

'He may be a jerk. Doesn't excuse what Owen did to him.'

Mr Peterson had been the basketball coach at Jared's and Owen's high school. She knew some of the Mr Peterson story, but not everything. Now Jared told her how Mr Peterson had continually picked on a black kid called Klevon

83

and how this had enraged Owen. How one day Mr Peterson had gone into the locker room to find his sports kit cut into ribbons and an anonymous note left saying that he was a racist and he was being watched. The next time Mr Peterson picked on Klevon he found the tyres to his car had been slashed and a second anonymous note warning him to stop being so racist. Jared had been scared of Owen then, not recognising his friend. He seemed to be in the grip of an obsession that was pushing him towards ever more extreme acts. In the event Mr Peterson got spooked and left the school at the end of the semester.

'He was sticking up for Klevon,' she said. 'And I'm proud he did that.'

'Goddammit you're deluded. Can't you see he was dangerous? He was out of control,' he shouted at her.

It was shortly after this conversation that Jared sought out Owen and told him to keep away from his kid sister. The intensity of Owen's reaction had been terrifying and this was the beginning of their great falling out.

Up on deck Owen and Rob had now sailed close in to the atoll and they dropped anchor where the boat would be sheltered by the mangroves. They took the sails down. In the dying light, and at the same moment, they both spotted a black hulled motorboat on the horizon. They stood and watched in silence. The boat was larger than theirs and appeared to be moving on a course towards their mooring but it had no lights on. It was obvious from the bow wave that it was using its engine at full throttle.

'What the hell is that?' Rob said.

'A black boat out at night can only be one thing: drug runners.'

They exchanged worried looks. The loneliness of the Cay

added to the feeling of menace. A bird on a nearby mangrove let out a shriek. What made Rob feel afraid though was the expression on Owen's face.

'You sure?'

'I reckon. Very dangerous men on that boat. If they see us they'll take our boat,' he said.

'Do you have any weapons?'

'No, well a baseball bat...'

'What should we do?'

'We need to tell Kimmie and Anna to kill the lights. They may not see us. Our sails are down and it's dark. And they may be in a hurry to get to their destination.'

They hurried down into the saloon. Owen knew how vicious the men on that boat would be. He'd heard of such things happening in these waters before, a skipper and his crew vanishing without trace. If they spotted them and boarded the boat they would rape Kimmie and Anna before they slit all their throats and tossed them overboard. It would be sport to men like that. Rob went into the forecabin and turned the small light off.

'I'm writing,' Anna complained.

'There's a boat headed this way that looks bad. We don't want them to see us.'

He found that he was breathless as he told her this. Her eyes widened in alarm.

'What do you mean bad?'

Owen called to them:

'Can you both come in here now?'

Anna quickly pulled on her jeans and T-shirt and followed Rob into the saloon. Owen had turned the stove flame and all the lights off. He looked grim and spoke urgently in the darkened cabin.

'There's an unlit boat headed this way. I reckon they're drug runners and they'll be armed. They may not have seen us. They were some distance away when we took the sails down. That's our best hope. If they have seen us we're in trouble.'

'What kind of trouble?' Anna asked.

'They might come in and take the boat.'

'You mean pirates?'

'It happens out here. Not very often, but it happens. Rob and I are gonna check again now. If they get any closer we're gonna have to decide what to do.'

Anna had never seen Rob looking so frightened before. Owen and Kimberly looked grim too. Owen picked up two flares and took out a baseball bat from the small berth at the back of the boat knowing how futile a gesture this was.

He and Rob went back into the cockpit and peered out. The light was poor; the moon was behind thick cloud. They could barely make out the dark bulk of the black boat and yet it seemed to be coming closer to them. Kim and Anna came up and sat with them in the cockpit. They had both put on oilskins and Anna was shivering in spite of the warmth of the night. They sat in strained silence and watched the dark shape intently. Dread was growing in all of them and the thought that the men on that boat might hurt Anna was making Rob feel physically sick. He would fight them to the death if they went near her or Kim. He wished he had a proper weapon with him. He hugged Anna to him tightly and she buried her face in his shoulder in a hopeless kind of way as if she understood how truly dangerous their situation was.

'Are they getting any nearer?' Kim asked quietly.

'Yes they're nearer. I think they might have seen us,' Owen said.

'Should we get off the boat and hide in the mangroves?' Anna whispered.

'Aren't we doomed if we get off the boat?' Rob said. 'If they take the boat no-one would ever find us here. It's in the middle of nowhere.'

Owen had been in difficult situations before but this time he was scared for their lives. They could get off the boat on the blind side, but even if by some remote chance they were able to hide in the mangroves the men would take the boat. They were not insured and he and Kimmie would lose everything. There were ten cases of rum, gin and whisky and four kilos of cocaine stowed in the back berth. It would be quite a haul for the smugglers. Raul would come after him if he didn't deliver the package to Money Joe. Raul had always been an ally but he was the kind of man who would turn nasty very quickly if anyone let him down. Rob was right too. If they were left on this atoll without a boat they would be as good as dead. But he couldn't bear the thought of sitting on the boat passively awaiting their fate.

'Anna's got a point. You three get off the boat now and find a place to hide. I'll stay here,' he said.

'No!' Kim said.

'If they come in I'll convince them that I was alone on the boat. Now go.'

'They'll kill you,' she said.

'Better than killing all of us.'

'Why are you even suggesting this?'

Owen stood up.

'We have to split up. It's our only chance. Rob, don't you agree? You three get off the boat and hide.'

'I don't like the idea of us leaving you here,' Rob said.

'I need you to stay with Kim and Anna. Now go!'

They had never seen Owen so fired up before. They stood up and clambered onto the deck on the blind side with Owen almost pushing them along in his haste to get them off the boat. Rob went first, sliding over the side of the boat into the sea. The water came up to his waist. He was followed by Anna. As Kim was stepping over the side Owen whispered to her:

'Give me your knife Kimmie.'

'No, I'm not gonna let you have it.'

'Bullshit!'

Kim slid into the water without another word. Anna had heard this urgent exchange and didn't understand it. Why hadn't Kimberly given her knife to Owen? They waded away from the boat in taut silence, Rob leading the way. There was a sucking sound as they slogged through the muddy water. The mangroves were low and scratchy and they had to twist and bend to move around them. Kim was finding it particularly hard as she was shorter than the other two and the water was deep. Rob, seeing how she was struggling, grabbed her arm and helped her along. Eventually they found a small patch of earth, large enough for the three of them to sit down. Rob sat in the middle and put his arms around the two women who were both shivering.

'If they come in we'll hear them. Sound carries on a still night like this,' Kim said.

They strained their ears for the slightest sound. Anna was thinking it was strange what a paralysing effect great fear had on your body. She felt as if all her strength had drained away. It was like in those nightmares where you're being chased and you need to run fast and your legs become so heavy that you can't lift them at all.

'Why did Owen do that?' Anna whispered.

'He thinks he can save us.'

Kim's voice was angry, almost dismissive and Anna felt the need to defend Owen.

'It was brave of him,' she said.

Rob was torn. He didn't like the feeling that Owen had assumed the role of the Alpha Male, the Have-A-Go-Hero. He had been given the role of the secondary male, left with the women, and it made him feel small.

Kim had also heard stories of pirates in these waters boarding boats and killing all the crew and passengers, and she knew these stories were true. Her overwhelming feeling though was one of anger towards Owen. She had known it would come to this one day, that they would lose everything. They should never have left Belize City this last time. He should have listened to her. Owen was not careful enough about their future and he seemed to be getting more reckless.

They sat on the small patch of mud and could hear the faint stirrings of the mangrove branches and the scrabbling of a small mammal moving across the ground. Anna wondered if it was a rat. The strange unearthly shriek of the bird that Rob had heard before repeated its call and made them all jump.

Owen sat in the cockpit tensed and hyper-alert. This time he would not hide from any attackers. He would take them on. Kim should have given him her knife. Her obsession with hiding knives from him was getting on his nerves. Once he had seen it as an act of love. Not any more. She insulted him with her over-protective attitude. He had the baseball bat by his side and he looked at the two flares. Maybe he could use them as weapons too? He could light them and throw them at the men if they tried to board. He put the flares in easy reach and went below to fetch a box of matches. As he came back into the cockpit he heard a disturbance in the water near the boat. His heart jumped. He climbed onto the deck and moved forward carefully on his hands and knees. There it was again. Something was moving in the water at the front of the boat. There was a swishing of water and a knocking sound. It wasn't the motorboat; it was something smaller. Had they sent an advance guard in a dinghy? He inched forward on his stomach, hardly breathing. Another knock and another swish in the water. Someone *was* approaching. This was when he needed that knife. He reached the bow and strained his eyes and ears to identify who was out there. And then he saw it. A large piece of driftwood had floated in and was knocking against his dinghy. He laughed out loud and his laugh sounded like what it was – the frightened laugh of a man on the edge. His father had laughed like that sometimes, laughed when he wanted to cry. He leaned forward and pulled his dinghy in, away from the floating lump of driftwood.

He got back to the cockpit. He sat very still and listened to the sounds of the sea. There was the rise and fall of a low swell but no sound of a boat coming in. A lump of driftwood had terrified him but now his fear had gone. Slowly hope was beginning to grow in him. Their sails were down, it was a dark night and their boat was partially obscured by the mangroves. They hadn't been spotted after all and the black boat had passed them by.

Time passed slowly as Rob, Anna and Kim sat motionless and silent on the tiny patch of earth, each with their thoughts and fears and weaknesses, each straining for the sound of any disturbance in the water that would herald a boat coming in.

'I think we can go back,' Kim said at last.

Quietly and soberly the three of them got to their feet and made their way through the mud and the water to the boat. One by one they climbed wearily on board with Owen helping them up. They huddled in the cockpit, dripping water all over the floor, too drained by the experience to make a move for many minutes.

'It's gone. I reckon it's on its way up the Honduran coastline now and will head to Belize or Mexico under cover of darkness,' Owen said.

Rob squeezed Anna's hand and she squeezed his back.

'We can eat now. No lights on please. Just use the stove.'

Kim and Anna went down into the saloon and got out of their wet clothes. Then Kim fired up the stove and finished cooking the fish stew. Anna fetched the bowls, too depleted to make any conversation. Kim ladled the fragrant stew into the bowls and she and Anna carried these up into the cockpit. The four of them sat in the darkness glad to be alive and to be eating fish stew.

Owen was still apprehensive.

'I think Rob and I should keep watch through the night, to be sure,' he said.

Anna felt a deep need to lie down and find some refuge in sleep. She offered to wash the dishes but Kim said no, it would calm her down to do it. Anna could not be bothered to struggle with the pull-out washbasin or to clean her teeth. She stretched out in the forecabin and tried to sleep but her mind kept replaying the events of the night.

Kim washed the dishes and tidied the galley. She rubbed rich Vaseline into her hands. Like many cooks she had stopped noticing the burn marks on her fingers a while ago. She made up her berth and climbed into it. Her anger towards Owen would not go; it was like a hard little undigested ball in her stomach. She remembered a skipper they knew on Roatán. He was a Texan and had once owned a fifty-foot boat, which he chartered and which made him a good living. Then one winter his boat was blown by a hurricane and now lay under a hundred feet of sand. Like them he was not insured. He had to work as a freelance skipper on other people's charter boats now. He'd said to her:

'I used to be fat and dumb and happy. Now I'm just fat and dumb.'

At the time she had marvelled at his attitude, to have lost so much and to be able to joke about it. She knew she would never be able to joke about losing their boat. It was their only asset, the key to her café, the key to their life on land. How she longed for them all to reach the safety of Roatán.

Through the night Owen and Rob sat on deck alert to the sound of any approaching boats. They passed a rum bottle back and forth and kept each other awake with their talk. Rob explained how you made good beer. Owen explained the differences between sailing a sloop and sailing a ketch.

Anna was lying below in the forecabin, unable to get to sleep. She could hear the low rumble of their voices from their desultory chat and understood how close Rob had grown to Owen. Belize City, which had seemed threatening at the time, now seemed a lot less dangerous than these treacherous waters.

DAY SEVEN

Many hours later the sun rose above the rim of the horizon and the sea was empty.

'Blessed light,' Owen said.

Anna and Kim slept on later than usual, exhausted by the events of the night before. When they got up they took the day slowly, lingering over a breakfast of bread and jam and coffee. Kim was quiet as Owen outlined the next stage of their sailing. She looked down at her plate and wouldn't make eye contact with him.

'We're still a day-and-a-half sailing from Roatán. I can't pinpoint exactly where we are because this tiny place isn't shown on my chart.'

He went down to the saloon and used his GPS to re-calculate their route and they set off again.

As they sailed past the atoll they could see how small and exposed it was. If the men in the black boat had come looking for them there would have been no escape. This made Anna feel shaky and Kim feel angry. Owen in contrast was buoyant; they had escaped any harm and he still had his boat, the cases of liquor and Raul's package. But he was worried that this was their seventh day on board and they should have reached Roatán by now. Raul would have been in touch with Money Joe to check on the delivery of his package. Well there was nothing he could do about it. They would get there in the next day or two.

*

Anna sat on the deck with her back to the mast, out of the way of the others, and wrote in her notebook. She couldn't write if she felt she was being watched because her journal was the place where she put down what she truly thought about things. Too often, when she spoke her deeply felt opinions aloud, she noticed that they jarred with other people, as if she saw the world differently from them. It sometimes made her feel like an outsider. Now she took time to describe the terrors of the night before and Kimberly's strange reaction to Owen asking for her knife. They had all been deeply shaken but so far had said little to each other about it. She wrote:

Maybe we are afraid to talk about our fear of death; about how we would confront it if we knew we were going to die last night. I keep thinking that once we reach Roatán these difficulties will fade and it will make this journey seem worthwhile. I'm hanging onto that thought. Today has been pleasantly uneventful and we've all needed a day to calm down. Sunny all day and the wind picked up this afternoon and we've had the best day of sailing so far. We're headed for a larger Cay, which Owen showed me on his chart. He said it will be our mooring for the night.

There is such an easiness now between Rob and Owen and Kim. You can see it in the way they banter together. It doesn't extend to me and the fault lies with me I'm sure. I must be projecting my uneasiness. I guess it's not easy for them being around someone who is not completely trusting and accepting.

I like Owen a lot. He's an interesting man, a deep man. And I feel for him because he suffers so from his insomnia. Sometimes he just goes missing. We can all be talking about

94

something and he's sitting there with us but his mind is some-where else completely and it's somewhere that makes him unhappy. A look of suffering comes over his features, like a little boy who is hurting badly. I think Owen has moments of calm but never true contentment. I can't shake off the feeling that he may do something that will endanger us all.

Kimberly has picked up that I'm not completely trusting of them and it's awkward between her and me. She is so loyal to Owen and would see my uneasiness as a reproach. We've hardly said a word to each other today. The truth is I feel under a lot of pressure. Usually I would tell Rob how I'm feeling but this time I'm not. He was irritated when I tried to voice my fears before.

She closed her journal and looked over at Owen who was sitting in the cockpit steering the tiller. His handsome face was impassive.

Owen was thinking about his father Jim Adams. His father had joined the US Air Force when he was eighteen years old. He was proud to be a serviceman and believed a man should be self-reliant, discreet and know how to defend himself. So when Owen was eleven years old his dad had signed him up for a course of Karate lessons in Clearwater. Owen had enjoyed the classes and shown an aptitude for the martial art. When his dad was home on leave he would go with Owen to the classes and watch his progress, taking great pride in how well his son fought. After the class his dad would often take him for a burger and then they'd walk down and look at the boats in the marina. He'd rest an arm around Owen's shoul-ders as they discussed which boat they liked the best.

Anna stepped carefully across the deck, hanging onto the lines, to join Owen in the cockpit. Over the last week they had fallen into a rhythm where Owen and Rob did the sailing and Kim did the cooking. Anna did not have a role as such. She sometimes did the washing up, but she felt she should contribute more to life on the boat. She sat down next to him.

'Is there anything more I can do to help on the boat Owen? I feel I'm not pulling my weight.'

'It's not a problem.'

'I feel I should do more.'

'You can be Keeper of the Boat Journal,' he said nodding towards her notebook.

'I've had plenty to write about.'

'Do you write all the time?'

'No, not when I'm at work; too busy. But I always start a journal when we go away and this is turning into my most dramatic tale by far.'

'Glad we could oblige,' he grinned at her.

She smiled back at him. Kim had come up and was hanging a towel on a line to dry and she watched Anna talking to Owen. Anna had this habit of catching a hank of her long dark hair and twisting it round and round down its length and then curling the hair at the end around her fingers as if she was going to make a plait. But she never followed through. She would shake her twisted hair out and start at the top again. The gesture irritated Kim intensely for some reason, maybe because Anna only did it when she was talking to Owen. She had read in one of her magazines that it was a sign of attraction when a woman played with her hair while talking to a man. Here she was telling Owen she wanted to contribute more to life on the boat. And Owen had said there was no need for Anna to do anything more, just write your journal he had said. What he meant was be decorative and write your dumb journal. She was so out of sorts today, everything was making her pissed. She left them to it and went to find Rob in the saloon. He was making coffee.

'Do you want one?'

'Thanks.'

She sat down at the saloon table. He thought she looked tense, almost unhappy. He handed her a cup.

'You OK?'

She guessed her face was giving her away. She couldn't tell him that his girlfriend was getting on her nerves big time. She liked him too much to hurt his feelings in any way.

'It was horrible last night and it spooked me,' she said.

'It was scary. Modern-day pirates, eh?'

'There are some dangerous folks around these parts.'

'You ever had any real trouble?' he asked.

She looked thoughtful.

'We've had a few close shaves. When we first came out here we didn't know the score and we got ripped off a few times. And you have to be careful on Roatán. Everyone is connected one way or another. We've wised up over the years.'

'But you still like it out here?'

'Less than I used to if I'm honest.'

'Why is that? It's so beautiful here.'

'You get so you don't notice the beauty any more, you just notice the difficulties. And I think Owen and I want different things. He loves this life but I'd like more security. I'd like a proper home I could make pretty and comfortable for us both.'

'But I love life on your boat,' he said.

She smiled at his enthusiasm.

'Mr Positive you are. Now I'm trying to decide what to cook for us tonight.'

In the early evening a fisherman rowed close to their boat and Kim beckoned him over. He had a good catch of lobsters

97

and Kim bought seven small live ones from him. She was excited with her haul. Rob helped her carry the lobsters down into the galley and they put them in the sink where they writhed and crawled over each other with their claws opening and closing. It was difficult to stop them climbing out of the small sink.

'I should cook these straightaway,' Kim said. 'Can you give me a hand Rob?'

Anna had followed them down into the saloon and she saw Rob trying to keep the lobsters from escaping from the sink. Kim was filling her large stock pot with seawater.

'Seawater?' he said.

'Always use seawater to cook lobsters if you can,' Kim said.

Anna fled from the saloon. She didn't want to see the lobsters being boiled alive. She went into the cockpit and then, because she was still able to hear the noise and the hilarity of the cooking below, she removed herself further away and went and sat at the front of the boat.

Down below it was mayhem. Four of the lobsters were about a pound in weight and the other three were larger. With Rob's help Kim was able to get the three larger lobsters into the heating seawater. Rob held the lid down as the lobsters struggled to get out. Kim was standing guard over the four smaller ones in the sink and they were joking and laughing.

Kim let the big ones cook for eight minutes. She took the three cooked red lobsters out of the pot with a pair of large tongs. Rob placed each of the four smaller lobsters into the boiling seawater and held the lid down again.

'They'll need six minutes,' Kim said.

'We're in for a feast,' he said.

Up on deck Anna had opened her notebook again and started to write:

I can hear Rob and Kimberly shrieking with laughter below as they boil the live lobsters. It makes me feel uncomfortable. I know I'll eat the lobsters with the rest of them so I'm being a big hypocrite. Kimberly is quite clinical about it. She used to work in a restaurant and must have seen lobsters cooked many times I suppose. I can see that Rob admires her gutsy attitude to gutting fish and cooking lobsters. And they seem to be getting even more matey recently. Owen is staring out at the sea. He's said nothing for ages. There is something so contained and secret about him.

The sun was setting as they ate the lobsters with melted butter as the only accompaniment.

'This lobster flesh is so sweet,' Rob said.

Butter was dripping down his chin.

'I have to agree,' Anna said. 'This is one of the best things I've ever tasted.'

When the last piece of lobster flesh had been consumed and Kim had collected and thrown the shells over the side of the boat and Anna had washed out the big stock pot and the plates, they sailed the last stretch to the uninhabited Cay where they were going to moor for the night. Owen put the engine on to bring them in and he heard the engine stutter again. It choked, spluttered and died.

'Aw goddammit the engine's gone again,' he said to Rob.

He banged the side of the boat with his fist in frustration.

'I spent an age fixing it in Belize and now it's died, after only seven days. That storm would have churned up the gunk in the bottom and it's blocked the injectors again.'

'Can we manage without it?'

'We'll have to. We've done it before.'

He reached for his chart and showed Rob.

'Here's Roatán. With a good wind like today we could reach there by tomorrow evening.'

He shrugged.

'It's a challenge when you've got no engine to fall back on. We'll be reliant on the wind and the sails.'

They sailed the boat into position. It was a larger Cay than the night before and presented a long stretch of sand, abundant palm trees and the usual cluster of straggling mangroves.

'Still I guess sailors made do without engines for hundreds of years,' Owen said once they were safely anchored.

Later the moon climbed the sky and there was a track of silver light across the calm water.

'That is so beautiful,' Anna said.

'Let's have a swim, now,' Rob said.

'It's so late.'

'Oh come on, a swim by moonlight, let's do it.'

Owen and Kim were in the cockpit and he was rolling a joint. Kim said she wouldn't join them. Anna and Rob went to their cabin, got into their swimming things and dived into the water over the side of the boat.

'The water's still warm,' she said as she swam towards the track of moonlight that rippled in front of her. They kept close to each other as they moved through the water. Then they flipped onto their backs and floated in the sea and looked up at the sky which was a black meadow picked out with stars.

In the cockpit Kim sat opposite Owen. He handed her the joint and she didn't look at him. They had hardly spoken all day. She took a deep draw from the joint.

'So what gives when we get to Roatán? Do we say goodbye to them there?' she said.

'I guess we let them live on the boat until they fly back, don't you think?'

'Why do you say that?'

'We took their holiday money didn't we? Do you have a problem with that?'

She handed the joint back to him and their eyes met.

'Would it matter if I did?'

'They're good people.'

'Rob is and I like him. He makes an effort to help out. Anna less so.'

'Kimmie,' he reached for her hand. 'Don't be cross...'

'We coulda lost the boat last night.'

'We coulda, but we didn't. It was a scare that's all.'

'I'm tired of living on the edge, Owen. I'm all worn out with it.'

'You had a bad night. You'll feel better tomorrow.'

She threw the joint stub over the side of the boat.

'I'm turning in.'

She went down into the saloon. Owen stayed in the cockpit. She must have been more shaken by the incident of the night before than he'd realised. Usually she bounced back more quickly. Anna seemed to be copping it as a result. And he knew that once Kim started to dislike someone then it followed that everything they did started to annoy her. He looked over to where Anna and Rob were floating in the sea. They looked happy he thought.

They swam back and he helped them aboard. He put the washboard down.

'Kim's turned in already. Last night took it out of her. There's a towel under the seat if you guys need one.'

Rob reached under the seat and pulled out a threadbare towel. He handed it to Anna.

'Don't you need it?' she said.

He shook the water from his hair the way a dog does who's been in the sea.

'No need, it's such a lovely warm evening.'

Anna dried her face and wound the towel around her long hair.

'It's beautiful and so calm. I would love sailing if it was always like this,' she said.

Owen started to roll another joint. He licked the Rizla paper along its sticky edge and rolled it neatly into place. His joints always looked remarkably professional Anna thought watching his long fingers at work. He lit it and passed it to Anna.

'Give it a try. Perfect night to get gently stoned and look at the stars,' he said.

She took the joint from him and this time she took in a breath and let the smoke travel down to her lungs.

'And lo the lady hath inhaled,' Rob said.

She raised her eyebrows at him and with a defiant toss of her towelled head she took another draw. This time she could feel something. This must be strong dope; it was making her feel woozy. Usually she felt nothing which was why she'd always thought it was all a big fuss about nothing. Owen watched her blow the smoke out through her lips. With her hair knotted up in the towel the mole between her eyebrows became more prominent, almost as if she had a mono-brow like Frieda Kahlo and it made her look kind of exotic. She was still in her bikini and seawater was trickling between her breasts. The moonlight caught the outline of her collarbones. She handed the joint to Rob with a giggle.

'I'm definitely feeling something.'

She was the one who got them started on the subject of *The Wizard of Oz*. They had all seen it of course, and it was part of their shared mythology. Anna seemed to have watched it many times.

'I want you to say which character you like best and why: Tin Man, Scarecrow or Cowardly Lion.'

'You go first,' Rob said.

'Well I should probably identify with Cowardly Lion because I'm a great big coward myself,' she said.

'A Great Girl's Blouse,' Owen intoned solemnly and they all laughed for an age at this quip. Rob liked Anna being more relaxed like this. The others had only seen the uptight Anna up till now.

'What was I saying? Oh yes. Well, I'd have to give my vote to Scarecrow.'

'Why?' Rob asked.

'He's such a great character. He thinks he's dumb and needs a brain but he's the smartest one of them all.'

'They're all lacking something, aren't they,' Rob said. 'Yes, your turn now, Owen' she said.

'Tin Man wants a heart right?' Owen said.

'Yes, even though he's the soppiest of the lot of them.'

'I like him,' Owen said.

'So why do you like him?'

'Because he knows something is missing and he needs it to be complete so he goes looking for it.'

'Yes and when he does get a heart he starts to cry and then he's worried that his tears will make him rust up. Rob's turn,' she said.

'Can I choose Toto? I like him the best,' Rob said.

'Shall we allow that?' she leaned in towards Owen conspiratorially.

'I think we can bend the rules on this one occasion. What kinda dog is he anyway?' Owen said.

'I think he's a terrier isn't he, clever little dogs,' Rob said.

And their conversation meandered on to dogs and what breed they would choose. Rob said he loved Fox Terriers. They had such boxy faces and were intelligent. Owen said he liked bigger dogs, a dog that you could pat on the head as it walked along by your side. A Collie or a Labrador is what he would choose. Anna said no it had to be a Spaniel. They had such beautiful silky ears and the sweetest temperament even if they occasionally acted loony.

'You know I always wanted a dog since I was a kid but I never had one yet,' Owen said.

Kim was lying below in the saloon and she was wide awake. She had heard Owen slide the washboard into place to keep the sound out but she could hear them anyway. They sounded like they were having a good time. Anna was laughing along with the men. It was too late to join them and anyway she was in no mood for it. She wished they'd shut the fuck up.

DAY EIGHT

Shortly after sunrise, the *El Tiempo Pasa* started to roll and the motion woke Rob. He dressed and joined Owen up on deck. The sea was getting rougher and Owen pointed to clouds building in the east.

'The barometer's dropping and it looks like we're in for a blow. Just a short summer storm I reckon but let's get a move on.'

The two men hauled the sails up and sailed towards the anchor and pulled it up. Kim was stirring below, putting water on to make coffee. Anna was in the forecabin and she rolled onto her stomach and pulled open the curtain covering their porthole. She saw a square of darkening grey sky and rolled onto her back again.

They were sailing away from the Cay when they were hit by a sudden vicious squall. There was a ripping sound and Owen swung round. The mainsail had caught the full force of the gust and to his horror he saw that some stitches had given way and the sail had started to rip along one of its longer seams down near the boom.

'Goddammit!' he shouted.

They could do nothing and had to stand and watch while the next gust of wind caught the tear and ripped at the rotting sail stiches until the mainsail was gashed open from side to side at its widest point. The torn sail flapped madly in the wind. Kim had hurried up from the saloon. She'd recognised that sickening staccato sound; their sails had ripped before.

'We'll have to sail back to the Cay,' Owen shouted above the noise of the wind and the flapping sail.

It was hard work sailing back to their anchorage of the night before with the ripped sail giving no drive to the boat. The wind lashed the boat and they struggled to stay on course with only the foresail intact. Owen, Kim and Rob worked in unison and after forty minutes they reached the Cay. They dropped anchor and it took the combined effort of the three of them to take down the damaged mainsail. Finally the boat was anchored and the immediate crisis was over. Anna had got dressed down below. She had heard the sound of the sail ripping and Owen's despairing shout. She wondered if she should go up, but knew that she would probably only get in the way. She put the kettle on and got the mugs and the coffee out. She joined them on deck now and saw their serious faces. Owen looked the most upset.

'I'm making some coffee,' Anna said.

The dark storm clouds were directly overhead and large rain drops started to fall so they went into the saloon and sat around the table. They sipped the hot coffee.

'I've got the kit to mend the sail. I've done it before. It's gonna be a big job. It's a big bugger of a sail and the whole damn seam has gone,' Owen said.

'How long will it take?' Anna asked.

'A day and a half I reckon. I'm gonna reinforce all the seams. I don't want this happening again. We'll moor here while I work. It's a good enough mooring.'

'We've got plenty of water and cans and rice,' Kim said.

'This bad patch of weather should pass soon,' Owen said.

'Let's have pineapple for breakfast,' Kim stood up. 'There's one rather over ripe pineapple left.'

They were trying so hard to be cheerful in the face of yet another disaster.

'I'm sure it will be fine,' Anna said.

'Course it will,' Rob said. 'We have food and rum and Kim's magic pot.'

Rob actually liked the thought of being stranded on the unpopulated Cay. It would give them time to explore it. And he was relieved that Anna seemed to be taking it well. Owen was right about the storm; the rain lashed down and the boat pitched for about forty minutes while they ate slices of sweet ripe pineapple. Then the storm moved on and the sea settled.

Owen wanted to spread the sail out on land as it would be easier to mend it that way. He and Rob undid the clips and detached the main sail from the mast and the boom.

'Could do with some help now,' Owen called out.

Anna joined them on deck. They folded the sail and put it into its bag so they could transport it. They got into the dinghy and Rob rowed them the short distance to the Cay. They spread out the ripped sail on a clear stretch of beach. It was a big bugger as Owen had said, and heavy to carry. A weak sun had started to filter through the clouds. Anna and Rob stood and watched as Owen took out a sailmaker's palm which he pulled onto his right hand and secured. He selected one of the thick sail needles and took out the white waxed thread and a pot of beeswax. He sat down with his back to a palm tree and waxed the needle. Then he started to stitch the seam with his strong needle, using the existing holes. Anna and Rob watched him working for a while and then wandered away.

As he worked Owen thought about how often he had done this. Every inch of the *El Tiempo Pasa* had seen his loving care at some point over the last three years. He saw the boat as his life companion that needed his unique love and attention. He hated the thought of having to sell her to a stranger. What worried him most though was the delay this latest problem was gonna cause. They should have reached Roatán by now. Raul and Money Joe would be questioning why Owen hadn't showed up with the package. They might think he'd done a runner. He'd have to call Money Joe as soon as they reached Roatán, let him know he had the goods, let him know he hadn't reneged on the deal.

Kim stayed on the boat. She wanted to assess the food situation properly and work out what could be eaten each day. She took everything out of the food locker and the cold store and put them on the saloon table. This was fine, they wouldn't starve. When a problem like the ripped sail happened she and Owen would slip into a default position of making the best of it. They had their familiar roles and it was moments like this when she felt a strong sense of purpose and unity with Owen.

Rob and Anna explored the Cay. It was about a mile in length and it had a sandy beach and the clearest water. Mature palm trees bordered the shoreline.

'It's our very own paradise island,' he said.

'You and your Robinson Crusoe fantasy.'

It was a perfect spot, the sort of place you see in holiday brochures and never quite believe that the sand can be that white or the sea that turquoise. Even the palm tree leaves were a glossy brilliant green. It was getting hotter. The sun had burned through the clouds and was now high in the sky. They both stripped off to their swimming things and swam in the warm shallows.

When they came out of the sea they noticed that there were a lot of dead palm fronds that were lying crisp and dry on the sun-baked sand. Rob kneeled down and examined one.

'You know I think I could make us a windbreak out of these,' he said. 'Back where Owen is working.'

Anna helped him drag some of the large dead fronds back. Owen looked up when they arrived.

'I need a break from this. What are you gonna do with those?'

'I want to build a shelter between two of the trees. Maybe these two?'

For the next hour Anna handed the dead palm fronds over to Rob and Owen who wove them into a passable roof between two of the shorter palm trees. They stood back and surveyed their work.

'I need to get back to the sail. But if you and Anna want to go snorkelling I've got a mask and fins on the boat,' he said.

'Yes maybe I'll do that. Thanks Owen.'

Owen went back to his sewing and Rob continued to weave and improve the roof of his shelter. Anna went to see how Owen was getting on. He showed her how far he had got.

'Your stitches are so neat.'

'It comes with practice and I've had a lot of that.'

She left him to walk up the beach to look for driftwood, on Rob's instructions. He told her he wanted to build a fire on the beach that they could light that evening.

'I'm glad you created this shade,' Anna said when she arrived back with her arms full of driftwood. 'It's so hot and I'm getting quite burnt.'

She pulled down the top of her bikini pants and showed Rob her tan line.

'Nice,' he said.

She stretched out on the ground and closed her eyes and drifted off to sleep. Rob's next task was to stack the wood that Anna had collected. He built a small neat bonfire, a pyramid of twigs and branches, ready to light that evening. He was in his element. With these tasks completed, he swam back to the boat and got Owen's fins and mask and had a long lingering swim along the shoreline.

Later, Kim joined Anna under Rob's roof and they sat opposite each other each with their backs against the trees.

'It's good to have this shade,' Kim said.

'It is. When we were travelling down on the coach from Mexico there was this woman with her three little girls and a new-born baby. She'd draped this white cloth from her shoulders to her knees so that the baby was lying in a clean white tent on her lap. Her three little girls were so excited and they kept getting up from their seats to take a peek at the baby. She would lift the cloth for them to look in and it was so sweet to watch. And I wondered whether the new baby was a boy or a girl. She already had three daughters and she probably wanted a son.'

Kim nodded.

'You see such large families out here and so much poverty,' she said.

'Yes.'

Anna stretched her arms above her head.

'I want to have children,' she said. 'And so does Rob, one day.'

Kim said nothing.

'Do you want children?'

'No, definitely not...'

'Really?'

'Owen and I are agreed on that.'

'Why is that?'

Rob had told her not to inquire too closely about intimate things, but she wanted to know because Kimberly had been so emphatic in her response.

'We feel the same way about it. Too many kids have miserable lives. We just wanna be responsible for ourselves and our own happiness.'

Kim got to her feet.

'I'm gonna go check on Owen,' she said.

She went over to Owen who was bent over the sail and she kissed him on the top of his head. Then she headed down to the edge of the sea and a great wave of sadness washed over her. She remembered a close friend asking her if she ever regretted committing to Owen. It hadn't made for an easy life had it, her friend had said. Kim had replied that her relationship with Owen was not like other folks'. They were completely for each other. She had loved and admired him since childhood and she felt that her purpose in life was to look after him. Yes, she had given up a lot to be with him. Their coming together had caused much conflict in her family and Jared's deep estrangement from Owen. Her parents were also anxious about Kim being with him. It was her deep intuitive feeling that she and Owen should never have children. Her hands were full enough looking after him and she accepted it. Now she was thirty-one though, she found herself thinking about this life choice more often than she used to. Her thoughts turned to Anna. She didn't really get Anna and she envied her calm assertion that she would have a family with Rob one day. How could she know that? How could she feel so secure? Did Anna know how lucky she was to be with such a relaxed kind man as Rob? In every relationship Kim believed there was one person who was the adorer and one who was the adored. She was the adorer and Owen the adored. And Rob was the adorer and Anna the adored. She felt that Anna took his devotion for granted. And a bite of doubt she hadn't felt before started to gnaw at her. Did Owen take her devotion for granted too?

That evening they ate their main meal in the cockpit of the boat. They hadn't eaten much all day and Kim had made them spicy vegetable chilli with beans and rice. She went down into the saloon to get the rum and limes for their usual evening drinks and Rob suggested they go back to their base on the Cay. They could have their rums there he said, and he would light the fire he had built that afternoon. They rowed back in the dinghy and sat under Rob's shelter. The evening was mild but he felt a fire would complete the day somehow. He held a match to the twigs at the base and the flames crackled into life. They sat around watching the flames consuming the dry wood and enjoying the attendant sounds and smells while they shared in the ritual of their evening rums.

'I do like your roof,' Kim said looking up at Rob's handiwork.

'I may extend it tomorrow. And I want to go fishing too. You've got a fishing rod haven't you, Owen?'

'A very basic one and a rather meagre tackle box. Are you into fishing?'

'I used to be. When I was in my teens I'd go to Southend with a mate and we'd fish off the pier there. We'd catch mackerel. Then we'd make a fire on the shingle and eat them, lovely fish, mackerel.'

Owen passed the rum bottle to Anna.

'Thanks.'

She poured more into her glass and handed the bottle back to him. Owen wore his hair quite long, not shoulder length but beneath his jaw line and he had pushed his hair behind his ears. This emphasised the leanness of his face and she watched how the flames of the fire lit up his cheekbones. He was staring into the fire as if lost in thought.

'How's the sail stitching going?' she said.

'It's going fine but it's slow work. I'm gonna try to get it finished tomorrow. We need to get to Roatán.'

'Does it hurt your fingers?'

He looked at his hands, stretched out his long fingers.

'It can get crampy when you've been doing it a while. I like the work though.'

He had always found the task of sewing a sail to be calming. He liked to retreat from people into a world of objects. Physical objects had a reassuring solidity and predictability about them that attracted him. He liked thinking about the shape and design of boats, about the different types of rope you could use, about the intricacies of a sail.

DAY NINE

It was their second day stranded on the Cay. When Anna woke up next to Rob in the cabin she noticed how he had sweat salt deposits under his eyebrows and she leaned over him and licked these off. He laughed in delight and kissed the mole between her eyebrows.

'Oh well, I guess we're going to have to get through another day in paradise,' he said with a theatrical sigh and she laughed.

Anna, Rob and Kim put on their swimming things and dived into the sea while the sun was rising above the horizon. Owen watched them splashing at each other and laughing. He was planning to work on the sail straightaway because he was feeling the pressure of Money Joe's package weighing him down. At the last moment he decided to join them in the water. He dived into the sea in his shorts and T-shirt and swam out strongly, leaving them behind. They were light-hearted, playing chasing games until the three of them tired and let the waves wash them onto the shore. They lay on the wet beach looking up at the bright sky and planning their day. Kim was going to sort through all the papers, books, bills and maps on the boat once and for all. She always did like to de-clutter she said. Anna was planning on snorkelling and collecting more firewood. Rob was going fishing.

Owen loved being in the sea. He was a strong swimmer and could swim for hours. He swam along the shoreline of the Cay getting a sense of its size and geography. It had been a good place to moor the boat. The Cay had a sandy beach except at the far end where a rocky outcrop extended from the land. He swam to these rocks, climbed up and made his way along them. The ocean surged in and out of the black rocks and looking down he saw brilliant translucent plants clinging to the sides of the boulders. He lay on his stomach and watched the tender green filigree plants moving with the rhythm of the waves. It was a calming sight and he lay there for a while. Then he scrambled to the farthest rock and sat and watched the sun moving up the sky. After a while, rather reluctantly, he dived back into the sea and swam back to his post by the palm tree. He waded out, shook himself and sat down, letting his wet clothes dry on his body as he took up his sewing needle.

It was even hotter than the day before and Anna and Kim stayed in their bikinis all day. Kim was already tanned and Anna's tan was deepening. Rob had stripped to his waist but Owen kept his T-shirt on. They had both given up on shaving and were sporting a two-day shadow. A sexy, relaxed atmosphere was growing between the four of them. Sitting cross legged under Rob's shelter they had a lunch of crackers and sardines followed by dates. By early afternoon Owen had completed his repair job on the mainsail. He had also reinforced every one of its seams against future rips. He put his needle and thread away with a feeling of satisfaction at a good job completed. He asked the others to help him roll and bag the sail and they rowed it back to the *El Tiempo Pasa*. It took them a while to re-attach the sail to the mast and boom. Then they stood back and looked at his handiwork.

'You did a fine job there,' Rob said.

'Thanks. And now,' Owen said 'I'm going on a long swim to celebrate. See you later.'

It was two hours later when Owen came walking out of the sea in his T-shirt and shorts carrying his fins and mask.

'Why does Owen always keep his T-shirt on? Even when he's swimming? Anna asked.

'Don't know, maybe to stop the sunburn?' Rob said.

'He's never stripped off once.'

Rob laughed and kissed her bare shoulder.

'You want to see his naked chest, don't you?'

She laughed back.

'No. It's kind of strange though isn't it?'

'Well I want to see your naked chest right now,' he said.

They both had the same thing on their minds. They walked until they were out of sight of Owen and Kim, shielded by some palm trees and a dune. They hadn't been able to have sex for nine days, constrained as they were by the proximity of their cabin to the others. They lay down by the edge of the sea and Rob kissed the mole between Anna's eyebrows, which was often the prelude to their having sex. He pulled her bikini bottoms off and threw them back up the beach. She took his trunks off and he had a big erection already. They made love half in and half out of the water. He lay on top of her and licked her breasts and her stomach saying she was lovely and salty. For Anna it was a kind of sensory overload, his warm sweaty body on top of hers, the feel of the sand under her body, warm and dry on her shoulders and back and cool and wet on her bottom as the small waves came rolling in. He got up on his knees to get inside her and she felt pleasurable intermittent shocks as the seawater touched her skin, the waves with their own rhythm alongside the rhythm of Rob's thrusting. As she reached a brilliant orgasm she could feel sea water tickling her bottom again. It was intense. And then Rob came and as well as his sperm she felt some sand get inside her, but it was good. It was the best sex they'd had for ages.

'Let's sleep under my shelter tonight, just you and me. It will be perfect,' Rob said.

Later a sleepy happy Anna lay on her stomach under the shelter and wrote in her notebook:

Rob has gone out fishing in the dinghy. I like it that he's trying to supply us with extra food. It makes me smile because I think foraging for food and building shelters and making fires are like a throwback to our primitive selves and this situation is bringing out the natural in all of us, in a good way.

She rolled onto her back and fell asleep.

As Rob rowed away from the shore in the dinghy he realised that this was the happiest he had felt for years. It had been such a good idea to get away with Anna for four weeks. He had chosen this particular time so that he could miss the wedding of his mum to that arsehole Elliot. His daft half-sister Savannah, who he loved dearly, had got it into her head that her parents should get properly married, even though they had been living together for twenty-five years. Savannah had so much money these days. She could get thousands for a single show or a shoot. She wanted to organise and pay for her parents' wedding herself. It was going to be at The House of St Barnabas in Soho, all very fashionable and media friendly. Rob had got wind of her plans and of the proposed date for the wedding. He booked the tickets for their flight to Mexico so that they would be away. He didn't tell Anna that this was why he had chosen these specific dates in June. She would probably have said that they should go to the wedding to support Savannah. But no way was he going to be there to witness Elliot marrying his mum. This way he was able to miss the wedding and give their regrets without causing a deeper family rift.

He rowed along the line of the shore till he spotted the outcrop of rocks which Owen had mentioned. He said he'd seen some movement of fish in the water at the base of the rocks. He rowed close and got himself into a sheltered position. Then he flicked open the lid on Owen's tackle box and peered inside. There wasn't a lot to choose from: some weights, some feathers, some old hooks, some steel line and a few battered lures. There was an old rapala lure striped in red and white. That might do in a while, but first he wanted to catch some smaller fish that he could use as live bait. Owen's fishing rod was about eight foot long. He rigged it up and sat and looked intently over the side of the boat down into the water around the rocks. He cast the rod. He was a bit rusty as it had been years since he fished. And yet the rod felt comfortable in his hand and his casting had been OK. He jigged the line up and down every now and then and watched and waited.

Within the next hour he had caught three small fish, only a few inches long. They would make good bait. He was sure there were bigger fish down there in the deeper water, lurking in the vegetation. He took the feathers off the line and put a new hook in place and speared one of the fish he had caught onto this. He cast the line and this time it worked. He felt the pull on the line after a few minutes. It was quite a tug. This was a bigger fish all right. And all his fishing instincts came back to him. He remembered how long to wait and when he should reel in the fish. His heart was beating so fast as he landed it. It was a good fish, maybe four pounds in weight. He took the hook out of its mouth and it flapped on the floor of the dinghy. Was it a snapper? He didn't care. It would be good to eat and he was euphoric.

Anna had fallen asleep on her back under the palm roof. She woke up feeling thirsty and looked out of the shelter to see Owen sitting with his back against the palm tree looking out to sea. She got to her feet and stretched and he looked over at her and said grinning:

'You were snoring.'

'Oh God... I always snore when I'm on my back. That's why my mouth is so dry. I need some water.'

'I've got some here.'

She sat down by his side and he handed her the bottle and she swigged at the warm water.

'That's better, thanks.'

She wiped her mouth with the back of her hand and handed the bottle to him. He took a swig.

'No sign of Rob, I suppose?'

'Fishing takes time,' he said.

Kim had had a good clear out and the boat was tidy and the glass on the lockers polished, just as she liked it. She often felt frustrated by how little she could do to make the boat look nice. She longed to use her home-making skills on a house. She dived into the sea and swam to the shore. She was going to walk the length of the Cay. They would never be here again and she wanted to hold it in her memory. The last two days had been better between her and Owen. Anna was being less uptight too and Rob was in his element. He was such a positive man, always trying to help out where he could. Somehow, though, she had to convince Owen that this was their last charter trip. She couldn't take living this way much longer because they were not masters of their own destiny. They kept being thrown off course by the failed engine, the ripped sail and their persistent lack of money. For her it had stopped feeling like an adventure some time ago, but how to persuade Owen?

He often said to her that people needed so little to be happy: a place of shelter, enough to eat and a passion: be it sailing or cooking or fishing or whatever. And a loving relationship she would add. Yeah of course, he would say, that was fundamental, but the American way of needing so much, of needing cars and swimming pools and technological toys was bullshit. It was an endless greedy pursuit that could never be satisfied and that left the pursuer feeling empty. She bought into his world view up to a point although she knew she wanted more things than he did. She saw some coconuts lying on the beach and shook several of them, holding them to her ear, and selected two.

Anna was telling Owen about her job. She had to teach her clients how to do vocal exercises and sometimes her old men felt foolish doing these.

'It's very important I get them to trust me and open up to me. That can be the most difficult bit. I'm working with this old man at the moment and we weren't making any progress. The turning point was after Christmas. He was trying to tell me something and had tears in his eyes and I thought it was because he couldn't find the right words. So we took our time and slowly I understood. He was saying: "Why would you buy a person a bad gift?" He was upset because his sister had given him a cheap and nasty gift. Why had she done that? Was it her way of rebuking him? Why had she given him anything at all? I said: "You're saying it's better not to give anything than to give something bought with such little love." He said yes, that was it exactly. He was so glad I'd understood him. It sounds trivial Owen, but it wasn't. He was talking about his feelings. Since then he's started to make good progress.'

'You like your old men, don't you?' he said.

'I do. I was always very close to my granddad, loved him to bits. I lived with him and my granny when I was little you see.'

'Why was that?'

'Mum and Dad were in an orchestra and had to travel all over the country. That's how they met, in an orchestra. So they left me with Granny and Granddad, in Norfolk. And then he died four years ago. It was dreadful, dreadful. He was the first person really close to me who died. May I?'

She reached for his water bottle and took another swig.

'He was a special man you see, a truly kind man. He worked most of his life as an ambulance driver. He was with people when they were struck down, and he said that even the most powerful man on earth was vulnerable when illness came. He liked that he could do something for people at that moment, when they needed it most.'

'He sounds like a good granddad to have,' he said.

'Oh he was.'

Her eyes filled with tears.

'Sorry,' she sniffed and flicked them away.

'And you didn't mind being left there, when you were so little?'

'Oh no, I loved it there. They had this small cottage with a large garden that seemed to go on forever. Granddad was mad on Sweet Peas. Do you know the flower? He grew them for competitions, in his greenhouse. I loved going in there; the smell was wonderful. And I *hated* it when I had to go and live with Mum and Dad. I much preferred being at the cottage.'

'When was that?'

She had started to twist a hank of her long dark hair.

'I was coming up to eight and my dad got this job in Canterbury. And my twin brothers came along a year later. Maybe I felt displaced by the boys, I don't know, but I was always asking to go back to Granddad's.'

She shook out the twist in her hair, running her fingers through it.

'I've often wondered if mum got pregnant with me by mistake. I know they loved their life in the orchestra. They loved the freedom of being on the road. When they talk about it they get all lit up. A small child is a hindrance to that kind of life.'

'So you're not a daddy's girl then?' he said.

'Oh no, I was a granddaddy's girl.'

They smiled at each other and he shared the last of the water with her.

'You know I used to do Karate lessons. My dad was so keen for me to learn how to defend myself and I was starting to win competitions in Clearwater. One Fall weekend there was a city-wide contest. It was a big deal. My dad was home on leave and he took me to the sports hall where the competition was being held.'

Anna nodded. She felt gratified that Owen was telling her about his father. Maybe it was because she had opened up to him.

'So we're heading to the hall when a car drives by and as it passes us it backfires so loudly. My dad flung himself flat on the ground and pressed his face into the sidewalk. He was trembling and whimpering and wouldn't move and I didn't know what to do.'

Anna nodded sympathetically.

'How awful,' she said.

'I was ashamed of him, my strong brave dad lying on the sidewalk and whimpering like a girl. We never made it to the competition that day.'

'Is your dad in the forces?'

'Why do you ask?'

'It's just that his reaction; well it sounds like Post-Traumatic Stress Disorder to me.'

Owen's face closed down.

'I don't know why I told you that Anna. I'm sorry but I don't like talking about it.'

She wanted to continue the conversation but she didn't push it. She knew it took time for people to open up. They saw Kim walking back towards them carrying some coconuts in her arms.

As Kim approached she noticed how Anna was sitting next to Owen, a bit too close she thought. She was talking animatedly to him and twisting her hair in that annoying way she had as she leaned in towards him. She had never once talked to her like that. Kim reached them and sat down on the other side of Owen. Whatever they had been talking about so intently had ended with her arrival. She put the two coconuts down on the sand with a thud.

'Nice walk?' Anna said.

'Yeah. There's a whole pile of these good to eat on the other side if we want more. I think two is enough. You can overdose on coconuts.'

And then they all saw Rob rowing back along the shore-line and he was waving excitedly at them and giving them a thumbs-up.

'He must have caught something,' Anna said.

They stood at the water's edge while he rowed over to

them. His face said it all. They helped him pull the dinghy ashore and in the bottom were two good looking fish.

'Awesome, they're red snapper. Gorgeous fish... we'll have such a feast tonight,' Kim said.

She was actually clapping her hands in her glee.

Anna laughed delightedly and looked at Rob with pride. He was beaming.

'Well done buddy,' Owen said.

An hour later Rob was sitting in the saloon and watching Kim cook his two fish.

'These are real beauties,' she said.

She cooked them whole in a little oil with a generous squeeze of lime juice. The galley filled with a wonderful smell. As she cooked she told him how much she wanted her own café, how the idea kept tugging at her and would not let her go.

'You can make it happen,' he said.

'You think so?'

'Yes, you're a brilliant cook.'

'Thanks. I could do the cooking all right, but it's the set-up costs and that kinda thing that concerns me.'

'Well if I could start a business with my two mates.'

'Your brewery?'

'Micro-brewery. We had very little business know-how when we set up. We got some help from my mate's dad who knew about cash-flow and stuff. But you know the most important thing was the wanting to do it and then sticking at it. Now we're making a small profit. If you really want to do it Kim I know you will.'

'Hey I could stock your beers,' she said.

'You could. That could be one of your special offers: bespoke British beers for the discerning palate.'

They giggled.

'I think I could do it. If there's something I wanna do I work hard at it. I guess what worries me is how Owen will adjust.'

'Would he be working in the café with you?'

'Jeez no, that would never work. He'll go back to working in a boatyard.'

'So what's the problem?'

'He's very into this way of life, picking up work when and where we can. He'd go on doing it for ever I think, if he could.'

'And you don't want that?'

'No I don't. Feels like it's time to go home.'

'Tell him that then Kim.'

'And there's another problem.'

'What?'

'He'd have to sell his boat so I can have my café.'

She used a spatula to take the cooked fish out and placed them side by side on a large plate. She placed a few thin slices of lime on the top. She wanted the others to see Rob's catch in all its glory.

'Food's up,' she shouted.

They sat in the cockpit and ate Rob's two fish until only the spine and the heads were left on the plate.

Anna and Rob were lying curled up together under his palm frond roof. They had brought the quilt from their cabin to lie on. Earlier they had lain flat on the sand and had watched the inverted bowl of the sky. They had never seen the sky like that, with no human light to diminish its majesty.

'The stars look like they're floating,' Anna said.

'We'll never forget this moment, will we? It will be one of

those moments that comes back to you on your deathbed,' Rob said.

'Shhh... death seems a long way away,' she said.

DAY TEN

It was just after sunrise when Owen and Rob hauled the sails up and watched them fill with the breeze. Anna and Kim came up on deck to say goodbye to the Cay that had been their home for the last two days. They were all deeply tanned, the men were unshaven and the mood between them was relaxed but tinged with regret to be leaving their paradise Cay.

'Today's the day we get to Roatán,' Owen said.

The weather was good with a fine breeze that helped them along. They had a full day's sailing ahead of them and sped through the sea without incident. Anna and Kim lay on the deck in their bikinis as the men worked the sails.

By early evening they were approaching the island of Roatán. At some point during the last ten days they had all wondered if they would ever reach their destination. It felt as if they had been tested and had known each other for a long time, longer than the actual time since their coming together on the boat. They sailed along the south side of the island. Anna had her notebook out and was jotting down her first impressions. It was a long thin island, forty miles in length and two miles wide. It was fertile, with lush green hillsides and abundant palms framing the shoreline. It was well popu-lated too. They saw white villas built into the hillside with terraced gardens. Along the shore were smaller traditional wooden houses, some built on stilts which were reached by duckboard jetties. They passed a number of small harbours with sailboats and yachts moored for the night. There were working boats too: fishermen's boats and tugs and small ferries that plied between the towns.

Owen was heading for a small pontoon near the town of French Harbour, which was about mid-way along the island on the south side. He was friends with the owner of a pontoon there, Brad, and he planned to moor there for the next few days.

'I'm so glad to be here at last. Shall we go to Vivienne's Bar tonight to celebrate?' Kim said.

She told them their friend Vivienne had a popular bar near where they were going to moor.

'She started with a small bar on the beach, not much more than a shack. She's worked so hard and now she's got this big bar and guest house and it's the place to go to in French Harbour.'

'She's Kim's hero,' Owen said.

'She is and you know why? She's done it all through her own efforts. She never had any help or any hand outs. Yeah, you've gotta meet Vivienne.'

They reached the pontoon and Owen and Rob had to sail the boat into the empty space without the aid of an engine. It took them a few attempts before they managed to drop the sails at exactly the right moment and drift up to the pontoon.

'We did it,' Owen said to Rob. 'It's not easy without an engine. You've become a fine sailor.'

Owen jumped off the boat and secured the mooring lines.

'I need to find Brad and tell him we're tied up here.'

He headed towards the harbour where he knew there were a number of cafés and bars. He entered one and paid to use the phone there. The phone was in a public space, right at the end of the bar. There were drinkers standing close by so he would need to be cryptic. He dialled Money Joe's cell phone number and after a few rings he heard his rasping voice.

'*Hola?*'

'Joe, it's Owen.'

'Where are you?'

'We just got into Roatán.'

'Raul and I were getting worried at how long you were taking. We thought you might be lost at sea.'

He laughed nastily.

Owen felt his face and his voice hardening.

'We hit a storm. I've got a gift for you and can bring it to your house tomorrow.'

'I'm in San Pedro Sula comrade. Bring it round in four days' time.'

'OK. See you then.'

Owen hung up and ordered himself a double whisky. He downed this quickly, thinking about those few words with Money Joe. The guy gave him the creeps. If Kim knew he was dealing with that lowlife as she called him she'd be furious. He had promised her he would stay away from him and his crowd. He didn't like dealing with him either, but needs must and his cut on the deal would keep them afloat for a while longer.

When he got back to the boat they had all decided it was too late to go out and they would bed down early. They spent a calm first night on Roatán being gently rocked by the *El Tiempo Pasa*.

DAY ELEVEN

They were in the cockpit drinking coffee and feeling light-hearted to have reached Roatán at last. They watched the chatter and activity in the other sailing boats moored along the pontoon. Several people walked by and shouted greetings to Owen and Kim who waved back. Rob recognised the feeling of community among these boat owners, much like how things had been in the commune when he was a boy. He could see the appeal of this life, could understand why Owen was reluctant to give it up.

'Is there a launderette here? I'm running out of clean T-shirts,' Anna said.

'And knickers,' Rob added loudly.

Owen laughed out loud:

'I love that word "knickers". It's so very English – "knickers".'

'There *is* a launderette in town, if you can face it,' Kim said.

'I know what you mean. I hate launderettes. Have you noticed how they make your clothes smell of potato?' Anna said.

Owen stood up.

'No laundry today. We're gonna have a day on Roatán's finest beach. But first I need to register the boat with the harbour master. Give me an hour.'

The men were swimming and Kim and Anna were lying

next to each other on a powder white beach in brilliant sunshine. They had helped each other apply sun cream and now lay in companionable silence as Anna read her way through *Bleak House* and Kim studied a glossy interiors magazine she had bought. It had photo features on the houses of the rich and famous. She turned the pages slowly taking in every detail.

'Oh this one is awesome. That's how I'd do my place if I had loads of money.'

She showed Anna the photos of a film star's beachfront hacienda. The designer had used natural materials, wood and stone and even driftwood, to create the floors and staircases. There were designer chairs and tables that looked roughly hewn but had probably cost a king's ransom. The window shutters were painted a Mediterranean blue.

'I love that shade of blue,' Kim said pointing at the shutters.

'It is beautiful, very beautiful, but I'd feel like I was living in a film set,' Anna said.

'I'd be quite happy to live in a film set. Just think – nothing chipped and nothing stained ever again,' Kim said.

'That would make a change,' Anna said.

'Do you and Rob live together?'

'Sort of, in a flat in North London, and believe me it looks nothing like that photo-spread.'

The men joined them and they picnicked on the beach on a large bag of shrimps and a fresh loaf they had bought on the way. They tore into the bread and shrimps. Then Kim took out her knife and sliced a large watermelon handing them pieces of the juicy red fruit.

'You need a brilliant sun to enjoy this by. Doesn't taste the same under a grey English sky,' Rob said.

The couples separated each to their own palm tree. Owen sat against a tree and Kim sat between his legs. He played with her hair and stroked her earlobes. Rob and Anna curled up close on the ground under their tree and dozed in the afternoon heat.

'Happy?' he asked.

'Yes, very.'

'I told you it would work out. It was worth the long sail,' he said.

It was a luminous evening. Owen and Anna were standing on the pontoon and he was showing her how to coil a rope. He swung the rope with immense grace, twisting it slightly on each revolution so it fell into perfect symmetrical hoops.

'You make it look so easy,' she said.

'You have a go now.'

The rope was heavier then she expected and her attempt was pitiful.

'Hopeless,' she said.

He showed her how to do it again. He was a tall man and sometimes he could look ungainly, but now he looked perfectly at ease with his environment as he swung the rope effortlessly.

'Come on, try again. It's a skill that comes with practice.'

Kim joined them on the pontoon. She sat and watched the two of them for a few minutes.

'Time to go see Viv,' she said.

Vivienne's Bar had a view of the harbour from which French Harbour took its name. It was a large traditional wooden building with a verandah built along its front. They pushed the door open and stood in a spacious comfortable saloon. There were men crowded around the bar and most of the tables were taken. Underneath the chattering and laughter they could hear blues music was playing. The tall windows had wooden blinds letting in slats of sunlight and these brought out the warm browns of the walls and the wooden floor. There were rattan armchairs grouped around tables at one end and tables for dining at the other. There was a second bar at the back more sparsely furnished which attracted the locals.

As they made their way through the crush Vivienne spotted them and moved from behind the long bar. She was a woman in her forties with thick dark hair looped up extravagantly with tortoiseshell combs. She had round brown eyes and exuded a warm friendly sensuality. She was wearing a red midi-skirt in soft material and it clung to her rounded hips. Her black top had a plunging neckline that offered glimpses of her magnificent breasts as she leaned forward. She hugged Kim tightly and then Owen.

'I didn't expect you back this way,' she said.

She spoke with a French accent.

'Our last trip,' Kim said. 'Rob and Anna here chartered the boat.'

Vivienne led them to a table.

'It's so busy tonight,' Kim said.

'Well I started this new thing. On midweek nights you get a beer or a small wine and a piece of tapas for two dollars. It's proving very popular.'

Vivienne was a good businesswoman but seemed to be universally liked on the island. It was true what Owen had said; Kim did look on her as a role model. Vivienne told them that Gary was holding his annual hog roast out beyond Oak Ridge the next night and they should go along.

'I don't think we can go uninvited,' Kim said.

'I'll call him and tell him you're back. And I'll say you've got two friends with you. You know Gary, he's so hospitable.'

Kim explained that Gary was a Texan who had settled here and his house was the centre of the ex-pat community on this part of the island. They ordered beers and some of the tapas dishes and Vivienne went back to the bar.

'She seems really nice,' Anna said.

'She's a total treasure. I love her. The food is always so good here too. She does the best fish soup,' Kim said.

'And her accent?'

'She's half French and half Garifuna.'

Their plates of tapas arrived, fried squid, fried shrimp, spicy chorizo on ovals of bread. Rob leaned back with his bottle of beer and as Anna looked over at him she saw how the sun coming through the slats was creating shadows of his long eyelashes onto his cheeks. It was the first thing she had noticed about him when he spoke to her on the tube, his ridiculously long and thick eyelashes. She felt a squeeze of love towards him. They ordered another round of drinks and then a third one as the level of voices rose ever louder in the bar.

'Do you know Rob's mum is called Robin and she called her boy after her so that they are Robin and Robbie,' Anna said.

Kim smiled.

'That's kinda cute.'

Rob grimaced.

'And I love how you two met. That's the *best* story,' Kim said.

It was a story Rob liked to tell. It was romantic when you thought about it.

'And she's still my beautiful vampire,' he said.

'I guess I should take that as a compliment...'

Anna leaned in towards Kim:

'How did you two meet?'

'Oh I was in love with Owen since I was ten years old. He was best buddy with my older brother Jared and used to come to our house all the time. They'd shoot hoops in our yard and I'd stand on a chair at the window and watch them. He never noticed me once. It took another twelve years till he even noticed I had grown up and we got together.'

'Best thing that ever happened to me,' Owen said.

When it was time to go back to the boat, Owen and Kim strolled in front while Rob and Anna dawdled behind holding hands.

Kim was stretched out on her berth alone in the saloon and was thinking about how she and Owen had got together nine years before. She was twenty two and had recently started work at an upscale restaurant in Clearwater. They had to wear a red uniform which did nothing for Kim's colouring, her dark blonde hair and slightly sallow skin. The head waitress there, Nicole, had short black hair, a shapely figure and she looked very good in the red uniform. Nicole had given Kim all the bad tables to wait on, the tables in the draughty spots or by the washrooms. Nicole of course had the best tables and made the most in tips. On her second Friday there the restaurant was full and everyone was ordering the Filet Mignon and Lobster Tail Special. Nicole came into the kitchen, saw two baked lobsters and steaks plated up and reached for them.

'That's Kim's order,' Manny the chef said.

She snapped at him:

'My two are here all the time and spend a lot. You know they get the VIP treatment.'

She gave him a hard stare, swapped the tickets around, took the two plates and manoeuvred the door into the restaurant with her hip. Kim came in to collect her dishes.

'Gonna be a few minutes more,' Manny said.

She knew what had happened. Nicole had taken her dishes and now her customers would have to wait. She was furious. She understood the pecking order, but still it burned with her and she gave Manny a look.

The next night Kim was watching Manny as he made a Béarnaise sauce.

'You like to cook?' he said.

'Yeah I do and I wanna know more.'

'So stay behind tonight and I'll show you how to make this sauce.'

She often stayed behind after that and over the months Manny taught her many things. When he got round to asking her out to the movies she was straight with him.

'I'm kinda crazy about this guy.'

'You dating him?'

'Not yet...'

'But you're plannin' to?'

'One day, if I can make it happen. I'm sorry Manny. You're the best. I'd never have lasted here without you.'

'It's OK,' he said, but she could see that he was hurt.

'Let's go to the movies anyway,' Kim said.

It was about three months later and Kim and an older waitress, Tina, were laying the tables for the evening rush. Tina was bitching about Nicole and her mean little tricks.

'She's a nasty one all right, and what bugs me is she's going steady with this good-looking fella. I saw her out with him.'

'Yeah?' Kim said.

She was checking the salt shakers and filling the half-empty ones.

'I expect she'll be flashing a ring soon. He works at the same boatyard as my ex. Owen something...' Tina said.

Kim's stomach contracted violently.

'Owen Adams?' she was almost whispering.

'Yeah, that's it.'

Nicole came into the restaurant to check what they were doing and the talking stopped. Kim felt dizzy with shock and pain. She hurried to the bathroom and was sick in the toilet. She hated Nicole, who was always in a vicious mood these days. How could Owen have chosen *her*? She was good looking but so what? She was a twenty-four-carat bitch. She felt ashamed of her secret feelings then. What an idiot she had been to think that Owen would ever look at her. And it would be even harder to work alongside Nicole now.

Six months after that, one warm evening, she was sitting on the steps of the yard at her parents' house crying bitterly. The gate opened and it was Owen.

'Is Jared home?'

Then he saw that Kim was in tears.

'What's up Kimbo?'

He sat down on the steps next to her. She told him her good friend Manny was being deported. Immigration officials had turned up at the restaurant and checked up on him. He was a Puerto Rican islander and he didn't have the right papers. He had told the boss he had a Spanish dad and an American mom and was a mainlander but it wasn't true.

'He's my best friend at work and now he's gone, just like that.'

'That's a tough rap. And does Nicole still work there?'

Her heart fluttered oddly. Surely he should know that?

'Yeah she does.'

Kim picked up a stick and started to stab at the earth of the yard, making a hole in the ground as she brought Nicole's face to mind.

'Making mud pies?' Owen said.

His voice was affectionate but Kim thought with despair he still thinks of me as Jared's sweet little kid sister.

She said, not looking at him:

'I've got no proof, but I've got this feeling and it's a very strong feeling…'

She stopped. Should she go ahead and say it? She took a breath.

'I think Nicole shopped Manny.'

She had to look up at him now. He registered what she had said and he made no defence of Nicole, just nodded. She felt an overwhelming need to rest her head on his shoulder, as lovers do. She fought the need and then she just gave in to it and rested her head in the hollow of his shoulder. He put his arm around her and pulled her closer to him and it was the happiest moment of her life.

DAY TWELVE

They were getting ready for Gary's hog roast after another day of lazing on the beach. Kim had put on her orange sundress and gold sandals. She was sitting on the berth applying mascara as Anna came down in to the saloon.

'You look so nice,' Anna said.

'Thanks, I don't often get a chance to dress up.'

Anna went into the heads and splashed cold water on her face. In their cabin she found her newly washed jeans and pulled out the best top she had brought with her. It was a floaty chiffon smock in purple with pale grey swirls on it. She put on a pair of drop earrings with purple stones that Rob had bought her. She brushed her long dark hair.

They paid for a taxi to take them the eleven miles east to Oak Ridge. Gary's house was a substantial Spanish style villa with a terraced garden extending nearly down to the shore. He seemed delighted to see them all. There were groups of expats standing around his garden, and a few local people there too. Gary, who had made a lot of money and wore it lightly, was well known on the island for his hospitality. He was also one of life's enthusiasts. He told them this was his third hog roast and he was getting better at it each time he did it. There was far more to roasting a hog than you would think.

'Is there?' Rob said.

'Oh yeah, a lot more. First I had to dig the pit. It has to be about one foot larger in every direction than the hog.'

He had addressed all this to Rob and now he went on:

'I lined the pit with bricks to hold in the heat, and then I filled it with logs first thing this morning. You need about a foot of burning embers before you even start the cooking.'

Rob nodded.

'Then I seasoned and wrapped my hog in layers of foil and wet burlap and put a heavy wire frame around it all. Three of my buddies had to help me lower it into the pit. He's some brute.'

'How long will it take to cook?' Rob asked.

'Twelve hours straight. Not long now and it'll be worth the wait. The meat will be awesome.'

Rob was amused. It had just been a polite enquiry on his part. Anna was standing at his side and they exchanged tolerant smiles. The guests were getting steadily drunker as they waited for the meat to be ready and the feasting to begin. They saw Vivienne standing under a tree talking to a tall man with coarse ginger hair that stuck up at all angles. Vivienne looked stunning in a simple black wrap-over dress which accentuated her curves. They joined her and she introduced Doug to them. He had that true redhead skin, pale and covered with freckles. Turned out he was from Virginia and ran diving courses out of Oak Ridge. Rob started talking to him and they quickly established that Doug had Scottish heritage.

'My ancestors were from the highlands,' he said.

'And you're a diver?' Doug asked Rob.

'Yes, I've got my PADI qualification. I've done a few sea dives and I want to do more.'

'There are some pristine sites along the Eastern reef here. I run a three-day live aboard course if you're interested.'

Rob shook his head.

'I'd love to but we're only here for another week.'

'If you fancied a day and a night on the boat we could do that.'

Rob looked over at Anna who was talking to Owen. One night away was possible.

'Can I have your number? I'll call you tomorrow.'

Vivienne and Kim were talking about Gary.

'He has this big old house all to himself,' Vivienne said.

'He must rattle around. He needs to find himself a woman,' Kim said.

'It's not so easy on the island, Kim. You know what it's like here. It's either long-term couples or people passing through.'

'But he'd be a catch, wouldn't he?'

Vivienne shrugged.

'Of course,' she said and then Vivienne's eyes widened in surprise and Kim looked round. A slightly older couple had arrived at the party. The man had dark blond hair brushed back from a high forehead and a slightly wolfish face. He was tall and thickset and had a presence about him. He was dressed more formally than most of the people there, in a cream linen suit. The woman with him was exceptionally well groomed. She wore a cerise pink dress, sleeveless with a peplum at the waist and a ruffle around the neckline. They watched Gary walk over to the couple to greet them. He seemed delighted to see them both.

'That's Barbara and Gideon Carter, richest couple on Roatán. He made his money in natural gas, an absolute fortune,' Owen said to Anna.

'They have this huge villa at Port Royal, in one of the best positions on the island,' Kim said.

They watched as the Carters worked their way around the

knots of people in the garden and were fêted wherever they went.

'He's got other properties here too which he rents out. You could say this is his little Kingdom on Earth,' Owen said.

'And hers too. She's real friendly though,' Kim said.

Owen turned to Vivienne who was also watching the Carters.

'Viv, I need a man with a car tomorrow. I've got a few things to transport.'

Vivienne pointed to a man standing by the food table.

'Ask Cesar over there. You can hire him for the day.'

'Did you see Barbara Carter's dress? I bet it's designer. She spends a fortune on clothes and gets them flown in from the shows,' Kim said.

'It's kind of dressy for a barbecue though,' Anna said and Vivienne nodded her agreement.

Owen came back.

'I've hired Cesar. Tomorrow I can sell the liquor.'

'I'll be glad to see the back of those crates,' Kim said.

'I'll come with you,' Rob said.

Gary was hitting a fork against a glass. He called everyone to gather round and partake of the hog. Two men were stationed ready to serve the meat. On a second table there was a tower of baguettes and bowls of potato wedges and green salad and a bewildering array of hot sauces and pickles. The party guests loaded their plates with the tender pulled meat. Bottles of beer floated in a plastic barrel of melting ice cubes.

They sat on the chairs ranged around the garden and ate the sweet meat and the salty fatty crackling. It was very good. After she had eaten Anna left the others and walked up to the verandah of Gary's house. She had spotted a lovely old wooden garden swing seat with fat cushions, surrounded by plants in pots. She sat on the swing seat and rocked herself back and forth with her eyes closed. She could hear a faint rustling from the trees in the garden and the hum of voices from the guests. It was so peaceful and so comfortable here. She couldn't resist it, she had to lie down.

Gary came over to Kim and Vivienne with a tall woman and introduced her to them as Gail.

'I've seen you around the island a few times,' the woman said to Kim.

She had an Australian accent and clear hazel eyes. Kim remembered seeing her at Gary's place once before. Gail was working as a waitress in Port Royal.

'I used to work as a waitress, in Florida,' Kim said.

'Who did you hate the most – the ones who challenge the bill and never say sorry when you show them the total is right? Or the creeps who leave their phone numbers wrapped in their dollar tips?' Gail asked.

'The cell-phone creeps. They honest to God think you're gonna ring them. And they're always ugly, with paunches and loud voices.'

The three women laughed. Gary was watching them, especially Gail, and he joined in the laughter and stroked his small beard nervously. At the end of the garden he had set up a wooden platform for dancing and a sound system with big speakers. This was now playing classic dance tracks at full volume. People were waiting for the first couple to take to the floor.

'Can I persuade you lovely ladies to dance?' he said.

'You go with Gail,' Vivienne said.

They watched as Gary and Gail took to the floor and the stage started to fill.

'She's probably out of his league in the looks stakes,' Kim said to Vivienne.

'It's a shame. Gary's a decent guy.'

Owen had wandered off and Kim wanted to dance now. Rob was standing nearby but there was no sign of Anna. She waited out another track but when Shakira's 'Hips Don't Lie' came on she had to dance to that, so she asked Rob if he'd be her partner. They got up on the stage and started to dance.

Anna woke up. She had had the most delicious sleep. How long had she been here? There was music coming from the garden and small lights twinkled all around the grass, making it look enchanting. She lay on the seat and swung herself a bit more as she came to. Below her she saw a group of people, about ten of them, standing in a circle. The group lifted their glasses at the same moment and drank their Jägerbombs and whooped. To their left she saw Vivienne talking to that man in the cream suit, Gideon something. Vivienne looked beautiful, her eyes shining as Gideon said something that made her laugh in delight. Beyond them she could see a stage and guests were dancing. She headed towards the music and saw Rob was dancing with Kim on the stage. Owen was standing under a tree, tall and aloof, looking on. She had noticed that people treated Owen with respect, or maybe it was caution. He certainly had an innate authority about him. She joined him by his tree.

'Where did you get to?' he said.

'I fell asleep on this old swing chair.'

'You can't beat a swing chair.'

'It was lovely. You not dancing?' she said.

'Not my thing.'

'Can't I persuade you?'

'I wouldn't if I were you. I have two left feet.'

They watched the dancers on the stage. Michael Jackson's 'Billie Jean' came on the sound system. The Jägerbombers were trying to moonwalk to it on the grass and one of them fell over and they all laughed raucously.

'Oh come on, I'll take my chances,' she said.

They joined the dancers on the stage. Kim had her head thrown back in ecstasy with her eyes closed. She opened them and seeing Owen and Anna she laughed and moved towards them, her hips swaying. Rob moved over too and the four of them danced and circled each other on the stage as the music throbbed louder and the scents of the trees and the plants grew stronger on the night air.

DAY THIRTEEN

Rob and Anna were still asleep and Kim had joined Owen up on deck. They sat cross legged and watched people stirring on the adjoining boats.

'You know what struck me at Gary's party last night, there's a lot of money in Roatán these days. I'm thinking we could sell the boat here instead of in Belize.'

'That wouldn't work Kimbo,' Owen said.

'Hear me out hun. We're gonna be here for the next couple of weeks so I've been thinking we can use the time to smarten up the boat. I'll make new drapes for the portholes. I can paint the lockers too. And maybe you can re-varnish the saloon floor and table; they're both looking very scratched.'

'That can't be done while we're living on the boat.'

'I thought about that. Maybe we can get some cabins on the cheap for a few days. I'm sure Rob and Anna would welcome a bit more privacy. We do the boat up and sell her here.'

Owen was unprepared for this conversation. Kim had obviously been thinking this through, planning their move back to Florida.

'I don't wanna talk about this right now Kimbo.'

'Why not?'

'We just got here. Let's enjoy a few days without worrying about money.'

When Anna woke up Rob was sitting up looking out of the porthole with a regretful expression on his face.

'What's up?'

'We've only got eight days of our holiday left. And there's no way we can sail back in time so we'll have to get a flight out of here,' he said.

'I guess so,' she said.

'Are you feeling like I'm feeling?'

'How are you feeling?'

'Sad at how little time we've got left.'

He sighed. She leaned forward and put her arms around his middle.

'We'll make the most of it.'

Over coffee in the cockpit Rob mentioned their need to buy air tickets to get them to Miami in time to pick up their flight connection to London.

'The airport's a mile from Coxen Hole. That's the capital and you need to go there to buy your air tickets,' Kim said.

'I can't go today. I'm going with Owen to sell the booze,' Rob said.

'Cesar will be here any minute,' Owen said.

'I could check the flights out of Roatán and book our tickets,' Anna said.

'I'll go with you. We can take the bus to Coxen Hole,' Kim said.

Cesar arrived and the three men loaded the ten cases of booze into his battered saloon and they set off for West Bay on the other side of the island.

Kim and Anna were sitting at the back of the bus as it trundled along a paved road. It was seven miles to Coxen Hole from French Harbour and it was hot and sticky in the crowded bus. They had passed the busy harbour and were now driving through the centre of French Harbour. Anna saw a basketball court, a supermarket, a library and four churches. The churches were modest white clapboard buildings with spires rising from squat towers and a picket fence around each of them. It reminded her of the churches you saw in Westerns. Four churches and this was a small town. They all looked cared for and recently painted. Religion must still be a potent force in this community she thought. It often was in poor communities. She saw a scooter chug by the bus with a family of four somehow hanging onto it. They passed a shanty town which sprawled from the road into the interior. She saw makeshift dwellings with corrugated roofs and washing strung on lines between them. Two little girls were squatted on the earth playing some kind of game with stones. They were throwing and catching the stones on the top of their hands. Anna pointed them out to Kim.

'See those two little girls? No shoes but their hair plaited so neatly. It makes you feel sad, doesn't it?'

'Yep it's a sad old world. Why bring a child into that?' Kim said.

Now they were moving through a rural district. Wild orchids grew on the banks of earth like daisies.

The bus pulled into Coxen Hole and stopped at the post office on Main Street, which was a busy, dusty street with weather-beaten shop fronts. Kim showed Anna where she could get the air tickets and they arranged to meet back at the post office in an hour.

Kim made her way to a small hotel on the edge of town where she knew the proprietor. She paid him to use his phone to call Florida. This time she got through to her mom.

'Oh thank heavens you called sweetie. I've been so worried as I haven't heard from you for a while.'

'Didn't Jared tell you I called a few days ago?'

'He didn't mention it, hun.'

'I don't believe it!'

'He's a bit unglued at the moment.'

'I know but... but he shoulda told you Mom. He knows you worry.'

'He's drinking too much and he's messing up at work and your dad and I are worried about him.'

Kim bit back her irritation. Jared had always got the lion's share of their parents' attention.

'He's just adjusting to the break-up mom and whatever you say I think it's good he's seen the back of Shelley.'

'But she's not letting him see much of Taylor and you know how he dotes on that child.'

Kim wished she could like her niece Taylor more than she did, but she found the child long on demands and short on thank-yous.

'It'll work out, you'll see.'

'I sure hope so. How are things with you sweetheart?'

'All good. We're back on Roatán again and we brought some nice English folks here. How's Dad?'

'He's missing you so much. You will be back for Thanksgiving won't you?'

'I hope we will be. We're gonna have to sell the boat soon.'

'And how is Owen?'

Her mom always sounded stiff when she asked after Owen.

'He's good. Did you see Cally recently?'

'A couple of weeks ago, in town, and she said she'd heard nothing for a while.'

'It's not so easy to get in touch from out here.'

'I know, I know. We can't wait to see you, darlin'.'

As Kim headed back into town she was seething. Sure her brother Jared had his problems and his horrible ex-wife Shelley wasn't letting him see his little girl, but he should have told her mom she'd called. She was sure this was partly Jared's mean way of getting back at Owen. Her brother had made a bad choice in his wife Shelley who was a lazy, needy do-nothing kinda woman. It mattered a lot who you chose as your life partner. Choose a lazy-ass like Shelley and there was bound to be trouble.

She arrived at the post office and there was no sign of Anna. She watched as a long limousine drove up and parked in front of the building. The driver got out from his seat and opened the door and Barbara Carter got out. She saw Kim and waved to her. Kim waved back noticing how Barbara's peach linen dress hung perfectly from her slim frame.

'How nice to see you, Kimberly. Now I'm hoping something rather special I've bought for Gideon has arrived and is still in one piece. I asked them to send it here because it's a surprise gift.'

'Is it his birthday?'

'It's our wedding anniversary, twenty years...'

'Well many congratulations to you both.'

'Thank you. I'm having a party to celebrate, in four days' time at our villa. I do hope you and Owen can come?'

Kim flushed with pleasure.

'We'd love to. Thanks so much. So what did you get him?'

'I found the most exquisite porcelain figure, for his study.

It's china gifts for twenty years you know. You will keep my secret, won't you?'

Barbara Carter smiled conspiratorially and walked into the post office.

Anna arrived five minutes later.

'Did you get the tickets?' Kim asked.

'Yes thanks; got us onto a connecting flight.'

'Owen and I just got invited to a fancy party, by Barbara Carter.'

'The woman at the hog roast?'

'Yeah, and I'm gonna need to buy a dress for it.'

'I'll help you choose one.'

'Great. But not here.'

They walked up Main Street and Anna saw a large handicraft shop and made a move to go in.

'I want to get something quickly, can you wait?'

Anna stepped into the shop. It was full of locally made artefacts: carved wooden bowls, hand-thrown pottery and brightly coloured blankets. She spotted a picture frame which had a mosaic pattern around its edge in a vibrant blue, similar to the colour Kim had liked so much in the photo-spread. Anna picked up the frame and looked at it more closely. It was more expensive than some of the other picture frames. She bought it and the shop assistant wrapped it in tissue paper. She came out of the shop and handed the package to Kimberly.

'To replace the frame I broke,' she said.

Kim unwrapped the paper and took the frame out.

'Aww, it's real pretty.'

'I know you like that shade of blue.'

'I do. Well thank you kindly. You shouldn't have,' she said.

They headed off to find a café.

It was early evening when Cesar dropped Owen and Rob off near the pontoon. They were both mildly drunk. They had spent the day going from bar to bar in West Bay and then West End, the area of the island with the spectacular beaches. This was where the cruise ships brought in large numbers of day trippers and where the bars charged tourist prices. They had been offered drinks while making their sales and had hardly eaten all day. Anna and Kim were sitting in the cockpit and Anna was rubbing after-sun lotion onto her arms and shoulders.

'Hey. So did you guys make a good profit?' Kim said.

'Oh yeah, we both did fine,' Owen said grinning over at Rob who shot him a quick warning look. He had been feeling guilty because he hadn't told Anna he had used their 'escape money' as she called it. Kim now shot Owen a look too and the atmosphere in the cockpit became tense. Anna realised that the three of them were in on something that she knew nothing about. She felt left out, angry and hurt. She couldn't bear to go on sitting with them for a minute longer. She put her bottle of lotion in her bag, stood up and said curtly:

'I'm going for a walk.'

She stepped off the boat and charged along the pontoon. Rob followed her. When they were out of earshot she turned to him.

'What was that profit comment all about?'

'I should have told you,' he said.

'Told me what?'

'I bought five of those cases of booze when we were in Belize. Owen said we could make a good profit by selling it to the bars down here. And we did.'

'So why didn't you tell me?'

'I used our escape money and I thought you'd disapprove. I'm sorry.'

'You know the thing I really hate is you having secrets with *them* and keeping *me* in the dark.'

Rob took a half step back. Anna was right to be angry about him not telling her, but as it happened it had increased their pot of money substantially. And it hadn't been illegal.

'I said I'm sorry. Don't go giving me the third degree,' he said.

'Can't you see how we just do what they want us to do all the time?'

'That's not true.'

'It took us ten days to get here, Rob. Ten days of our holiday.'

'So what? We had the best time getting here. Why do you have to be so difficult about it?'

'Oh go back to your precious friends. I want to be on my own.'

She strode away from him as fast as she could. She did not know where she was headed but her anger buoyed her up. After she'd been racing along for a while she decided she would go to Vivienne's Bar.

Rob let her go with a heavy heart. He thought she had started to relax into their life on the boat. He thought she had grown closer to Owen too and had started to like and trust him. He had even wondered if she was attracted to him. Owen was the kind of man that women found attractive: tall, strong, practical, a man of few words who had an air of mystery about him. He knew that Anna still felt a bit awkward around Kim, but they'd been getting on so well the last few days. He felt mildly attracted to Kim himself and wondered now if Anna's resistance to her had an element of female rivalry to it. The two women had such different approaches to life. Anna was physically afraid of so many things although, paradoxically, she was strong emotionally and would face up to difficult personal situations. She was afraid of flying, of drowning, of cockroaches, of walking under a scaffold. Kim was less afraid of the world. He found himself increasingly admiring her courage. He liked the way she could gut a fish and cook a good meal even in choppy waters. She was resourceful and made the best of things. When they ran out of stuff she improvised to make life as comfortable as possible for them on the boat. Rob watched Anna's retreating figure. She was headed towards the centre of French Harbour. He walked back to the boat slowly.

'I landed you in it, didn't I?' Owen said.

Rob nodded glumly.

'Sorry buddy.'

Kim brought up two bottles of beer and handed one to Rob and then one to Owen.

'I saw Barbara Carter in Coxen Hole today and we're invited to a swanky do at their house in four days' time. They've been married twenty years and...'

'Do we have to go?' Owen said.

'Of course we do. I always wanted to see inside their house. And I'll need to buy a new dress.'

Owen rolled his eyes.

'There goes my small profit,' he said.

'You beast, when did I last buy a new dress?'

Kim went back down into the saloon. Anna had over-reacted and her sympathies were with Rob. Jeez he had sold the liquor to make them some money. What was the problem here? Anna could be uptight sometimes. She rummaged in her make-up bag and took out her nail polish and her twee-zers. Now they were going to be on Roatán for a while she wanted to spruce herself up. She painted her toenails a bright glossy orange and plucked her eyebrows as her toenails dried.

In the cockpit Rob and Owen were drinking their beers.

'I love Anna more than anyone, but she has this strong thing about telling the truth. And I guess I grew up not think-ing it mattered that much.'

'I'm with you there.'

'She has an uptight dad you see, and even though she's not close to him she's taken on his attitudes.'

'She told me about her granddad.'

'Oh yes, he was a good bloke and a much easier man than her father. She was inconsolable when he died. I don't like her father if I'm honest. You know one of the most difficult con-versations I ever had was when I had to tell her I'd done time in a Young Offenders' Centre. I was scared she was going to dump me.'

'What happened? Wait. I'll get us another beer.'

Rob told Owen his story. After his hated stepfather arrived in his life Rob had become a troubled kid. When his mum got pregnant with his half-sister, Elliot had moved them out of the commune and into a flat. Rob was ten at the time and had only ever known life in the commune which was like being part of a large extended family.

'So now it was just the four of us, after Savannah was born, and Elliot was a devious prick from the start. He acted all reasonable towards me in front of mum, but when we were alone he was always digging at me and accusing me of stuff. He would call me a loser. I got into the habit of going back to the commune and staying with my mates. I only came home when Elliot was away on tour with his band.'

'How did your mom take that?'

'Mum is a very feminine woman and she needs to have a man around. She said I shouldn't try to break her and Elliot up; that she had plenty of love to go round. I knew she'd never leave him.'

Rob swigged at his beer.

'I smoked weed at the commune, we all did, but none of us were dealers. Then someone tipped off the police that there were drugs there.'

'Yeah?'

Rob nodded.

'I'm sure it was Elliot. The cops did an early morning raid and they found some stuff. When they tried to search my rucksack I struck out at two of them. That's what got me into trouble, my fighting them. I punched one in the face. Well, I was an angry kid. They found a few ounces of weed in my rucksack and I was sent down.'

Owen went below and got them two more beers. Rob was breaking his own rule, but it was cathartic to tell Owen what had happened all those years ago and he knew Owen wouldn't judge him.

'My mum was beside herself when I was sent there. She came to see me, on her own, and said it meant I had a record now and it would affect me for the rest of my life.'

'Tough rap buddy.'

'Yes. So I told her it was Elliot who got me sent there, that he was the one who had shopped us. She didn't believe me. She was crying and trying to convince me I'd got it all wrong. I told her she never saw the real Elliot and he had *always* wanted me out of the way. I never lived at home again so I guess he won.'

'I would have hit the bastard,' Owen said.

156

'I wanted to, very much, but that would have backed up his story that I was a delinquent kid and out of control. My mates at the commune stuck by me and they're the guys I set up the brewery with.'

'And Anna didn't dump you did she?'

'No, she didn't. I told her the whole story and she took my side, bless her. She said she could tell Elliot was a liar. You know I ought to go look for her. It's been a while.'

'I reckon she's gone to Vivienne's Bar,' Owen said.

Anna was getting steadily drunker. When she'd arrived at the bar she had bought a bottle of red wine, found herself a corner table and taken out her notebook. She had written a lot of her anger against Rob out of her system. The bar wasn't as busy as the last time and she was oblivious to any looks she was getting as she sat there drinking and writing. After a while she noticed that her writing was getting uneven and she closed her notebook.

Vivienne had recognised Anna as Kim's friend and she was keeping an eye on her. She was a pretty young woman and she was alone and getting drunk. It was a dangerous combination in this place. She saw a couple of men looking over at Anna and one of them she knew to be predatory. A while later she saw this man walk over to Anna's table and speak to her. Was he offering to buy her a drink? Anna looked up at the man and shook her head vigorously. The man slouched back to his table. Vivienne waited a moment and then joined Anna at her table.

'You all right *cherie*?'

Anna was drunk and had lost her inhibitions.

'Not really no; I had a row with Rob, a bad row.'

'Was it so bad?'

'Yes I think it was. They were all in on this deal to sell the booze. And I knew nothing about it. It made me feel awful and I had to get away from them.'

'They're on the boat?'

'Yes. The three of them. This holiday was going to be our great treat, but it's not worked out like that.'

'You all seemed so sympatico the other night.'

'Rob was very keen to go on the boat, but I didn't want to.'

'Why not?'

'I was worried about living up close with two strangers. I'm not good with new things. Rob is. He always fits in so easily. And I've been useless on the boat, clumsy and scared and no help to man or beast.'

'I'm sure that's not true.'

'Oh it is. I've found it difficult.'

'Well I find nothing ever comes off except buttons,' Vivienne said.

'What a funny saying.'

Vivienne's smile broadened.

'I suppose it is. My grandmother used to say that to me a lot.'

'*Nothing ever comes off except buttons*. I must remember that,' Anna said.

'Have you two been together long?'

'Five years. And I hate fighting with him.'

It was comforting to talk to Vivienne. She had such kind brown eyes and a way of listening that felt truly sympathetic.

'I'm being awfully self-pitying, aren't I?'

Vivienne patted her hand.

'We all have our insecurities,' she said.

The combined effect of Vivienne's kindness and drinking a bottle of red wine made Anna start to cry.

Rob came into the bar. He saw Anna sitting with Vivienne and as he approached the table he could see she was very drunk and in tears. The moment she saw him she stumbled to her feet and fell into his arms. He nodded to Vivienne and helped walk Anna back to the boat and put her to bed.

DAY FOURTEEN

Now that they were at a busy mooring Owen had tried to sleep next to Kimmie on the berth in the saloon. It was no good; he had been restless all night. He got up, trying not to disturb her, took his hat and a bottle of water and went up on deck. All the other boats were silent, shrouded in sleep. He sat and watched the sun come up. This was the morning he had arranged with Money Joe to deliver the package from Raul. Money Joe lived at Sandy Bay on the west of the island. He went back down to the saloon and looked at Kimmie lying curled and peacefully asleep. The night before he had taken the package from the back berth and put it into his rucksack. It was important she know nothing about this. She murmured sleepily as he kissed her and said he was going out. He walked for an hour through the cool of the morning and caught a bus to Sandy Bay.

An hour later Kim was up and boiling water for coffee. There was no sound from Rob and Anna's cabin. Rob had come back late and put a very drunk Anna to bed. Kim was going into French Harbour to buy material for the new drapes. She'd told Owen this the night before and he'd made no comment. As she headed into town she was thinking about his silent resistance to her plan to smarten up the boat.

Anna was lying next to Rob feeling very ill. The boat was

a horrible place to suffer the sickness and achiness of a full-blown hangover. How she longed for a proper bathroom with a deep bath where she could have lain and soaked her aches away. Or a high-powered shower she could have stood under for half an hour. She took two paracetamol with the water Rob handed her. She couldn't remember anything about getting back from the bar or undressing. He must have put her to bed.

'Sorry about last night,' she said, shamefaced.

He kissed her pale face.

'I'll make us some coffee.'

Later he offered to row her around the bay to find a place where they could swim. Owen had said they could take the dinghy for the day and as there was no beach to speak of at French Harbour he had recommended visiting some of the lovely small bays nearby that were accessible by boat.

'I don't think so Rob,' she said.

'Swimming might make you feel better, get your body moving.'

'I feel too sick to get into the dinghy. You go. I'll rest up here today.'

He took the mask and fins and left feeling irritated with her. She was wasting one of the few precious days left on this holiday. He slung the mask and fins into the dinghy and checked he had enough dollars in the fabric money bag he wore under his T-shirt. He rowed out to deeper water and then along the shoreline to the east of French Harbour till he found an outcrop where he thought the swimming would be good. He pulled on Owen's mask and fins and dived into the sea. He swam for about an hour in wonderfully clear water and enjoyed the brilliant flashes of colour from the small fish around the rocks. He trod water as some longspine squirrelfish darted in front of his mask, and a crowd of tiny blue chromis glittered at the periphery of his vision.

Anna dressed herself and went to sit in the cockpit with a large bottle of water. She was glad the others had gone out. Worse than the nausea and her aching limbs was the feeling of shame at her behaviour last night. She had thrown a strop and stormed off. And what had she said to Vivienne? Had she been terribly indiscreet? She seemed to remember she had cried at one point and said they were all ganging up on her. How embarrassing and childish.

The bus had reached the outskirts of Sandy Bay and Owen got off. Money Joe's house was built on stilts above the water and a small jetty led up to it. Owen walked up the jetty and knocked on the door. Money Joe's woman, Maribel, a local woman, opened the door and took him through to the sitting room. Money Joe did not get up from his chair; he nodded to Owen to come in and pointed to the chair in front of him. He had long grey hair which he wore in a ponytail and a Jesus beard. He was dressed in jeans, sandals and an Iron Maiden T-shirt that stretched over his paunch. Some people were taken in by his hippy style of hair and dress. Owen was not. He knew that he was completely ruthless and was also prone to episodes of paranoia. Owen sat down on the raffia chair opposite him.

'Greetings comrade... Would you like a gin?' Money Joe said.

'A bit early for me, a black coffee would be good.'

Money Joe would sip gin all day but he never seemed to get drunk. Maribel, who had been waiting to get instructions, now went out and returned a few minutes later carrying a mug of black coffee and a glass of gin on a tray. Owen stood up and took the tray from her and placed it on the mirrored table between them.

'Gracias,' he said to her.

As far as he knew she spoke little English even though she had been with Money Joe for many years. It seemed to be a relationship of few words. Maribel left the room and shut the door behind her. Owen unzipped his rucksack and handed over the large package. Money Joe took it from him and went over to his desk. He took out a penknife and cut away the gaffer tape until he got to the smaller packages inside. He slit into one of these, dipped a wet forefinger in the powder and rubbed this over his gums. He smacked his lips as if he was eating something very tasty. Then he opened a drawer in his desk and took out an envelope. He gave this to Owen and slumped back into his chair. He flicked open a box of cigars by his elbow.

'You want one of these?'

'No thanks.'

Money Joe rolled his fingers over the cigars, selected one and lit it. Owen was counting the dollars in the envelope. It was enough to keep his boat for a few more months. He zipped the money into his rucksack.

'How long are you staying this time?' Money Joe asked.

'Not long.'

'I may need a package taken to Belize City in a few days. You up for that?'

Owen hesitated.

'It may not work; we have to be here for a week or so.'

'Let me know comrade.'

Owen nodded and drank his coffee. If you spent too much time with Money Joe you inevitably got caught up in things and they were usually things you'd rather not know about.

'I was wondering if you had any cabins available for a few days? I'd need two.'

Money Joe had invested in some hillside cabins across the island which he rented to tourists.

'How many nights do you need?'

'Five nights ideally.'

'That's OK, day after tomorrow. You know my cabins out near Oak Ridge?'

'Yeah. You'd be doing me a big favour.'

'I don't want rent, but you can give me something for the electricity. You wouldn't believe the cost of electricity on the island these days.'

'No problem. Thanks.'

Owen put down his mug.

'I need to get back to the boat. A guy's coming over to look at the engine.'

Money Joe let out a malicious laugh showing teeth stained by years of his cigar habit.

'You still having trouble with that shit engine of yours?'

They shook hands and Owen left the room and headed for the back door as he needed to use their bathroom. He passed the kitchen where Maribel was sitting at the table filling in a puzzle book. She did not look up at him. The word on the island was that she had once belonged to the Mennonite community in Belize but had broken free from them. She was strangely self-contained and seemed to have no curiosity about the visitors who came knocking on Money Joe's door at all hours. It was safer that way of course.

And then through the kitchen window he saw Teyo walking up the jetty towards the house. Teyo was a strongly built man with thick black hair slicked back from his forehead. He wore a gold chain around his neck and looked strangely like a Central American version of Elvis Presley. He had an easy smile and was a rotten man. Owen did *not* want to greet Teyo. He did not even want him to know that he and Kim were back on the island. They had met at Money Joe's house some months ago and Teyo had taken a strong fancy to Kim which had alarmed Owen. He went into the bathroom as he heard Teyo banging on the front door. He waited until Teyo had been let into the house and he and Maribel had gone through to the sitting room. Then he slipped out of the bathroom and into the kitchen and opened the backdoor which led to the duckboards at the rear of the house. He sidestepped a sprawl of rusting tools and a coil of rotting rope and lowered himself carefully off the jetty and into the water holding his rucksack above his head with one hand. He would wade under the stilts of the house and get over to the jetty without being seen by Teyo.

He moved through the water slowly and as silently as he could. Part of him knew this was a foolish thing to do. Why had he feared meeting Teyo? He inched forward carefully and now he was under the sitting room of the house. He could hear the low rumble of Money's Joe's voice and the more staccato responses of Teyo. He was worried he would be heard and discovered and if he was how on earth would he explain being in the water? Just then Money Joe opened a window above him and threw out a lighted cigar which fizzed in the water and bobbed along in front of him. He heard Money Joe saying irritably:

'Shit cigar...'

He heard Teyo say:

'So she noticed his wandering eye?'

'Yeah, finally...'

'She'll pay for that,' Teyo said as Money Joe shut the window.

Owen heard Joe's slouching steps as he crossed the sitting room and his voice rumbling again but he couldn't catch any more words. He waited a moment longer to steady himself and then pushed through the water to the jetty out of sight of the windows of the house. He pulled himself up and took his trainers off and emptied them of water. He checked the envelope and the dollars in his rucksack were not wet. He felt faintly ridiculous but also relieved. He calmed himself by walking along the quay and looking at the boats moored there. It was then that he saw the black hulled motorboat out in the distance. He stopped and stared. There was no doubt: it was the same boat they had seen on their journey to Roatán.

Rob hauled himself back up into the dinghy and rowed towards a tiny beach that could only be reached by water. He pulled the dinghy onto the sand. He had the beach to himself and thought it would have been so much nicer to have shared this spot with Anna. There were a lot of sand flies around and at the top of the beach he found the rotting corpse of a seabird. For some reason he felt the need to bury the bird. He used his hands to dig into the sand until he had made a hole deep enough to be a grave. He lifted the bird using one of Owen's fins and rolled it into the hole. He covered it with sand and patted the mound and put several large pebbles on top.

'To mark the spot,' he said aloud feeling back in touch with his childhood self.

An hour later he rowed back to French Harbour and secured the dinghy. He needed to eat and he wanted fish. He had spotted a place earlier, a restaurant built out over the water. And then he saw Kim walking down towards him from the town, carrying two bags. He took these from her.

'How's Anna?' she asked.

'Sleeping it off,' he said with a conspiratorial grin. 'Will you join me for lunch?'

'Well I'd love to,' she said.

'What about going there?'

He pointed to the restaurant built out over the sea.

'It's kinda expensive there.'

'Let's go there. My treat, to thank you for all those great meals you've made for us.'

They picked a table out on the back deck which was built over the water. He ordered the King Crab Special and Kim chose yellow tail snapper wrapped in a palm leaf. He ordered a bottle of white wine and she shook her head at the prices.

'See the material I bought,' she said.

She pulled out the fabric she had chosen for the porthole drapes: thick cotton with bold blue stripes on a white background.

'I wanted Mediterranean blue but they didn't have it. I think this blue and white looks neat though. And I'm gonna paint the lockers the exact same shade of blue.'

'It'll look good. So you're going to sell the boat here?'

'I think so.'

'You don't see so many wooden boats any more.'

'No, but the folks that want one really want one and they'll pay for it,' she said.

'It's a handsome boat all right.'

Their food arrived on large plates and the fish portions were generous. He poured more wine into her glass.

'This is such a treat,' she said.

Their eyes met and they smiled warmly at each other. She was a plucky woman, Rob decided, and it was what he liked most about her. She always tried to make the best of things.

It couldn't be easy living in this hand-to-mouth way with Owen.

'You looking forward to life back on land?'

'Oh I am, and to seeing my darlin' mom and dad. It's been a long time.'

She cut into her fish and chewed it slowly.

'I like the way they cooked this. Anna told me you guys live together in London.'

'I spend most nights at her flat. And I keep my music collection there so that makes it home, but for the sake of appearances I keep a daybed at my mate's place.'

'For the sake of appearances?'

'Anna's father, he'd give her a hard time if he knew we were living together.'

'So he's a straight kinda guy and he'd like you guys to get married?'

'Not a reason for doing it Kim. He's a bit of a bully, in a very civilised way of course.'

He put a forkful of crab into his mouth.

'Well maybe bully is too strong. He's a snob. And I'm sure he wishes Anna was with one of the sons of his golf-playing crowd in Canterbury. And she chose me instead.'

'She chose well,' Kim said.

'Thanks. You know Anna and I come from very different backgrounds, but the strange thing is we both grew up in homes full of music and musicians, very different musicians though.'

'In what way?'

'My step-father Elliot plays in a rock band. Anna's father teaches at some famous church school that's big on choral music.'

Kim sipped at her wine.

'And my biological dad is a rock musician, but I don't know who he is, or even if he's still alive,' Rob said.

'How come?'

'My mum got pregnant at a music festival when she was only nineteen and I'm the result.'

'And she never told the fella?'

'No. Or even her mum and dad though they wanted to know who he was. She's kept the secret so long and she's very attached to it. I've asked her but she won't tell me, says it's best I don't know.'

'Would you like to track him down?'

'I would you know. He's American. I didn't care when I was a kid. Mum and I were so close and it was always the two of us against the world. But the feeling's been growing in me for a while that I need to know who he is.'

'He may not be good father material.'

'Probably not, but I'd still like to know something about him, to know more about where I come from.'

'I can understand that,' Kim said.

Rob poured more wine into her glass and his.

'Thanks. Now I wanted to get married to Owen so much. And my wedding day shoulda been a happy one, but my brother Jared didn't show up. My mom was waiting and waiting for him and the day became all about Jared not showing.'

A shadow crossed her face.

'Why didn't he show up?'

She hesitated.

'He and Owen fell out badly years ago. So he decided to make a big point of it and not show at our wedding.'

'I'm here now to avoid a wedding,' he said.

He regretted it the moment the words were out of his

mouth. Too late to unsay them. So he told Kim about Elliot and his mum as they watched the waves roll in under the wooden decking beneath their table. She had picked up some of his story the night before, when he'd opened up to Owen.

When Owen got back to the boat he found Anna sitting in the cockpit looking ill. It was getting hotter so he fitted the canvas cover over the cockpit to give her some shade. He went to work on his engine. She watched as he dismantled and meticulously cleaned each piece of the machinery. She sipped her water feeling too ill to write in her notebook or even to read. Her scalp felt tender. That was the problem with a hangover; you had to live through the wretched hours until the alcohol poison had worked its way out of your system.

'Sorry I was such a grouch last night,' she said.

'It's OK.'

'I felt left out you know. I didn't know Rob was in on selling the booze.'

'We made a good profit, and he did it to help your situation.'

'I know, I know. It's just I hate secrets.'

'Everyone has secrets Anna.'

She felt rebuked. She realised she cared about having his good opinion.

'I probably do set too much store on being told the truth. It's hard for me to think it doesn't matter.'

'There are many ways to be good and even more ways to be bad in this world,' he said.

She had noticed that Owen had a way of saying things that had the ring of authority about them but that also closed down conversations. She offered to make him a coffee. She squeezed past him into the saloon and put the kettle on. She made black coffee for him and tea for herself and put a big spoon of sugar in her tea. He sat with her at the saloon table and wiped his oily hands on a rag before picking up his mug.

'I like Vivienne so much. She was very kind to me last night,' she said.

'She's a good person.'

'She is; a lovely warm woman and I'd like to thank her somehow. Maybe take her some flowers.'

'She wouldn't expect that.'

He finished his coffee and looked at his engine and his expression darkened.

'Can't you mend it?' she said.

'Probably not. I think folks throw things away too easily and most things can be mended. But there comes a point when something has reached the end of its life and I think my engine has reached that point.'

'But you don't like that idea.'

'What?'

'The idea of things wearing out...'

'You trying to psychoanalyse me?'

'God no, my head aches too badly for me to analyse anything.'

'You should eat something,' he said.

'Maybe.'

He stood up and looked in the cold box.

'I could fry us some eggs?'

'Thanks for the offer but I couldn't eat fried eggs.'

'There's some ham.'

'Better. I'll make us ham sandwiches. You get back to work on your dying engine,' she said.

*

171

They had finished the bottle of wine and the plates had been cleared away and they'd had coffee and it was late afternoon as Rob and Kim went to find the dinghy. As Rob rowed them back to the *El Tiempo Pasa* Kim noticed the shape of his arms. He had nice shoulders and arms and a thought flashed into her mind which made her blush and which she pushed away at once. She had wondered what sex with Rob would be like.

Anna made herself get off the boat and walk down to French Harbour in the hope that some exercise might make her feel less ill. When she got into town she went into Eldon's supermarket and bought herself a large carton of coconut water and sat on a wall and drank the whole thing. A man went by on a bicycle balancing a crate with two live chickens on the handlebars. A short way along the road she saw the yellow building with the sign French Harbour Public Library, which she had seen from the bus. It was a modest but cheerful looking building and she decided to take a look inside. She pushed the door open and saw children's artwork stuck up on the walls and a poster asking for donations towards the cost of children's school uniforms. Then she heard a voice she recognised coming from the depths of the room. She peeked around the corner of a bookcase and saw Vivienne sitting on a beanbag with a circle of young children seated on the floor around her listening as she read them a story. She couldn't see Vivienne's face, only her back, but she heard how she was using her voice expressively to make the story come alive. She repeated some words several times with relish and looked around the circle as the children wriggled and smiled. They looked like children from the shanty town. Vivienne was wearing a navy top and a full patterned skirt, also navy blue with a design of brilliant orange and white fans all over it. One little girl was nestled up close to her and kept stroking the fabric of her skirt. Anna stood and watched for several minutes as Vivienne turned the pages and the children sat entranced by her voice and her story-telling. She decided to slip away without speaking to her.

In the evening the four of them sat together in the cockpit having their rum and limes. Anna was drinking pineapple juice. The sky was streaked with clouds of palest pink and silver.

'I got us some cabins for the next few days, over in Oak Ridge, up the coast from here. We can move into them day after tomorrow,' Owen said.

'What a great idea,' Anna said.

'But how much will it cost?' Rob asked.

'Almost free, just a contribution towards the cost of electricity. Someone I know. He said we could use them.'

'Thanks Owen,' Rob said.

'I thought you two might appreciate more privacy,' he said.

Kim leaned over and kissed the side of Owen's face.

'Thank you for doing that darlin'.'

DAY FIFTEEN

Anna came out of the forecabin. She was wearing a long T-shirt over panties and Kim noticed again, and envied, her long tanned legs.

'What are you two gonna do today?' she asked.

'Rob said he'd take me out in the dinghy to a small beach he found yesterday. Do you want to come?'

'Thanks but I'm gonna stay here and start work on the drapes.'

As Rob rowed them over to the beach Anna could see how his arms had got more muscular over the last two weeks and he handled the dinghy well.

'You're getting good at rowing.'

'I may take it up when we get home.'

'I'm so glad about the cabins.'

'They may be a bit basic Owen said.'

'They'll have a shower Rob, and a bedroom, away from the others.'

They reached the small beach and there was no-one there.

'Brilliant, we've got it to ourselves,' he said.

They pulled the dinghy ashore and when they were sitting on the sand Rob said:

'So at the hog roast I was talking to Doug who runs a dive boat out of Oak Ridge.'

'Which guy was that?'

'The tall guy with the red hair, did you see him? He said he could take me out for a day and a night and we could get in two big dives around the reefs.'

'And you want to do it?'

'I'd love to. But it means my being away for a night on his dive boat. Are you OK with that?'

'You really want to do it don't you?'

He nodded.

'OK. I think you should do it.'

He kissed her.

'Sweet face, thank you. Owen and Kim will be close by if you get lonesome. Now why don't we sunbathe naked? We've got the beach to ourselves.'

She grinned at him and took her book out.

'Sorry, I'm near the end and I've got to finish it.'

He persuaded her to take off her top but not her bikini panties. She lay on the beach on their towel and opened her book and he rubbed cream into her back and over her shoulders and down on her thighs as she read on. He stretched out on his back next to her and closed his eyes. He was hot and happy and had a half erection. He was going to dive the reefs. He heard her turning the pages of her book. She was a passionate reader; had studied English at university and could have gone further with her studies. Her father had wanted her to stay on and do a post-graduate degree, but she was committed to the idea of becoming a speech therapist. That was the legacy of her granddad who believed in public service. Unlike Anna's, his own education had been a fuck up. It hadn't been going well even before he got sent to the Young Offenders' Centre. But after those bruising months he had lost all interest in studying. When he returned to school he started to miss classes and later became a hard-core truant. If he hadn't set up the brewery with his mates he wasn't sure what he would have done workwise. His qualifications were meagre. Anna believed in him though. She was convinced he was clever and should go back into education. She was always bringing home brochures for evening classes. One day he'd follow up on one of them.

He heard a faint buzzing and opened one eye. An aggressive looking insect like a June bug had landed on Anna's bottom. She was oblivious to it and would freak out if she knew. He got up onto his side and looked at the bug with curiosity. It had a long proboscis that it used to pierce skin. He flicked it off her bottom before it could do her any damage.

She closed her book with a happy sigh.

'Brilliant. He's the master.'

'I'm glad to hear it at 900 pages. There's something I need to tell you.'

She sat up. She was still deep in Dickens' world but this sounded serious.

'What is it?'

He took a deep breath.

'I should have been more open with you. I know that now and I'm sorry.'

'Tell me Rob.'

'I booked our holiday so we could miss the wedding.'

'Your mum and Elliot...'

'I couldn't stand the idea of being there, watching that arsehole going through the ceremony with my mum.'

She nodded, taking it in. Anna didn't see his family very often but she liked his sister.

'Was Savannah OK about us missing it? I mean it was her idea wasn't it, the wedding?'

'I said I'd got our plane tickets ages ago and couldn't change them.'

'Ahh, I see.'

'I didn't want a big scene.'

'I can understand, after what he did to you.'

'I thought you'd say we should have gone.'

'No. He hurt you. He's a liar and a nasty bit of work.'

He should have known she would be on his side. He should have trusted her. She reached for his hand.

'Sometimes I think you hold back on telling me stuff, Rob, and I think it's because you got into that habit with Elliot, hiding stuff, keeping stuff in.'

'Maybe I do. I love you sweet face.'

'I love you too and you can tell me stuff.'

Kim opened the saloon table to its full extent so she could work on it.

'I'm gonna start work on the drapes now,' she said to Owen.

He was stretched out on the berth with a book but now he got up and went up on deck. She took down the old drapes from the portholes. They had rotted and faded in the sun. She measured them carefully and wrote down the dimensions. She got out the new blue-and-white striped fabric. She kept a pair of scissors with her private things. She was singing to herself as she cut into the crisp new fabric.

She heard Owen talking to someone up above and a minute later he called down into the saloon.

'Gary's here.'

She left her work reluctantly but needs must. Gary was always so hospitable to them. He was sitting in the cockpit with Owen.

'Now what can I offer you Gary, coffee, rum or a beer?'

She got them a couple of beers and put some pretzels in a bowl.

'Join us Kimmie,' Owen said.

She sat with them although she wanted to be down below making her drapes.

'That was a great party,' she said to Gary.

'Glad you had a good time. What did you think of Gail?'

'She seems real friendly.'

'She's great, isn't she?'

Kim smiled.

'You gonna ask her out?'

'She's kinda independent you know. And I don't think she's done with travelling yet.'

Gary's mouth drooped at the thought that the highly desirable Gail would leave the island one day soon. Kim was looking at him and thinking that's the problem for Gary, he's stranded on the island because he's got so much money and doesn't have to work. His only role was to be the generous host and to hold his parties for the ex-pat community. Even if he got it together with Gail she couldn't see it working long time. A woman like Gail still had lots of challenges ahead of her.

'So, the reason I dropped by. Kim mentioned you're looking to sell the boat. I met this guy who's looking for a wooden boat. He's set on it being an old wooden boat like yours. He'll pay good money and I thought you'd like to know,' Gary said.

Kim waited for Owen to say something, but he didn't.

'Good of you to think of us Gary. Who is he?' she asked.

'A Dutch guy, Sander, I don't think you know him. He knows about boats and he came into some money recently.'

'It would be good to meet him, wouldn't it?' Kim said looking at Owen.

'Sure. Leave me his details,' Owen said.

Kim found a piece of paper and Gary wrote down the Dutch guy's name, Sander Haak, and his number and gave this to Owen.

'And we sure do appreciate your thinking of us,' Kim said since it was obvious Owen was not going to thank Gary.

After Gary had gone Owen and Kim sat on in in the cockpit.

'Before you say anything I don't wanna sell the boat here,' Owen said.

'There was no need to be rude to Gary.'

'And there was no need for you to tell him we wanna sell the boat. That's our business. Why did you do that?'

'Why not? He's a buddy and we have to sell her sooner or later don't we?'

'Not yet.'

'By my reckoning we've only got a few weeks' money left.'

'We've got enough.'

'You can't have made that much on the liquor sale?'

'Don't put pressure on me. You know it has the reverse effect.'

She sighed with frustration and shook her head.

'I thought you liked this life,' he said and his voice had a hard edge to it.

'I did, for a long time. I'm finding it harder now.'

'Why? What's changed?'

'It's the never knowing where the next dollar is gonna come from.'

'Well I didn't have you down as a nine-to-fiver,' he said.

'That's not fair and you know it. I've been with you every step of the way.'

'I'm hearing a "but"…' he said.

'It feels like we've reached the end of the line. And I'm missing my mom.'

To her surprise her eyes filled with tears.

'OK, OK, I get it.'

His voice was sharp and he stood up and jumped off the boat.

'Where are you going?'

He didn't answer her.

He strode away along the pontoon and down to the harbour. A fisherman was sitting with a mound of yellow nets in front of him and was mending one with care. Owen sat on the wall and watched the man at work. In this part of the world you looked after the tools of your trade. There was none of the wanton waste you saw everywhere in Florida, objects discarded the moment there was a chip or a stain, surplus food chucked into bins. Kimmie had told him how much got thrown away at the restaurant where she worked and it disgusted him. The fisherman secured the final knot and put down his net.

'Nice work,' Owen said in Spanish.

The fisherman nodded at him.

He wandered into the town. He was going to send a card to his aunt Cally. He didn't remember to do this very often, maybe twice a year, and it had been a while. He chose a card with a picture of working boats on it and went to a café and got himself a coffee. He wrote that they were both in good health and he hoped his aunt was doing well. He did not say they would be coming back any time soon. The feeling was growing in him that he couldn't go back to Florida.

*

It was rare for them to fight outright like this. Kim felt miserable as she went down into the saloon, picked up her scissors and continued to cut the fabric for the new drapes. She was sure Owen would throw the piece of paper away with the Dutch man's name and cell number on it, a man who would have bought the boat and cared for it too. It didn't make sense. She thought about Gary and Gail again and how a couple needed to want the same things in life in order to make a go of it. She had always thought she and Owen wanted the same things, but recently they seemed to be pulling in opposite directions.

Later she heard Rob and Anna rowing up in the dinghy. They secured it and joined her in the saloon as she was clearing the table of her sewing things.

'Hi there,' Anna said.

'Looks like you've been busy,' Rob said.

'Yep, I've been sewing all afternoon. Owen's out and I've got a bit of a headache now.'

'I'll make dinner if you like,' Anna said.

'Well thanks. I'd appreciate that.'

They kept waiting for Owen but he didn't show up. Eventually Anna went below and she cooked them pasta with tomato and red pepper sauce and grated cheese on top. It was a simple dish.

'Comfort food,' she said as she served it up to them.

'It's nice to be cooked for,' Kim said.

Later, lying in their cabin, cuddled up to each other, Rob said quietly:

'Something's up. Owen's not back yet.'

'And Kimberly seemed low tonight. I wonder if they had a fight?'

'It's a shame. This is our last night on the boat with them.'

'Well I'm looking forward to the cabin and a proper shower,' she said.

It was well past midnight as Owen walked back to the boat following the line of the harbour wall. His feeling of lowness had grown all evening and he'd been drinking at a dive bar for hours. He saw a couple in front of him who were taking the same walk back. They stopped to embrace and it made him feel sad watching the couple hold each other so passionately. After a long moment the couple pulled away from each other and sauntered on. He needed a slash and found an alcove in the wall. He unzipped and relieved himself. He looked down at his penis in his hand. He didn't use it much for sex these days, in spite of having a wife he loved and who the lowlifes on Roatán referred to as a pocket Venus.

Kim was still awake in the saloon waiting for Owen to come back. She had taken the fabric out again and had carried on with her sewing until the work was done, straining her ears to hear his footsteps on the pontoon. Finally she heard him approach the boat. She left the saloon and dropped the washboard into place so as not to disturb Anna and Rob. She watched him approach in the darkness and his steps looked unsteady.

'Where've you been?'

'Out…'

'Oh Owen, it was our last night on the boat with them.'

He moved from sadness to anger in a flash.

'The boat you're so keen to sell,' he said.

'Don't start that again. Please.'

'I'm gonna sleep on deck.'

'Well there's a surprise,' she said.

DAY SIXTEEN

The next morning they assembled for coffee in the cockpit, as they always did first thing. Kim looked tense and Owen said very little. It was to be Anna's and Rob's last morning on the *El Tiempo Pasa*. They went below to pack their belongings. Rob sat on the bed looking out of the porthole as Anna packed her rucksack quickly.

'You go on deck and help Owen with the sailing and I'll pack your stuff,' she said.

Owen and Rob sailed the boat the eleven miles eastwards from French Harbour to a mooring in Oak Ridge on a buoy. Oak Ridge was a working town built around the harbour. Many of the houses and shops were built on stilts and reached by boat. There was a large fish and shrimp processing plant, the largest on the island. They stood on deck and watched the small boats which were used like buses to ferry the workers back and forth to the factory. There was not much of a beach to speak of and little sign of tourists. They got into the dinghy and Owen rowed them ashore.

Money Joe's cabins were on a hill on the outskirts of the town, a short walk up from the scrubby beach. Owen led the way, striding ahead of them till he found the two they had been allocated. They were simple wooden cabins and stood next to each other. He handed over the keys to Rob and they agreed to meet up later.

Rob unlocked the door and stepped inside. It was basic in design and finish and there was no glass at the windows just mesh and slats you could open and close. There was a main living area containing a small hard sofa and two chairs. Off this there was a kitchen and a small bathroom. The furniture was cheap and flimsy throughout. There were four white plastic chairs in the kitchen around a small metal fold-up table. The cabin had been given a perfunctory clean and Anna saw a procession of ants climbing the wall behind the stove. She checked out the bathroom.

'Oh bliss, a proper shower,' she said.

There was a separate bedroom with narrow twin beds.

'Singles,' Rob said mournfully.

'We can push them together to make a double.'

They did this. Rob picked up the two mosquito nets, one for each bed.

'We'll need these,' he said looking up at the squashed mosquitoes all over the ceiling and walls. He spread the nets over the beds as best he could. He was already missing the boat. Anna unpacked her rucksack.

'I'm going to take a nice long shower.'

Owen and Kim stood in the main room of their cabin and looked around.

'Typical Money Joe,' Owen said. 'Cheapskate bastard...'

'It's only for a few nights.'

Kim was troubled that Owen had got the cabins from Money Joe, even though she had been the one to ask him to get them. Why had he gone to him of all people? She made a point not to mention the varnishing of the floor of the saloon, although this was the sole reason for the move to the cabins. When Owen was in one of his moods it was wise to say nothing. If it came to it she could do the varnishing herself.

'At least we've got a double bed,' she said.

'It's so airless in here,' he said.

She opened the slats at the bedroom window to their full extent.

'I'm going over to West End in a bit, with Anna, to buy a dress for the party.'

After a long shower Anna came into the bedroom, sat on a towel on the bed and rubbed body lotion onto her legs and her arms.

'That was nice,' she said.

Rob watched her rubbing in the cream. She had shapely legs and he especially liked her thighs. He could feel himself getting aroused.

'You're all lovely and slippery.'

He pushed her back onto the bed and kissed the mole between her eyebrows and moved his hands down her stomach and onto her thighs.

'I can't now. I told Kimberly I'd go to West End with her.'

'Can't it wait?'

'Later. We're going shopping.'

He sat up looking disgruntled.

'Shopping trumps sex, does it?'

'We've got the cabin now. There's plenty of time,' she said.

She dressed and went next door and thanked Owen again for securing the cabins for them.

'Glad I could oblige,' he said.

He looked glum. The women headed down the hill to the beach. It was a dirty scrubby kind of a beach and there were a few loungers laid out but these were unoccupied.

'Not the prettiest place, is it?' Kim said.

'No; French Harbour is nicer. But it was kind of Owen to get us the cabins.'

'And it's kinda interesting around here. There are mangrove swamps along the road where you can take tours. We did it once and you see all kinds of wildlife there.'

'I'll tell Rob. We should do that,' Anna said.

They walked along to the bus stop by the fish processing plant.

Rob tapped on the door and Owen let him in.

'Bit of a shithole, ain't it? Owen said.

Rob nodded his agreement.

'Anna's happy to have the shower.'

'I feel so shut in here. Strange I know because it's bigger than the space we've got on the boat.'

'Can't you and Kim sleep on the boat?'

'She wants me to varnish the floor of the saloon.'

'Ahh, when a woman wants a man to do something it usually happens.'

Owen looked rueful.

'She's trying to wear me down. Do you fancy a swim?'

'You're not working on the boat today then? I could give you a hand?'

'I wanna find a little bay I used to go to near here. We can go in the dinghy.'

Owen picked up his two oars and a bottle of water and they made their way down the hill to the beach. He rowed for about twenty minutes going east and then Rob took over.

'It's worth the row, you'll see,' Owen said.

They reached a tiny bay protected by rocks on either side with a triangle of the clearest water and a small sandy beach. They pulled the dinghy up onto the sand.

'Nice spot,' Rob said.

'It's good swimming too because of the rocks.'

Owen reached for his rucksack and took out the makings for a joint. He sat on the sand and rolled it, lit it and drew on the joint deeply a few times before handing it to Rob.

'I'm away tomorrow night on Doug's boat. Will you keep an eye on Anna?'

'Sure.'

Rob inhaled on the joint.

'Thing is she can get fearful when she's on her own, on account of her over-active imagination.'

'Ahh, they can be troublesome.'

He handed the joint back to Owen who drew on it deeply again. As they got stoned Rob talked about Anna, the things he loved about her. She really didn't care about material things and she clashed with her father a lot because he was very status conscious. She had told him how she hated her father's pretentions: the large and manicured garden with the matching teak garden furniture which was so different from her granddad's lived in and worked upon garden. She was much more like her granddad, who was the son of a farm worker.

'Yeah, she talked about him with great affection,' Owen said.

'He was the greatest influence on her life.'

Owen was rolling a second joint.

'When Anna went back to live with her parents she felt like a fish out of water. No-one in her family has ever really *got* Anna except her granddad.'

'And you; you get her,' Owen said.

'I guess I do. She's physically afraid of every damned little thing but emotionally strong. She doesn't back away from difficult truths.'

'You sure do love her. Don't worry I'll keep an eye on her.'

They smoked the second joint in silence looking at the sea in front of them. The colours in the water moved and shifted from green to turquoise to midnight blue. Owen sighed as he stubbed the smoked down joint into the sand.

'You OK?'

He shrugged.

'I've been better.'

'Are you and Kim all right?'

'She's mad at me, keeps going on at me to sell the boat.'

'You don't want to sell your boat do you?'

'No I don't. Can't bring myself to do it. I don't know how I'm gonna do it but I'm not going back to Florida.'

As the bus pulled into West End Anna could see why this was the divers' and surfers' mecca on Roatán. The town fronted a spectacular beach. Dive shops lined the main sandy road which ran along the shore and there were posters everywhere offering diving classes and sea kayaking and glass-bottomed boat tours. Kim said further along there were two clothes shops they should check out. In the first one she found a turquoise sun dress with a deep frill around the hem. She liked the colour and tried it on.

'It's pretty and it suits you,' Anna said.

Anna felt the fabric between her fingers. The dress was made of cotton.

'Are you thinking it's too casual, more of a day dress?' Kim asked.

'I think so. I don't think it's dressy enough for a big do.'

They found the second boutique where the clothes were more expensive. Kim went through the rails at the front of the shop. She made a beeline for dresses in bright, bold colours: acid yellow, turquoise and orange. Anna went to the back of the shop and started to go through the rails there. Most of the dresses were too bling for her taste; they had gold beads or appliquéd flowers on them. She found one she liked. It was a simple white satin dress with a halter neck. She called out to Kimberly.

'Come try this one on.'

Kim looked doubtful.

'I don't usually wear white you know.'

'I think it will look good on you.'

Kim went into the changing room and took off her bra because the dress was backless. She pulled the zip up and looked in the mirror and was surprised. She came out of the cubicle.

'That looks fantastic on you,' Anna said.

'You think?'

'It's perfect, especially with your tan.'

'I could put my hair up.'

Kim held her hair up and looked in the mirror, then turned to look at the revealing back of the dress.

'Can't wear a bra with this,' she said.

'It's perfect on you, honestly, do get it.'

'I think you're right.'

Kim bought the dress. The shop assistant folded it in tissue paper and put it into a waxed paper bag and they came out of the shop into the brilliant sun of the street.

'I'm gonna buy you a Margarita for finding me that awesome dress.'

They headed back towards the bars on the seafront and Kim caught sight of Vivienne coming out of an office. She looked striking in an amber-coloured dress and was carrying a box carefully in front of her. Kim called out to her and she came over to them, put the box down on the sidewalk, and embraced them both. She always smelled so wonderful Kim thought. She used a perfume, Jicky by Guerlain, which Olivier her son would buy for her in France.

'How lovely to see you both,' she said.

'Come join us. The Margaritas are on me,' Kim said.

'I'm driving, so just a coffee for me.'

She picked up the box carefully.

'What's in the box?' Kim asked.

'It's an old clock which I had mended; it belonged to my grandmother.'

They went into a bar and found a table and it was pleasantly shady after the heat of the street. Kim went to the bar. Anna noticed that Vivienne was wearing large amber drop earrings and these exactly matched the colour of her dress. They were quite flamboyant and on most women might have looked out of place, but on Vivienne they looked just right.

'I want to thank you so much for the other night, for looking out for me,' Anna said.

'My pleasure *cherie*.'

'It was very kind of you.'

'Is everything all right now?'

'Oh yes, things are great thanks. We moved into some cabins in Oak Ridge today. We'll make it our base until we leave.'

Kim came back with the cocktails and the coffee.

'*Merci* Kimmie. I hear you're in Oak Ridge now.'

'For a few days, Owen and I need to do some work on the boat.'

Kim would have said more if Anna had not been there.

Vivienne was one of the few people to whom she ever confided her troubles with Owen.

'What did you buy?' Vivienne nodded at the waxed bag.

'I got this dress for the Carters' party.'

She reached into the bag, shook off the tissue paper and held the white dress up.

'It's a wonderful dress. You must tell me all about it afterwards,' Vivienne said arching her eyebrows expressively.

'Don't worry; you'll get all the details. I've wanted to see the inside of their house for a long time.'

'I'm told it's quite something.'

'She's his second wife, isn't she? Someone said she used to be his secretary.'

'I believe so,' Vivienne said.

'She's sure got expensive tastes now,' Kim folded the dress carefully and put it back into the bag.

Anna sipped her Margarita.

'This is a good one. Thanks Kimberly,' she said.

Vivienne told them she was in West End to pick up the keys for a villa rental. Her son Olivier was arriving that night with three of his friends and she'd rented a villa for them for two weeks.

'They're all mad keen surfers. I offered them rooms at my place but they want to be in West End.'

'I guess it's where the main action is,' Kim said.

'I got them a villa right on the beach.'

'Is it one of Gideon's properties?'

'It is as it happens.'

'He's got all the best properties. Did he charge you the full rate? I hear he's a tough nut when it comes to rentals.'

'Well I wasn't going to ask him for a mate's rate,' Vivienne said and gave an ironic laugh, but it sounded a bit unnatural.

Kim thought, Jeez I shouldn't be asking Viv about money, but I guess she's doing really well if she can afford one of Gideon's beachfront villas for the boys.

'They'll be staying at mine tonight, so I should be grateful for that at least.'

'I'd love to see Olivier while he's on the island,' Kim said.

While they were talking Anna had noticed a man who was standing at the far end of the bar. He was flashily handsome in a slightly gross way. He had thick black hair slicked back from his forehead and a chunky gold chain around his neck. In the slightest way he reminded Anna of Ricky, her first love. It was this man's thick black hair and the cocky look he had about him which had triggered the memory. Ricky had always gelled back his black hair from his pale face and had the same masculine swagger about him. She had been powerless in the face of his sexual confidence when she was fifteen years old. This man was older. He had been watching them since they sat down and he made Anna feel uncomfortable. It wasn't just the faint resemblance to Ricky; it was something else that disturbed her. He moved his eyes and saw her looking at him. She dropped her eyes quickly feeling unnerved. She waited until Vivienne had stopped speaking before saying in a low voice:

'Don't turn around too obviously but do you know that man, at the end of the bar? Black hair. He's been staring at you both.'

Kim put down her glass and bent as if to adjust her bag. She took a peek over her shoulder and saw Teyo walking out of the bar. His glossy black hair was unmistakeable.

'That's Teyo,' she said.

'Who is he?' Anna asked.

'An island lowlife...'

'One to be avoided,' Vivienne said.

Anna looked from one of them to the other.

'He made me feel uneasy.'

'Owen says he's a whack-job. He came onto me once when we were over at Money Joe's. Said I looked so hot I was smokin'. I thought Owen was gonna punch him.'

'What happened?'

'I made us leave at once. He's not the sort of guy you get into a fight with.'

They had finished their drinks.

'Do you want a lift back as far as French Harbour? I can drop you in the town by the bus stop,' Vivienne said.

The sun was setting as they climbed the hill to their cabins and Anna asked Kim if there was a Mr Vivienne.

'There've been a few. Olivier's dad, but they split up years ago and she brought Olivier up pretty much on her own. She had a relationship with a French businessman who spent time on the island. It's been over for a while and I think she's between men.'

'She's very attractive.'

'She's gorgeous. But you know I always feel with Vivienne that she's fine on her own. She's so strong and resourceful. She doesn't need a man.'

'And Olivier?'

'Oh he's the light of her life. They adore each other.'

They parted at the cabins and Kim unlocked the door to theirs. Owen was out and she hoped he had come round to her way of thinking and was working on the boat. She took her dress out and hung it up in the bedroom closet and stroked the silky fabric. She felt excited to have bought it. She went into the kitchen and put some rice to soak in a bowl, took out her knife and started to slice an onion. She heard Owen's voice outside the cabin and he was saying something rather loudly. She pulled the front door open and saw Owen and Rob both doubled over and holding onto their sides as if they were hurting as they laughed and laughed. Anna came out of her cabin and she too watched the men unable to speak as they gasped with laughter.

'Oh I get it,' Kim said looking over at Anna.

'What is it?'

'They're both stoned out of their heads!'

Later, Kim and Owen sat in the kitchen and ate the risotto she had made. She told Owen she had seen Teyo in West End and this seemed to sober him up at once.

'I didn't want that whack-job to know we were back on the island. Did you speak to him?'

'No. We were in this bar and Anna spotted him and said he was staring at Vivienne and me.'

'I bet it was you he was staring at. I don't like the idea of him looking at you.'

'Nothing happened. He just creeped us out. You know Viv must be doing well. Olivier's arriving tomorrow and she's rented him one of Gideon's beachfront villas in West End. They cost a lot.'

'Maybe he's paying?'

'I don't think so. Do you wanna see my dress?'

'Put it on for me.'

Kim took the dress into the bathroom and put it on again. It was rather seductive especially as she had to wear it without a bra. She checked in the mirror. Her nipples didn't show through the fabric. She had a feeling that Owen would not like her nipples to show. She loved the way the fabric fell and revealed most of her back. She piled her hair on top of her head with a hair clip and sashayed into the bedroom. Owen was fast asleep on the bed.

DAY SEVENTEEN

It was early when Rob set off for his day and night of diving with Doug. Anna had offered to get up and see him off but he'd told her to go back to sleep. He picked up his rucksack and locked the cabin door behind him as she'd asked him to do.

When he arrived at the dive boat Doug was sitting in the cockpit with a lot of diving gear around him. He helped Rob onto the boat and showed him where to stow his things.

'I've checked the weather and it looks bad later on so we should start soon if we want to get two dives in.'

'Fine by me.'

He picked up a wet suit and handed it to Rob.

'Try this one on. I think it will fit you.'

Owen hated sleeping in the cabin and had spent a disturbed night in the double bed next to Kim. That dream had come again, the white-faced killer about his filthy business. What was it about that bloodless face that was so terrifying? He woke up with a start and once his heart had settled he lay looking up at the ceiling of the cabin. The stains of mosquito blood had turned brown. Images of his father kept coming. Jim Adams hadn't got better. He had seen the change in his father from when he was about twelve years old. Owen never knew which father would come back on leave. Would it be the kind loving dad or the scary silent dad? He could tell simply by the sound of his step on the stairs which dad it was. And so could his mom. He remembered how she used to creep around the house when his father was sleeping during the day. The slightest noise would wake him as if he was always on the alert for danger. He would burst out of the bedroom and scream at them and it was as if he couldn't see it was his wife and his children he was screaming at. He never raised his hand against them, not once. That was his father's code. You never hit a woman or a child. But Owen started to fear that one day he might. He remembered his mom telling him about her terrifying Valentine night ordeal.

Jim Adams was cutting her new dress, the one she was going to wear to their Valentine dinner. He had grabbed his hunting knife and started to slash at the fabric shouting it was a whore's dress and he would never let her wear it. She ran and locked herself in the bathroom with trembling fingers and thought at least he was focusing his rage onto the dress. Thank God the kids weren't here to witness this. They were staying over at Cally's. Cally had said let the kids sleep over so the two of you can have a good night out together, to celebrate his coming home for good. Celebrate! His mood swings were getting worse and she was frightened at how quickly he could become explosively aggressive, often at something so trivial. Her new dress tonight had been one such provocation. His reaction had been sudden and violent and crazy. Once she had been able to help him when the darkness came over him. She would make him go out with her and they would walk and walk until he had calmed down. Not any more. He had been a good man but the darkness inside was taking him over. She knew Cally was worried about him too. The air force had been his life since he was eighteen years old and now he had left it for good or, to be more exact, *it* had left *him*. It was some time later when she heard him slamming out of the house. She knew he would get on his motorcycle and ride his rage, going too fast and taking corners at dangerous angles. Sometimes she wished he would crash his motorcycle. It would be a quick adrenaline-fuelled death and he would be out of his torment.

After a few more minutes she unlocked the bathroom door and checked he had indeed gone out. She went into their bedroom and saw the remains of her new red dress. He'd slashed it to ribbons. She took down the large case from the top of the closet and packed some of her clothes. She went into Owen's room and packed his jeans, T-shirts, fleeces and his basketball, then moved on to Megan's little box room which was a riot of pink. She sat on Megan's bed with its Barbie duvet cover and matching pink pillow slips. She looked at the posters of ponies and rabbits on the wall and Megan's collection of *My Little Ponies* ranged along the shelf. She must remember to pack Megan's favourite ponies. She was momentarily blinded by tears. She stood and put some of the miniature pastel ponies into the case. Her children deserved a good childhood. The military had destroyed Jim and now they had spat him out. Where was the follow-up counselling; where was the aftercare to see how he was coping?

She caught the bus to the Marina where Cally lived. As soon as Cally saw her with the large suitcase she knew things had come to a head. She took her into the kitchen and shut the door. Megan was lying on her stomach watching cartoons in the living room and Owen was out with his best friend Jared. She told Cally how he had slashed her dress with his knife and that she was very frightened of him these days.

'I've got to get the kids away from him. He's dangerous now.'

'But he's ill,' Cally said. 'Please don't give up on him.'

'I can't get through to him any more Cal. I have to put the kids first.'

Owen sat up in bed, filled with a vast and deep emptiness. He told Kim he was going for a swim and carrying his fins and mask he hurried down to the beach. There was no-one about and the morning had an early freshness to it. He swam out into deeper water and gradually the sound of his breathing and the sights below the surface calmed him. He was alone in the water, away from the world of people and the hideous messiness of emotions. He swam amid a shoal of yellowtail damselfish and the myriad of fish moved through the water as if they were a single body and a single mind in perfect harmony with their environment.

He was walking up the beach later when he heard his name being called and he turned to see Money Joe waving to him. He had been talking to a group of men on the beach and now he walked over.

'Greetings comrade, how are the cabins?' he said.

'It was good of you to let us have them, Joe. You got business here?' Owen nodded towards the men on the beach.

'Some poor sods are about to be baptised. I'm up here to collect rent.'

They went up the hill together. Money Joe seemed to be having difficulty with the incline of the hill, so they stopped talking until they reached the summit when he said:

'So you'll do the Belize job for me?'

'Sorry Joe but can't be done. We've decided we're not leaving for a while.'

Money Joe stopped walking. Owen wasn't sure if it was his anger at his refusal or the steepness of the hill which made him stop in his tracks and breathe heavily. He waited for him to recover himself.

'You with me or against me?' Money Joe said finally and his voice was cold.

'What do you mean by that?'

'You make it a habit to walk under people's houses?'

Owen's scalp tightened. So he had been seen.

'Only Maribel told me you left by the back way the other day. And I'm thinking why did you do that?'

Money Joe laughed nastily but the look he shot at Owen was deeply suspicious.

It was a day of torpid heat and it felt as if it was building to a storm. After breakfast Anna carried one of the plastic chairs from the kitchen and was sitting outside the cabin. She had started on her next novel, *The Crow Road* by Iain Banks, when she saw Owen walking up the hill with a man she hadn't seen before. The man had a paunch and a hippy gone-to-seed look about him. Owen must have been swimming in his T-shirt and shorts again because she noticed his clothes were wet and clinging to his body as he moved. She sensed he wanted to get away from the man at his side so she got up from her chair and moved towards them.

'Anna this is Joe and these are his cabins,' Owen said.

'Hello.'

She shook hands with the man and his palms were clammy.

'You're English,' he said.

'Yes.'

'How long are you staying on the island?'

'Less than a week left sadly. It's such a beautiful place.'

The man nodded and walked away from them without another word.

Owen watched Money Joe as he headed along the path that ran across the front of the cabins.

'Is everything OK Owen?'

'He can be such a paranoid jerk sometimes.'

'He was a bit abrupt.'

'Yeah, too much gin for too many years,' he said.

'Rob's gone to Doug's boat. Where's Kimberly this morning?'

'She's gone down to French Harbour to have lunch with Vivienne and Olivier. Do you wanna see a traditional island baptism?'

'Now?'

'There's a group of church folk gathering on the beach.'

'And we're allowed to watch?'

'Should be OK.'

'I'd love to. Wait while I get my sun hat. Some religious types think you should cover your head.'

She washed her hands quickly, grabbed her hat and locked the cabin.

There were about twenty people and some children standing in a group on the beach. Five men all dressed in matching pale blue shirts seemed to be in charge of the baptism. Anna approached the man in the group who was carrying a wooden cross in his hand.

'Is it OK if my friend and I watch the baptism?'

'You are most welcome and please join the family members gathered here to witness this joyful occasion,' he said.

He had an American accent and pale blue eyes.

Anna and Owen sat on the beach, away from the others. The people being baptised looked like a local family dressed in their Sunday best. There was a man and his wife and three young boys. The five men in blue shirts led the father down to the sea and they waded out until the water was up to their waists. He looked nervous. They clustered round him and then immersed him totally in the sea and held him there while they said in chorus:

'In the name of Jesus Christ for the remission of sins.'

As they pulled him up out of the sea he was shaking the water from his head and smiling and looking around.

'Is that joy or is it relief?' Anna said.

Owen shook his head.

'When people are desperate they turn to the church and you can make a person believe anything.'

The man Anna had spoken to now held the wooden cross up to the sky and looked at the baptised man and said in ringing tones:

'Your immersion in the sea symbolises the death of the old sinful you. Your sins have been washed away by the cross of Christ.'

'Amen,' said the other men and they clapped their hands.

'You're not religious then?'

'Nope. I don't trust religious folks. Religion is a story you tell to comfort a child who's afraid of the dark.'

'Well that's exactly the kind of thing my granddad would have said. He was an atheist, a militant atheist in fact.'

The men went through the same process with the mother. She looked deeply moved and tearful as they pulled her out of the sea. There were the same words followed by more enthusiastic clapping. Then it was the turn of the three children. One of the children, the smallest boy, had started to cry. He was clearly overcome by the occasion with all these grown-ups gathered together and his family the focus of the attention.

'Poor little kid,' Owen said as he watched the small boy cry out in fear as the men in blue approached him.

'They're very young. You'd think they'd wait till they were older, let them have some say in the matter,' Anna said.

'Powerless,' Owen said.

'Sorry?'

'You're powerless when you're a young kid. Your parents have all the control.'

Anna thought that this was quite a harsh way of looking at the relationship between a parent and a child. Then she recalled her own conflict with her father and decided that Owen had a point.

'Yes, and you go along with what they want because you need their love and approval,' she said.

She was watching the little boy and she sighed.

'That sounded heartfelt,' he said.

'I was thinking about when my father and I fell out and how he clamped down on me. Mind you I was fifteen at the time, not a kid.'

'What happened?'

'There was this boy, Ricky, and he ran the rides at the funfair and I got into what my father called a deeply inappropriate relationship with him.'

'That sounds a bit strong.'

'Well I had sex with Ricky on our last night together; just the once. I can't begin to tell you how amazing I thought he was. His life seemed thrilling. He travelled all over the country with the fair and I saw him on the first night they came to Canterbury. You know those rides, the ones with the carts that swing round so fast, waltzers I think they're called? Well Ricky hung onto the front of ours while my friend and I were cowering back in the seat. I went along every night after that so I could see him.'

'And your father didn't like that?'

She nodded.

'He was horrified. I was under the legal age, but it wasn't the only reason. He can be a snob sometimes. He grounded me; actually locked the door to my bedroom. I couldn't say goodbye to Ricky and it caused a major rift between my father and me.'

She laughed suddenly.

'What's funny?'

'I wrote tons of terrible poetry about how I felt.'

The man with the wooden cross came over to them. The baptisms were over and the little boy was being comforted by his mother.

'I'm John Morgan. Do you have any questions? I'd be happy to explain the work of our ministry here in Oak Ridge.'

'I was interested in the total immersion. At home we just sprinkle water on the baby's head,' Anna said.

'We believe total immersion is important. It symbolises the death, burial and resurrection of Jesus Christ. You come out of the water freed from the dominion of sin.'

Dominion of sin; she didn't know what to say to that. Owen was standing next to her and she felt, rather than saw, him shiver.

'The little boy seemed a bit overwhelmed by it all?' she said.

'Yes it is a very big thing for the children. But look at him now. He's so happy he did what his big brothers did.'

It was true; the little boy was running along the beach with his brothers, shouting with pleasure.

'We'd best be getting back,' Owen said.

She thanked John Morgan and his pale blue eyes beamed a kind sincerity at her as she shook his hand. Owen had turned away. They headed back up the hill to their cabins and he shivered again.

'Are you OK?'

'I'm starting to feel strange, kinda shivery and achey. Think I'll lie down for a while.'

He went into his cabin and shut the door.

Anna went into her cabin. The heavy heat was making her feel depleted and a bit low as she contemplated an afternoon and an evening on her own. She wondered why she had told Owen about Ricky. She rarely confided to anyone about Ricky even though her memory of him was still so vivid. She thought it always would be because you remember the first one. Those strong arms emerging from the rolled up sleeves of his black T-shirt, his smell of diesel oil mixed with Lynx aftershave and an edge of sweat. She hadn't been able to look away from the bulge at the front of his jeans as he hung onto the front of the waltzer cart staring at her. His confidence was sexy. He knew how to do it and he had initiated her into sex on the bed in his mobile home as the tinkle of the fairground music came through a half open window. Her father had raged it was a cheap sordid encounter. It wasn't like that at all. Her feelings for Ricky had soared and for her it was a glorious initiation. But her father's disgust had troubled her.

Olivier looked even more French than his mom, Kim thought, as he opened the door and welcomed her into Vivienne's private quarters above the bar. His dark hair flopped over his forehead and he had her round brown eyes. Kim had come to help prepare the food and join in the lunch for him and his three friends. They were setting off to the villa in West End that afternoon. Vivienne's flat was very much like the woman, welcoming and warm. It was richly coloured with an abundance of cushions and throws on the two purple sofas and a red glazed vase of irises standing in the middle of the dining table. Olivier led Kim through to the kitchen and the two women hugged.

'Olivier got promoted last week. He's team leader now,' she said.

'Don't go on *maman*,' Olivier said rolling his eyes in embarrassment.

'What great news, congratulations,' Kim said.

She smiled over at Vivienne and seeing her face shining with pride and joy as she looked at her son made Kim's heart ache a little bit. Olivier left them.

'He's so handsome,' Kim said.

'Would you like some wine *cherie*? I'm going to have one glass of white.'

'Thanks.'

Vivienne handed her a glass. She pointed to the old clock which she had put in pride of place on her dresser.

'My grandmother's clock is working perfectly now. It has the sweetest chimes on the hour.'

Kim looked at the clock. Vivienne had put a photo of her grandmother, who was Garifuna, right next to it. The photo was in a silver frame.

'I'd love to make a home all pretty and comfortable like you've done Viv. Now what do you need me to do?'

She helped Vivienne prepare Olivier's favourite dishes: mackerel with horseradish sauce, green beans cooked with shallots and sprinkled with almonds, a large bowl of cous cous enlivened with black olives, spring onions and red peppers and a generous cheese board. As they worked side by side Kim told her how frustrated she felt at Owen's attitude.

'It's like he's changed his mind about selling the boat

without any discussion and I'm supposed to go along with it. And he's sulking now and won't even talk to me about it.'

'He's always been very attached to his boat.'

'Sometimes I think he loves that boat more than he loves me.'

'You know that's not true.'

'If I'm so important to him why can't he see I wanna go home?'

Her eyes filled as she chopped the spring onions finely.

'How long have you two been together now?'

'Nine years.'

'He needs reminding you have needs too.'

Vivienne topped up Kim's glass.

'Thanks, we were right out of money when we reached Belize City last time. If we hadn't met Rob and Anna we'd have sold the boat then.'

'So he will sell when you run out of money again. And you can go home.'

'He'll have to. But he could sell it now for a good price. Gary knows a Dutch guy who's looking to buy a wooden boat. Owen hasn't even called him.'

'Men can be so stubborn.'

'Somehow I've got to bring him round Viv.'

Kim laid out the cheeses on the board.

'We're gonna sail over to Port Royal tonight for the party.'

'To the Carters' jetty?'

'Yeah; we'll moor there and sleep on the boat.'

'Look out for some friends of mine tonight. They've been booked to do the music and they're very good.'

'If they've been together twenty years how old do you reckon she is?' Kim asked.

Vivienne was chopping a red pepper into thin slices.

'I'd say she's a well preserved forty-eight.'

'And Gideon?'

'A bit older.'

Vivienne turned and washed her hands under the kitchen sink, letting the cold water run over her wrists. She dried her hands and held them against her cheeks to cool her face.

'Well I'm sorry you won't be there tonight,' Kim said.

They carried the platters of food through and laid them out on the table and called for the boys to come eat.

Kim left two hours later after helping to clear up. Vivienne was driving the boys over to West End. As they parted on the street she hugged Kim.

'Have fun tonight. And stop worrying. Owen will come round.'

Kim caught the bus back to Oak Ridge. The Carters had a private jetty with plenty of moorings and she reckoned a lot of the guests would sail to the party. Their villa was not an easy place to get to by road. She was going to shower and do her hair and make-up in the cabin but she wouldn't put on her dress until they had moored at the Carters'. She would wear her gold sandals and gold earrings with the white dress and she needed to check what Owen was gonna wear. He was a reluctant party-goer and he never liked dressing up smart. As she headed up the hill she was singing under her breath. The sky didn't look so great. Thick clouds tinged with grey and purple were massing above and the air felt heavy as if a storm was brewing. She remembered that Rob was diving with Doug today and sleeping over on his boat. She'd told him to take some Dramamine tablets with him, in case he got a recurrence of his seasickness. She opened the cabin door and Owen was lying stretched out on the sofa.

'Hey hun. I didn't think you'd be here already. I thought you'd be on the boat,' she said.

'I'll start work on it tomorrow.'

'And did you get round to calling that Dutch guy?'

'There's no need. Like I said before we've got enough to live on for a few months.'

'How do you reckon that? We must have spent most of Rob and Anna's money?'

'The sale of the liquor…'

'It can't be that much. Not to live on for a few months.'

'It's enough Kimbo. Stop worrying.'

There was something he wasn't telling her.

'Did you get something from Money Joe?'

He said nothing but she knew the expression on his face so well, the tell-tale tightening of his lips.

'Did you carry a package to Money Joe? From Raul? Like you did before?'

'Will you stop trying to control my life.'

He got up and went into the bedroom and shut the door behind him with an emphatic click. He flung himself down on the bed.

Kim followed him in there ten minutes later, wanting to make it up.

'What's up Owen?'

Her voice was gentle.

'I've been feeling achey all afternoon.'

'You gonna be OK for tonight?'

'I don't know. My arms and legs ache pretty bad.'

'I'll make you some coffee.'

She went into the small kitchen and boiled water and she was fuming. She was sure he was going to say he felt too ill to go to the party. She remembered his reaction when she'd told him about it. He'd been against the idea all along. She wanted very much to see the inside of the Carters' mansion and she wanted to wear her new dress. She took a mug of strong black coffee through to him.

'I'm gonna start getting ready,' she said.

She went into the shower and stripped off. As she washed she was thinking I'm damned if I'll miss the party. I'll go anyway, even if he says he won't. I have needs too. She took her time in the bathroom and then she stood in front of the mirror in the bedroom with her hair in a towel and started to apply her make-up. She painted black eyeliner along her upper lids and applied mascara carefully. Owen was lying on the bed watching her.

'I'm not up to it tonight Kimbo,' he said now.

'I knew you'd say that,' she snapped.

He did look pretty rough, but he was always trying to get out of parties and his illness seemed all too convenient to her.

'I didn't get ill on purpose.'

'If it was something you wanted to do you'd find the energy to do it.'

'No-one's stopping you going,' he said.

'Too right!'

'No need to shout.'

'It's like we're always living your life Owen, the life you want. But I want to do one thing, have one night off, and hey you're not up to it.'

'That's bullshit and you know it. I feel ill.'

She brushed her hair vigorously and tied it up pulling out some tendrils around her face. She stepped into her new dress, put her dangly earrings on and strapped on her high gold sandals. She put money and lipstick and the keys into her purse and left the cabin closing the door behind her without another word to him. He made her wild! She would get a taxi the six miles to Port Royal. She teetered down the hill to the town in her high heels and wished she'd brought another pair with her for the walking. But she wasn't going to go back to the cabin, not now, no way.

In the taxi she cleaned the heels of her sandals with a tissue. It would have been more comfortable to arrive at the party in their boat. Now she'd have to get a taxi back later. In her head she was still carrying on an angry exchange with Owen telling him she was thirty-one and she still wanted a bit of fun in her life and was that so wrong? It felt like she'd been battling with him for a while, since they'd left Belize City the last time. It was as if her wishes didn't count for anything any more. He'd got stoned with Rob yesterday and still hadn't started work on the boat. What was he thinking? That they would just go on as they had before? He was acting as if they had enough money to live on for a while. She knew he'd been to see Money Joe at least once in the last week. The thought that he'd done some deal behind her back made her even more furious.

The taxi drove down a private road and pulled up in front of the ornate iron gates of the Carter residence. The villa was surrounded by a high wall and a man standing by the gates indicated that Kim should follow the track of the lights. She walked up the illuminated path and this led to the atrium of the Carters' palatial villa. She entered a large high-ceilinged room where all the guests had assembled. Everyone had dressed up for the occasion with a lot of the men in tuxedoes and the women in cocktail dresses. There were long pink candles glittering in every corner of the room. The flickering light of the candles was reflected back by the many mirrors hanging on the walls. Posies of pink and white roses stood in crystal vases on occasional tables and in one corner a five-man band in white jackets and black bow ties were playing rhythm and blues. Those would be Vivienne's friends she thought. There was a long linen draped table with ranks of polished glasses and ice buckets filled with foil topped champagne bottles. Waitresses dressed in black skirts and white shirts were circulating with silver trays of drinks and canapés. Excited voices and laughter competed with the music from the band.

She sighed with pleasure as she moved into the room. This was wonderful. What a delightful change it made to be dressed up, made up, light-hearted. With Owen it sometimes felt like she had been on suicide watch for years. She looked around the highly lit and perfumed room and recognised a few faces. There was Gary and his gang over there. A waitress held out a tray to her and she took a glass of champagne. It was Gail from the hog roast, the Australian woman Gary fancied.

'Hey Gail...'

'Hey Kim... You look great. Your hair suits you up like that.'

'Thanks.'

'Where's your fella?'

'Owen. He was gonna come tonight but he's got a fever.'

'Well it's gonna be some party,' Gail said as she moved away with her tray of glasses.

Kim joined Gary and his crowd and he whistled.

'Pretty lady. Now did your old man call Sander?' he said.

'The Dutch guy?'

'Yep.'

'He didn't call him yet and tonight he's got a fever and he's resting up.'

'Tell him it's worth making that call. I reckon he could get a good price. I talked your boat up to Sander.'

'Thanks Gary, you're a buddy. You know Owen. He works to his own timetable.'

She took another glass of champagne from a passing waitress. As she chatted to Gary she noticed Gideon Carter dressed in a white tuxedo was looking at her with unmasked appreciation. He was standing on the bottom step of the staircase and as their eyes met he smiled at her and raised his glass a bit. She raised her glass back at him and turned back to Gary feeling pleased. She knew she looked good.

Rob was sitting in the saloon of the dive boat as Doug cooked them their supper. It was going to be chilli con carne with rice. They had completed two dives and what a revelation the reef had been. It was as amazing as Owen had described it the first night they met in Belize. He had swum in the midst of a shoal of brilliantly coloured fish and on the second dive he had seen the huge sea sponges Owen had mentioned. A line from a poem he'd learned at school came back to him as he trod water and looked at the giant gently moving sponge in front of his mask: 'above him swell, Huge sponges of millennial growth and height'. It was a miraculous landscape beneath the surface of the sea, alike and yet different from the land forms above. There were valleys and walls of reef with jewel-coloured life forms darting everywhere. He had been thrilled to his core by it.

Now they were moored on a buoy and the sea was getting rougher. The wind was up and the boat was rolling and pitching. This time he had taken two Dramamine tablets and so far he was feeling OK, better than OK, he was feeling good, physically tired and ravenous after their two long dives.

'You know Roatán is not the paradise it might look to visitors,' Doug said as he handed Rob a beer.

'Thanks. It is paradise under the water,' Rob said.

'Yeah it is. We'll drink to that.'

They clinked their bottles together and drank. Rob wondered how Anna was doing alone in the cabin as Doug handed him a plate piled high with rice and meaty bean sauce.

Anna took a cool shower and changed into her white cotton trousers and a pale green T-shirt. She tied her hair back in a ponytail. It had been a sticky day, unpleasantly warm with too many insects buzzing around and trying to bite her when she'd sat outside after lunch. So she'd spent the afternoon inside, writing up her notebook and reading. She knew Kimberly and Owen were going to that big party tonight so she couldn't join them for dinner, but she felt the need to get out of the cabin. She would go down to Oak Ridge and have dinner out on her own, treat herself to something nice to eat and a glass of wine. She had her book with her and she would find a place where she could sit and eat and read.

She walked down the hill and into Oak Ridge which had the feel and the tension of a working town. She passed the fish and shrimp processing plant. What a stinking place it was. She couldn't imagine having to work there. She had seen lots of workers, male and female, coming out of the gates. That awful throat-catching smell must linger on your hair and your clothes when you got home. There was nowhere suitable to eat by the fish plant. Indeed she wouldn't have dared walk into some of the small bars she saw in this area. She continued round the harbour and even here she struggled to find a place where she would feel comfortable as a woman sitting on her own. She peered through the windows and doors and the bars were full of groups of working men. There didn't seem to be any women about and she wondered if she'd have to go back to the cabin after all.

Then she saw two women standing together down by the harbour wall. One woman, the older one, was dressed in a tight black top and a short skirt that rode up her legs. Her face was lined and her mouth had the slightly caved in look of a drug user who has lost some of her teeth. She was standing next to a younger woman with brightly hennaed hair who was wearing a micro-skirt, cropped top and high heeled sandals. They were both smoking and looking around in a desultory way. They had to be prostitutes. She hurried past them feeling a mixture of awkwardness and empathy. When she was a sixth-form student she had worked in a fruit-processing factory in Norfolk one summer holiday. She had stayed over at her grandparents' place for the whole six weeks. She had got to know the factory women well. They were a friendly and ribald group, always telling dirty jokes and laughing off their troubles although their lives were hard and money was short. One of their team had stopped coming to work and the other women speculated that she had gone 'on the game'. One woman said it was a mug's game and she would come to regret it. Another woman said 'you can't blame her. She'll get paid now for lying on her back, easier than what we do here.' Anna was a freshly minted feminist and had said if men weren't willing to pay for sex then there would be no prostitution. The first woman said 'the men pay with cash but the women pay in another way, a worse way, and no good will come of it.' The conversation had made a deep impression on her. Was it just her, or did other women also think about what it must feel like to work as a prostitute? What was it like to take all those different male organs into your body? Could you somehow detach yourself from your bodily sensations?

Five minutes later, she found a café where there was a woman serving behind the bar and she went in. She sat at a table in the corner, scanned the menu and ordered the dish of the day, a fish stew, and took out her book. But she didn't read. It had been a strangely disconcerting day from the moment she got up. She hadn't expected to miss being on the boat but she realised now that she did miss it.

Owen felt much worse. He was burning up and sweating and he needed water but he felt pinioned to the bed. Tonight in her anger and her haste Kim had left her money belt behind by the side of the bed. He reached for it, unzipped it and took out the small case. He opened this and held her sharp little knife and pressed the point against his forefinger until a tiny drop of blood appeared. He put the knife down on the floor by his pillow where he could reach it easily.

When Anna left the café it was dark and the weather had got worse. The wind was rising and the branches of the stunted mangroves were rocking back and forth. She hurried up the hill. She was not looking forward to the moment when she would have to unlock the door to her cabin. She would put on the lights and check all the rooms before she could relax. She wished she was a braver person, despising her feebleness at times like this. Then she saw that there were lights on in Owen's and Kim's cabin. That was odd. She thought they'd be at the party by now. She tapped on the door. No answer. She tapped again, waited a minute, twisted the handle and walked in. Owen was lying in the bedroom and he looked strange and sick.

'You're ill?'

'Can you get me some water,' he said.

His voice was hoarse. She got him a glass of water which he drank down at once, and then gulped down a second glass. She felt his forehead which was burning hot and his cheeks were unnaturally flushed.

'You need to cool down,' she said.

She went into the bathroom and found a small towel which she soaked in cold water and she used this to wipe his face and his arms.

'How long have you been like this?'

He moved his head on the pillow.

'A few hours...'

'Did you take anything to bring your temperature down?'

'I took some Tylenol,' he said.

'I'll stay with you till Kimberly gets back from the party.'

He lay on the bed and she kept wiping his face and his neck with the damp towel. He looked vulnerable lying in the bed staring up at her. There had always been something about Owen's face that went straight to her heart. It was the look in his eyes which was the look of a hurt, suffering child in his long, rangy man's body. She started to tell him about her work and what had drawn her to it. She had been deeply moved as a teenager when she read about how they had treated soldiers in the First World War who had lost the power of speech.

'It wasn't physical; the cause I mean. It wasn't to do with damaged vocal chords or anything like that. They simply stopped speaking. They treated them so cruelly, as if they were cowards. The officers got better treatment but the rank and file men were tortured. One man had electric shocks fired into his vocal chords until he made a sound, until he screamed.

They had stopped talking of course because they'd seen unspeakable things.'

Owen listened, his eyes glittering, his body jerked by occasional spasms. She knew she was rambling on but Owen seemed to have this effect on her.

'My dad stopped speaking,' he said.

He murmured something else but she couldn't hear him properly and she leaned closer to him.

'What did you say, Owen?'

'She shouldn't have taken us back there.'

'Who shouldn't?'

'I said we shouldn't go back there.'

He said more, in a fragmentary way, frequently stopping and darting his eyes around the room and exhaling as if he was scared.

'We were in the motel. Mom always said: "don't let the sun go down on your wrath." She couldn't stay angry with him. It was my birthday and he said he had to see me on my fourteenth birthday.'

She didn't interrupt him. He needed to tell his story in his own way but she wondered if he was hallucinating. She wiped his face with the wet towel again and he closed his eyes.

Kim talked and laughed with Gary's crowd and drank champagne and ate the exquisite canapés. She stood and listened to the band playing the rhythm and blues and they made good music as Vivienne had said they would. When they stopped playing she spoke to the singer, said she was a friend of Vivienne's who had mentioned the band to her. The singer grabbed a beer from a passing waitress. His face had lit up at the mention of Vivienne's name.

'You a good friend of hers?' he asked.

'Oh yeah, I saw her today. Olivier is over for a couple of weeks with some friends and I went over to see them all.'

'He's a good boy and a credit to her. I must go over and say hi to him while he's here.'

'He's gonna to be staying over in West End for the duration I think.'

'Well you tell Vivienne when you see her next that Herman is gonna stop on by and take her out for a drink and a bit of supper. Now I guess I should rest up a while before our next set.'

He walked away and Kim thought fondly there goes another man smitten with Vivienne. And why not, she was a gorgeous woman. She noticed a table at the side which was piled with gift-wrapped presents and a stack of cards addressed to Barbara and Gideon. She had not thought to bring anything with her, not even a card. Well the Carters were a couple who had everything already. She went to find their swimming pool which she'd been told was sensational. It was in a purpose-built glass extension that ran down one whole side of the house. The pool was huge and kidney-shaped. More lit pink candles had been arranged around the pool. Thick white towels were laid out for the use of guests on wooden loungers. There was a Jacuzzi on a raised platform by the pool. The whole area was empty of guests and she sat down on one of the loungers and looked around. The pool was so luxurious and tempting and she wished she'd thought to bring her bikini with her. Then she saw Gideon Carter come in.

'Are you thinking of swimming?' he said.

'I don't think so. It's such a beautiful pool though.'

'I'm sure it will fill up later when the guests get hot and lose their inhibitions,' he said.

'I wish I'd brought my swimming things with me.'

He looked at her.

'You're smaller than Barbara but I'm sure we could find something to fit you.'

'Maybe later,' she said feeling shy about the way he had been appraising her figure.

'Can I get you another glass of champagne, Kimberly?'

'Well thank you kindly.'

He came back with a bottle and filled both their glasses. They clinked and drank.

'Where's Owen tonight?'

'He was feeling ill and had to rest up.'

'Do you want to see the garden?' he said.

'It's kinda dark,' she said.

'It's all lit up. Come on, I'll give you the tour.'

He led her out through the pool door onto a long covered terrace lined with terracotta pots planted with orchids and some other scented flower she didn't recognise. She liked orchids even though they were kinda hot-house and some folks might even say artificial looking. She liked the exotic shapes of their petals and their colours, pink, peach, creamy white. She noticed he was carrying the bottle of champagne with him. The lights were placed artfully all around the garden. She wondered if Barbara had planned for the party to spill out here, but the wind was rising and you could hear the sea soughing beyond the villa. Everyone else had stayed inside. She enjoyed the feeling of the breeze on her face and arms. She was feeling a little over heated having drunk four glasses of champagne too quickly. From the terrace he took her into a rose garden which had a central gazebo and two wooden benches. They sat on one of the benches and he filled her glass again. She told herself to drink it slowly this time, to sip it.

'Wow orchids and now roses. You don't expect to see roses growing on the island.'

'They take some special work to grow here,' he said.

'Who does the gardening?'

'We've got two full-time gardeners.'

Most of the roses in the garden were in shades of pink and peach.

'Barbara likes pink I'm guessing,' she said.

'Yes and I thought you girls were supposed to grow out of that.'

He grinned at her and she smiled back.

'Do you want to see the herb garden?'

He led her deeper into the garden through a bower to some square beds planted with herbs. She recognised various smells on the night air.

'This must be coriander.'

She bent down and rubbed the leaf between her fingers and smelled it.

'My favourite...'

She walked along the bed, identifying the plants.

'Sage, and rosemary of course, and this is some sort of mint.'

She picked a few of the leaves, rolled them between her palms and inhaled.

'Lemon mint I think, how awesome to have all these herbs to cook with.'

He was bending over her and filling her glass again and she sensed he wanted to kiss her. But it was his wedding anniversary party for Chrissakes! She raised her glass to her lips quickly and took a big gulp, then felt a couple of large raindrops plop on her shoulders. He put his hand on the middle of her bare back and his hand was warm.

'We best get back inside. Don't want you to get wet,' he said.

The rain started to fall faster and he took her hand and they hurried back to the house. He dropped her hand as they reached the door to the atrium.

'Now for the boring bit,' he said.

Anna got up and looked through the cabin window. The sky was flashing white with lightening and she could see the shapes of the mangroves and avocado trees outside and they were swaying crazily as rain lashed into the cabin. She closed the window slats firmly. She got a chair from the kitchen and sat at the side of his bed. There was no sign of Kimberly and she was so tired. Owen was getting worse; his temperature was still rising and he was sweating profusely. His eyes were closed and he moaned from time to time as if he was in pain. She tried to keep him cool by continually bathing his head and arms but his T-shirt was wet with his sweat. He snapped his eyes open, kicked off the sheet and said uneasily:

'Where is she? It's been hours. Is she hurt?'

'No, no, of course not; it'll be this storm that's stopped her coming back. She'll be here soon.'

She went into the kitchen and boiled some water, put sugar in it and brought it to his bed.

'Come on, you need some fluids inside you.'

She helped him sit up and he drank a mouthful; then lay back against the damp pillows.

'Take your T-shirt off. I'll get you a clean one.'

He did not respond. She looked in the drawers and found a clean T-shirt. She kneeled at his side and tried to take his sweaty T-shirt off him. He pushed her away with all his force. She fell on the floor and banged her elbow hard.

'Ouch that hurt!'

She got to her knees and rubbed her elbow and looked angrily over at him and saw how his body was going rigid. He was shaking with convulsions. Anna had seen patients with febrile convulsions before. She knew it was caused by his excessively high temperature and she stayed calm. Then he vomited. He leaned over the side of the bed and was sick down his T-shirt and onto the floor. He fell back onto the bed and closed his eyes. His body had stopped shaking.

She filled a bucket with hot soapy water and approached him cautiously. She was worried he'd push her away again. She washed the vomit off the floor but kept her distance from him. Then she saw Kimberly's knife lying by his pillow. What was it doing there? She reached for it and just as her hand reached the knife Owen's hand flew out and stopped her from picking it up.

'Leave it,' he said harshly.

She jumped back from him. He put the knife under his pillow then closed his eyes again muttering some incomprehensible words.

'You're being difficult. I *wish* you'd let me clean you up. And there's nothing left in your stomach. You need to eat something. You must let me help you.'

She went into the kitchen and looked through what was in the cupboard. There were some vegetables and canned goods. She had a packet of rice in her cabin. Yes a little bit of boiled rice would do the job and she would pick up her first-aid kit too. She looked at him lying on the bed and he seemed unaware of her presence, so she said nothing, unlocked the door and ran through the rain to her cabin. She found her first-aid kit, which she always carried with her whenever she travelled. She sat on the bed and went through its contents quickly: paracetamol, antiseptic lotion, plasters, bandages. In the kitchen cupboard she found the packet of rice and a small bottle of soy sauce and she took some tea bags too. She needed a cup of tea badly. Her elbow and arm were throbbing from her fall and she wanted so much to rest. She went into the bathroom and splashed cold water on her face. The rain on the roof of the cabin sounded like a hundred drumsticks beating on a hundred drums. This was not like English rain. There was something fierce and elemental about it. She wondered how Rob was doing on the dive boat. The sea would be rough and she hoped he was not being tossed by the waves and made sick by it. She wanted him here with her now very much. Her exhaustion and Owen's weird reactions were making her feel scared. She gathered everything together and headed back to Owen's cabin. The door was swinging open and banging shut in the wind. But she had closed it when she went. She hurried inside and Owen was gone. The sheet was flung back from the bed as if he had left in a rush. She saw his vomit stained T-shirt in the corner. She felt under the pillow and Kimberly's knife was gone.

Gideon Carter was standing on the fifth step of the staircase with a microphone in his hand. Gradually the hubbub in the room quieted and more guests pushed into the atrium. It was unpleasantly hot in there with all the bodies pressed together. The combination of the champagne and the heated and over-perfumed room was making Kim feel queasy. She had felt better in the garden. Gideon waited until he had the attention of the room. He scanned the crowd below him and launched into a witty speech about the charm and unpredictability of life on the island reflecting the charm and unpredictability of marriage. He got a lot of laughs. He said how much he appreciated the presence of so many friends and he thanked Barbara for organising such a great party. Shame about the weather but that was Roatán for you. Barbara was standing at the bottom of the stairs looking up at him and she smiled at Gideon and held her glass up when he said:

'To the next twenty years.'

It all felt a bit false to Kim as if it was a show put on for the benefit of lesser mortals like her and Gary and all the other people on the island who looked on the Carters as a kind of royalty. Gideon told everyone to enjoy the rest of the night and put down the microphone. The musicians started to play again and the guests moved away from the staircase. Some people started to dance. Kim walked to the door of the atrium and watched as the rain hurled down and exploded on the paved path outside. She wondered if all those orchids on the terrace would survive this onslaught. She would have liked to get more air but she couldn't go out in that rain. She walked through to the swimming pool room. Some guests were now in the pool shrieking with glee and she saw Barbara Carter at the centre of a circle of guests by the loungers, talking and laughing. Their voices were bouncing off the glass walls and ceiling and she decided to find a room where she could sit quietly until her dizziness and queasiness had passed.

Back in the atrium she pushed through the melee of guests and opened a door into a long room which was clearly the Carters' dining room. There were large canvasses of modern art hanging on the walls and a dining table which would seat twenty people with ease. She saw a high-backed chair in the corner of the room and she sat down on this, taking her sandals off and pulling her feet up under her. The large chair dwarfed her as she rested her head back. She closed her eyes and felt blood pulsing in her temples.

'Don't you like dancing?'

She opened her eyes to see Gideon Carter standing in front of the chair smiling down at her and holding her gold sandals in his hands. She hadn't heard him approach so she must have fallen asleep.

'I'm feeling kinda hot and dizzy at the moment.'

'Let me show you the rest of the house then. It will be quieter and cooler up there. Best put these on first.'

She found herself doing what he said. She strapped her sandals on and took his hand when he held it out to her. From the dining room he took her into an octagonal-shaped room with cream walls and a glass roof. He said this was the break-fast room. It looked more lived in than the rest of the house with a stack of newspapers and magazines splayed on the table. He showed her a photograph hanging on the wall. It was black and white and fuzzy as if it had been blown up from a much smaller picture and it showed a poor-looking house with a fence around it.

'You come from Florida, don't you?' he said.

'Yeah, Clearwater.'

'That's the house where I grew up. Kissimmee.'

She looked at the photograph. It was the house of a family without much money, a bit like the house where she'd grown up.

'I've never been to Kissimmee,' she said.

'I don't go back there any more.'

He took her hand again and led her into the kitchen where two waitresses were washing glasses. One of them turned and looked as he strode through the kitchen holding Kim by the hand. It was Gail.

'You're doing a great job gals,' he said.

He took her up the back stairs of the house. She let him lead her through the upstairs rooms, let him show her the rich carpets and the art on the walls. She could hear the music below and she thought I must tell him I'm OK now and I want to go downstairs and dance. He led her up to the landing above and the music was faint now. There was a sharp crack of thunder and the sky outside the windows was lit by a flash of static brilliance. They both stood and watched the storm from a window. The lights that were tied in the trees were moving madly in the wind and she wondered if they would break free and smash on the path below. So he had been a poor boy once. He came and stood behind her and stroked the back of her neck and her shoulders with his warm fingers.

'You can't travel back in this,' he said.

He turned her to him and started to kiss her gently and then moved one large hand up under her dress.

The thunder reverberated like two mountains coming together and Anna flinched. She was walking along the path leading from the cabins to the town looking for Owen. It was madness for him to be out in this storm with such a high temperature. The rain was hitting her face, getting into her eyes and she was cursing him. Could he have headed back to his boat? In his confusion and sickness would he go there? Probably. It was his haven. Now she could see right down the hill towards the shore and there was no sign of his tall angular frame moving below. She gave up and went back to his cabin. She stood inside the threshold and wondered what to do. And then she heard a strange thudding sound and it seemed to be coming from behind the cabin. She stood very still and listened intently. There it was again, a dull thudding, followed by a rustling sound under the cacophony of the rain. It was strange how sounds that seemed perfectly harmless in the daytime took on a sinister aspect when it was the middle of the night. Could Owen have gone back there and fallen down? More likely it was just the wind making some unsecured door bang somewhere nearby; one of the empty cabins perhaps? But she would have to check in case it was him. She had seen a torch in their kitchen and went to get it, switched it on and went outside again. She felt afraid of what she might find as she crept behind the cabins, shining the torch's beam onto the wet ground in front of her. There was the rustling sound again. She walked in the direction of the noise.

'Owen? Is that you?' her voice came out high and squeaky.

Another rustle. She swung round and saw it was the wind sweeping some fallen mangrove branches across the ground.

'Damn you Owen,' she said.

She marched back to the cabin and put the kettle on to make tea. The water came to the boil and she was pouring it into her cup when she heard footsteps behind her and spun around, the kettle in her hand. Through the kitchen door she saw Owen taking faltering steps towards her. He had no T-shirt on, just his boxer shorts and he was covered in blood. He was holding Kim's knife which was black and sticky. His eyes were unfocused as if he was sleepwalking. She saw lines of blood running down his chest and stomach like so many little rivers. He lifted the knife and cut himself again on his torso and fresh blood ran.

'Don't do that!' she cried.

He started as if he was waking up and his eyes came into focus. She put the kettle down with trembling fingers as he walked towards her and then stood perfectly still right in front of her.

'Why are you doing that?'

'He said he was saving us.'

It was as if he was seeing another scene, some scene of horror. Her heart was hammering but she saw the suffering man standing in front of her and he needed her help. She had a moment of insight.

'Did your father hurt your mum?'

His eyes jerked into focus again and now he looked at her intently as if he was seeing her properly for the first time. He reached out his other hand which also had blood on it. He touched the mole between her eyebrows with his forefinger.

'You have a third eye. You're one of the real people, Anna,' he said.

He looked down at the knife in his hand and dropped it.

'He stabbed my mom and sister and I did nothing to stop it.'

'Oh Owen...'

He went on in a great rush of words as if he couldn't stop them coming out now.

'I heard him come in and I heard my mom scream when she saw his hunting knife and he kept saying "I'm saving you, I'm saving you" and he stabbed her right in the neck and all this blood spurted out and Megan was there and she tried to run but he grabbed her and he stabbed her in the neck too and his eyes were crazy. I ran up the stairs and crawled under my bed and he came looking for me and there was blood all over him.'

He exhaled and rubbed his own bloody hands over his eyes leaving a smear of blood on his eyelids and forehead.

'He came into my room and saw my Silver Cup which I won for Karate. He picked it up and blood was smeared all over my Cup and he sat down on my bed and started to sob.

I was only feet away from him, lying under the bed and I heard him sobbing.'

'How terrible.'

'He put my cup down on the floor and I heard this horrible gurgling sound. He'd slit his throat. There was blood everywhere, everywhere and I did nothing to save them.'

He started to howl.

'Wash me clean,' he said.

Anna opened her arms to him and he moved towards her. She held him in her arms and rocked him and kissed his head as he cried and cried such bitter tears.

'What could you have done? You were just a boy, a young terrified boy. It wasn't your fault.'

'I should have saved Megan; she was my little sister. He stabbed her in the neck and her blood came spurting out so fast.'

She cradled him in her arms.

'It wasn't your fault.'

'I hid under the bed.'

'There was nothing else you could have done.'

It was an age before he stopped crying; there were years and years of pushed down tears that needed to come out. At last he raised his head off her shoulder and he seemed completely spent. She bathed the wounds on his chest and stomach and applied antiseptic lotion and he didn't resist her attentions this time. Beneath the new cuts on his torso she could see a myriad criss-crossing of scars, some recent, some much older. This was not the first time he had cut himself. She bandaged his chest. Then she washed his face and hands and dressed him in a clean T-shirt and boxers and got him back into bed.

'Come on, lie down now,' she said gently.

She helped him lie back against the pillows and pulled a clean sheet over him.

'Sleep now. I won't leave you.'

She stroked the dark wet hair back from his forehead and a painful shuddering sigh escaped from deep inside himself.

The rain was lessening at last but she knew Kimberly was not coming back and she could not leave the cabin with Owen so desperately in need of her care. He was sleeping now, the sleep of pure exhaustion after great emotion. The towel she'd used to dry him with was soaked in blood, wet with it. She ran a bucket of cold water and left the towel and his T-shirt to soak in the kitchen. She picked up Kimberly's knife and cleaned it and put it back into its case and then hid it in the kitchen cupboard behind the tinned food. Now she understood why Kimberly hid knives and why Kimberly was so afraid of broken glass. They would all be triggers for Owen's terrible memories. And they were the tools of his harm too. He must have been self-harming for a long time. It was why he never took his T-shirt off; he was hiding his scars. She looked down and saw Owen's blood on the front of her T-Shirt. She locked the cabin door and hurried back into their cabin. She found a clean T-shirt to change into and hurried back to Owen's cabin. The room felt stuffy so she opened the slats of the window. Owen was now deeply asleep. How she longed to stretch out on the bed next to him, to get a few hours' sleep. She knew he wouldn't hurt her now. She gave in to the impulse, took off her shoes, pulled the band from her hair and lay down next to him on top of the bed. She sank into a bone weary sleep as the wind outside dropped to a whisper and the trees were silenced.

And if Owen had been able to float above his body that night he would have seen Rob sleeping peacefully in the back berth of Doug's dive boat as it rolled and pitched gently now the storm had passed. He would have seen Kim lying naked and alone in a bed in the Carters' villa as the party guests departed. And he would have seen Anna lying next to him on the cabin's double bed with her dark hair fanned out on the pillow.

DAY EIGHTEEN

Kim woke up around 5 a.m. and her head was throbbing with a vicious champagne-induced headache. Her throat was painfully dry and her eyes were sticky as she pulled them open. She was naked and the bed she was lying in smelled of sex. She put her arms over her head and curled into a foetal position as the details of the night before came back to her. He had been kissing her, touching her and then leading her into this room. She hadn't resisted. There was no way she could pretend he had forced her. She had wanted sex with him and had orgasmed twice and that never happened.

She had to find her clothes and get out without anyone seeing her. She groped on her hands and knees around the floor and under the bed for her panties, dress and sandals. She slid her dress on before opening the door into the corridor. There would be a bathroom somewhere near here where she could wash herself. She crept along the corridor in her bare feet and found a bathroom with a shower. She slid the lock carefully behind her. First she drank handful after handful of cold water from the tap to slake her thirst. She splashed cold water on her face while trying to avoid her reflection in the mirror above the washbasin. She stepped into the shower. Her body felt a bit bruised and her nipples were tender. While she was soaping herself, and lathering again and again between her legs, she remembered Gail. Gail had been in the kitchen and had seen Gideon leading her through to the back stairs and up to the bedrooms. And Gail was friends with Gary, and Gary was friends with Owen. A wave of hot shame made her tremble under the shower's blast of water. She got out and towelled herself and pulled on her panties and her dress. Carrying her sandals she unlocked the bathroom door and crept back along the corridor to the back-stairs of the house. She couldn't remember where she had left her purse, which had her money in it. She'd have to leave it as she wasn't going to go searching for it now. She had to get away from this house as fast as she could.

The kitchen was in darkness and had been returned to order, although she could smell the lingering reek of wine on the air. Cardboard boxes full of glasses were stacked on the large central table and there were plastic recycle boxes stacked with empty champagne bottles. A cover had been put over what was left of the anniversary cake. It had been iced and tiered like a wedding cake. Looking at the cake she became aware of the enormity of his betrayal; for him to have done that on the night of his anniversary party. She tried the kitchen door into the garden. It was locked. She looked around the kitchen and spotted a bunch of keys on a hook by the sink. She tried the keys one by one till she found the right one and pulled the door open. As she sat down to put on her sandals she felt the early morning air on her face and the dew on the grass. She was trying hard to remember if the Carters had any dogs. She got to her feet looking around nervously but could see no sign of dogs who would give her away. She walked through the herb garden and through the rose garden till she found the main path leading to the gates. She was remembering how Gideon kept filling her glass as he led her ever deeper into the garden. And she had gone along with it.

She kept coming back to the fact that Gideon had done this on a night when he was celebrating twenty years of marriage to Barbara. It was the unbelievable arrogance of the man; that he could have whatever he wanted. And she had had sex with him so what did that make her?

The main path was in full view of the house and anyone looking out couldn't fail to see her. She hoped everyone still slept on. She picked her way along the edge of the path in the shadow of the trees lining its route. When she got to the large wrought iron gates she discovered they were locked. Of course, after the last guests had gone the staff would have locked the whole place up. The villa was surrounded by walls and gates, like a fortress. What were the Carters afraid of? And how had Gideon intended to explain her presence in the house, in the guest bedroom? He would find a way round it no doubt; say she'd got drunk and he'd got a waitress to put her to bed.

She was trying hard not to think about Owen as she retraced her steps back through the flower garden and through to the vegetable garden behind the villa. There had to be a way out of here somewhere, maybe an entrance the staff used. Beyond the vegetable garden she saw a wooden door cut into the wall. She headed for this and her gold sandals sank into the soft earth which looked as if it had been recently dug up. The garden door was locked. She remembered the bunch of keys in the kitchen. She hurried back to the kitchen, grabbed these and returned to the garden door. Time was passing and before long the staff might start to arrive. She tried all the keys on the ring. Not one of them opened the garden door. She would have to climb up over the garden wall and get out that way. The wall was high and there were no trees anywhere near the wall which she could use to get a foothold. She returned the keys to the hook in the kitchen; then headed for the large shed she had spotted. This at least had been left unlocked. She peered inside and behind the forks and shovels she saw a small metal stepladder. It wasn't very tall and wouldn't reach the top of the garden wall but it would get her within reaching distance. She manoeuvred the stepladder out and placed it against the wall and climbed to the top. She could see over the wall now. The surface of the wall was rough and she grazed the inside of her arms as she hauled herself up the rest of the way until she was straddling the wall. She looked down the other side and it was quite a jump. She took her sandals off and held the straps in her teeth as she jumped from the top of the wall onto the ground. She was winded when she landed and she sat on the ground for a few minutes and cried tears of guilt and shame and remorse. Her white dress was stained with soil and her grazed arms hurt now as well as her head. She got to her feet. She had a six-mile walk ahead of her.

She had been walking along the road towards Oak Ridge for about forty minutes before she heard and then saw a battered pick-up van drive by with two men and a dog sitting in the back. They had tools with them, farmworkers on their way to the fields. They called out to her but she wouldn't ask them for a lift. Her high-heeled sandals were pinching badly and her feet were swollen and sore. She took them off and walked on barefoot even though the road surface was rough. She was suffering and felt she deserved every bit of it. How could she face Owen and what could she say? Even if she said the storm had meant she couldn't get back to the cabin look at her filthy dress and grazed arms and her purse gone. How to explain all that? She thought back to her fight with Owen the evening before. She had felt she was entitled to a night of fun and, yes, she had wanted to get away from him for a few hours. She stood on a sharp pebble in her bare feet and cried out in pain, sat on the ground and saw the sole of her foot was bleeding. She put her thumb in her mouth and wet it with saliva and held it against the sore place. All kinds of men had come onto her over the years but she had never once betrayed Owen. What made her feel worse was that she had enjoyed the sex with Gideon Carter while it was happening. She remembered saying to him more, harder, more. He had pulled her on top of him like Owen used to do and had pinched her nipples. They felt sore now beneath her dress. She stood up and made herself walk on. She heard the sound of another vehicle, this time approaching from Oak Ridge, and as it came into view she saw it was a blue saloon car with large flashy chrome fins. It drove past her then slowed down and stopped. The driver got out. It was Teyo. He walked over to her grinning widely. His black hair was held back with a pair of sunglasses on the top of his head and his thick gold chain swung beneath his half opened shirt.

'Hola pretty Kimberly. Can I give you a lift?'

'But you were driving away from Oak Ridge,' she said.

'You need to get there?'

'Yeah, our boat is there but...'

'I can take you. It's a short detour.'

She was still over three miles from Oak Ridge and her feet were so sore.

'I don't wanna put you out.'

'It's no trouble,' he said.

'Well um, I guess, if you're sure, well that would be kind, thanks.'

He opened the passenger door for her with a flourish and as he walked round to get in the driver's side she was thinking fast. Get him to drop her down by the boat, not at the cabins, she wouldn't mention the cabins. He got in and looked over at her.

'Where can I take you Kimberly?'

She hated the way he said her name, Kim-ber-ly, as if he was tasting her name, rolling it around in his mouth. She should have refused the lift. He must have noticed her stained dress and dirty feet and wondered where Owen was.

'Our boat's moored on the far side of the harbour. Can you drop me near there please.'

He made a three point turn in the road and started to drive back towards Oak Ridge.

'You were at the big party last night?'

She needed to be careful. She knew that on Roatán everyone was connected to everyone else and there was always the bush telegraph humming around the island.

'Yeah I was.'

'And you just left?'

She resolved to say as little as possible, to give nothing away, so she merely nodded half smiling at him and put her hands in her lap and clasped them.

'I heard they ordered two hundred bottles of champagne,' he said.

She made no reply. Her temples were pulsing painfully. Every now and then he looked over at her as he drove along the road and his looking made her feel uneasy and ashamed. She in turn found herself looking at his hands on the steering wheel with a sick fascination. He had thick stubby fingers and the tops of his hands were scarred.

Doug sailed his boat back to his mooring at Oak Ridge and he and Rob exchanged email addresses and said they would keep in touch. Rob strode up the hill, looking forward to telling Anna about his wondrous dives on the pristine reef. Their cabin door was unlocked which surprised him. He went in and there was no sign of her. The beds were made and the kitchen was tidy. If she'd gone out for the day surely she would have locked up. He left his rucksack on the floor and went next door to Owen's cabin. This door was locked and he could hear no voices or movement from within. He walked around the side of the cabin and looked through the slats of the bedroom window. He saw Anna lying stretched out on the double bed. She was still in her clothes, her long dark hair was spread out on the pillow, her arm was resting on Owen's hip and he was asleep at her side. Rob stepped back from the window as if it had burned him. He went and sat on the doorstep and tried to calm the clamour of his jealous heart. He did not want to think badly of her. He had always loved that Anna was different to most of the women he met, he loved her uprightness, her lack of vanity, her straightness, if you like.

It was some time later when he steeled himself to tap on the cabin door. He waited, hearing movements behind the door and then Anna opened it. She looked half asleep.

'Oh Rob, thank God you're back.'

She went to hug him and he pulled back from her.

'What are you doing here?' he said in a hard voice.

'Keep your voice down. Owen's sleeping. He's been very sick.'

'Really?'

'We'll talk in our cabin.'

She turned and crept back into the bedroom. Owen was still asleep. He looked pale but less feverish. She picked up her shoes and closed the door gently behind her.

'The crisis has passed,' she said.

They were back in their cabin and Rob was standing with his arms crossed over his chest.

'What crisis?' he said.

'Owen was very sick last night. He had febrile convulsions and was vomiting and then he started to cut himself.'

'I don't understand what you're saying.'

She took a deep breath and tried to order her thoughts.

'It all came out last night. His father flipped and stabbed his mum and his little sister and then killed himself. Slit his throat. Owen saw it all. Can you imagine?'

Rob sat down and tried to take it in.

'His father?'

'Yes his father. He went berserk. Owen was fourteen and his sister was younger. Killed her and Owen's mum. Owen escaped. He was hiding under the bed.'

'Christ!'

'He has so much guilt Rob, that he did nothing to save them. He saw it all and he blames himself. So he's been self-harming for years, cutting himself on his chest and stomach. He used Kimberly's knife on his chest last night. It was horrible; so frightening and so sad.'

'Where is Kim?'

'She didn't come back from the party and I couldn't leave him.'

They sat in silence.

'I'm exhausted,' she said.

She did look done in and he felt guilty he had suspected her.

'You best get some sleep.'

She undressed and he tucked her into bed and kissed her face before arranging the mosquito net over her bed frame.

'Were *you* OK? We had an awful storm here last night and I was worried it might make you sick,' she said.

'It was rough but I wasn't sick this time. And the reefs were miraculous Anna, quite miraculous.'

'I'm so glad.'

But she didn't look glad. She had a troubled look on her face. He closed the bedroom door and left her to sleep.

It was two hours later and Rob was sitting outside when he saw Owen emerge from his cabin. He was shocked at how ill Owen looked. He hadn't dressed, was wearing a white T-shirt and boxer shorts and his feet were bare. He took unsteady steps over to Rob, who went and got him a seat from the kitchen.

'I just woke up. Where's Kim?'

'She's not come back yet.'

'She should be back by now.'

'Sit there I'll make us some coffee.'

Rob came out with two mugs of coffee and they sat and drank it.

'She may have gone back to the boat. We had words last night,' Owen said.

'I can go look for her in a bit.'

'I'm coming with you.'

'You don't look up to it. Really. Anna said you were very sick last night. I can go down to the boat for you.'

As he sat there Rob wondered if he should make any reference to what Anna had told him. He was about to say something when he noticed that blood was seeping through the front of Owen's white T-shirt.

'You're bleeding,' he said.

Owen looked down.

'Anna bandaged me up last night.'

He got to his feet.

'I'll get dressed and then we can go find Kimmie.'

Anna was still sleeping so before he left Rob wrote a note and left it in the kitchen. He felt reluctant to leave her and he locked the cabin door behind him. Owen had changed into another T-shirt and long shorts. They took the hill down to the shore slowly as Owen seemed to be in some pain. He scanned the beach and the sea. Through the hazy morning light they could see that his dinghy was on its mooring.

'It's still there, look. She can't have gone to the boat,' Owen said.

'Is it worth rowing over anyway, to check?'

'Yep, let's do that.'

Rob rowed them out to the El Tiempo Pasa and Owen waited in the dinghy as he climbed aboard the boat. He pulled up the washboard and checked the saloon. There was the pile of sewing Kim had left on the berth, the new curtains she had made, but she wasn't there. He slid the washboard back into place and shook his head at Owen and got back into the dinghy.

'Could she have stayed over at the Carters'? There was a big storm last night.'

'Maybe. I wanna check Oak Ridge first,' Owen said.

As Owen and Rob walked through the streets and alleys of Oak Ridge they both sensed that something was up in the town. The shrimp and fish processing plant was shut, the gates chained. Small groups of workers were standing outside the gates talking and smoking. They fell silent as Owen and Rob passed them. Owen was walking with difficulty – he was obviously in pain.

'Let's stop for a coffee now. You look all done in,' Rob said.

They found a bar, one of the rougher places where the fish

plant workers went, and Owen sat down, wincing and put his hand up to his chest. Rob went to the counter and waited while the woman made them two coffees. There was a group of local men standing there talking in low voices. They stopped talking as he reached the counter and looked at him suspiciously. He recognised the atmosphere. Something bad had happened, something that had disturbed these men, and they were tough men. He carried the drinks back to Owen.

'Something's up,' he said.

'I know; there's a bad atmosphere in here,' Owen said.

Owen drank his coffee down in one gulp.

'We should leave. I don't like the mood in here.'

The door opened and Cesar the driver came into the café and looked around. Owen called his name and he approached their table slowly, reluctantly even.

'What's up Cesar? What's happened?' Owen said.

Cesar wiped his hand over his mouth and looked over at the men standing at the counter.

'Sit with us. Come on. Let me get you a drink,' Owen pressed him.

Cesar would not sit down at their table.

'You haven't heard have you,' Cesar said.

'Heard what?'

He leaned in towards them and said:

'They found a woman's body at the fish plant, a few hours ago; murdered.'

At Cesar's words Owen leaped to his feet. His chair crashed onto the floor and he ran out of the café. Rob put money on the table and followed him. Owen was running towards the fish plant. He got to the gates and started to shake them violently. He was shouting at the top of his voice, howling for someone to come open them, but no-one came to the gates. The frantic effort of shaking the gates had made his chest start to bleed again. Rob saw a dark wet patch spreading across his T-shirt.

'It can't be her; it can't be her,' he kept saying as he rattled the gates.

'It could be anyone. Don't torment yourself,' Rob said.

Owen's face was waxy and he looked close to fainting. He slid down the wall and sat on the ground. Rob sat down next to him.

'You're sick Owen; you must go back to the cabin.'

'Where is she?'

'I'll go up to the Carter villa now, make some enquiries there,' Rob said.

'I'm coming with you.'

'No. She may come back to the cabin at any time. You need to be there.'

He wouldn't listen. Rob helped him to his feet and they walked away from the fish plant. Some way along by the side of a small chapel Rob saw an alley and a yellow sign at its entrance saying Mini Cabs and Water Taxis This Way. They walked up the alley and found a small dark office which had no entrance, there was a window with chicken wire over it. Rob spoke through the grille.

'We need to get to Port Royal as soon as possible.'

'The boats are out. We can take you by road.'

'OK.'

They got into the back of the car and it worried Rob that Owen was travelling with his wounds still seeping blood.

Anna slept deeply for several hours and when she woke up she lay in bed and went through the events of the night before. She got up and found Rob's note in the kitchen and showered and dressed. Rob and Owen were still out so she decided she'd take the bus over to Coxen Hole. She remembered seeing an internet café there, the only one she'd seen on the island, and she had to find out more about what had happened to Owen all those years ago. She couldn't stop thinking about it. She wrote on the bottom of Rob's note telling him where she was going but not why, in case Owen got to see the note too.

It was eighteen miles on the bus and it was hot and crowded with local people again. The internet café she had spotted was near the post office. She paid the two-dollar fee and found herself a desk at the back of the room. She typed in Owen Adams and the location: Clearwater, Florida, USA. A number of news reports came up on her screen. She clicked on one, a Florida newspaper, and read that Jim Adams had served in the US Air Force for twenty-two years and his last posting was at an Air Force base in Tampa, Florida. In 1988 he was discharged on grounds of ill-health, suffering from Post-Traumatic Stress Disorder. On 26 February 1989 he killed his wife and daughter by stabbing them repeatedly. His daughter Megan was seven years old. He then killed himself. His son Owen, who was fourteen years old, was in the house and alerted the police. There were photographs of Jim Adams and Owen's mum Bronwyn and his little sister Megan. She found the picture of Megan Adams particularly heart-breaking. A bright little face looked out from the screen, a face which shared some of Owen's features. Poor little tragic Megan, dead at seven. She remembered the words Owen had said to her while they were watching the baptism on the beach:

'You're powerless when you're a young kid. Your parents have all the control.'

It had jarred with her at the time but now it made sense. She went on to read the reports of the inquest. She was surprised and angered at how few column inches were devoted to it. Three lives ended violently and a fourteen-year-old boy left traumatised for life: surely it was worth more than the few inches she could find here? The last sentence said flatly:

The couple's son Owen was the sole survivor of the attack.

Survivor? How did you ever survive something like that? This was the horror Owen had been carrying inside himself for the last twenty-four years. She followed more links and came across a longer article, written by a journalist six months after the killings. She printed this article and left the internet café.

She realised she hadn't eaten all day so she found a café, ordered a tortilla and started to read the article. This journalist had dug deeper for details of the atrocity and had spoken to Jim Adams' sister Cally. He must have gained her trust because he got her to reveal much more about what had led to the frenzied attack. Cally explained that about a year before the killings there had been a freak accident at the air base; a spillage of fuel which had covered an airman. He had caught fire and burned alive in front of Jim. The dead man had been a friend of Jim's; they had joined the Air Force at the same time. Cally said her brother was never the same after witnessing that accident. He had broken down once and told her about it; had said the screams and the smell came back to him all the time. It was impossible to stop the images playing in his mind. But it was his memory of the smell that was the worst. It was for ever in his nostrils and the smell of a burning body was something you could never forget.

'*They didn't help him. The air force was his life and they abandoned him,*' she was quoted as saying.

Cally also shared Jim Adams' suicide note with the journalist. This had been found by the police in the pocket of his jeans. He had written that the world was an evil place where it was impossible to live a good life and be a good person. There was a battle going on between good and evil forces and the Devil had all the power and was going to triumph. His wife Bronwyn and his beloved children Owen and Megan were pure souls. He loved them and he had to save them from future sin and wretchedness by killing them. He knew God would forgive him and would gather them all to his bosom. Amen. Anna read the article twice and was close to tears. She folded it and put it in her bag. She left the café and headed back to the bus stop.

The taxi trundled down the path and pulled up in front of the gates of the Carter villa. Rob asked the driver to wait and he and Owen got out. Owen's T-shirt was now badly stained by the blood and he took faltering steps so that Rob gripped him by the arm as they approached the gates. They were locked and a guard was sitting on a stool on the other side fanning himself with a newspaper. He got to his feet and came to the gate.

'We need to speak to Gideon Carter at once,' Owen said through the bars.

'I don't think so,' the guard said.

'It's urgent.'

The guard shook his head.

'He's not seeing anyone today.'

Rob tried.

'We're worried about a guest who was at the party last night, Kimberly Adams. All we want to know is if she's in the house.'

'All the guests have gone,' the guard said.

'Can we speak to Barbara Carter then?' Owen said, his voice hardening.

'I've had instructions. They're seeing no-one today.'

Rob tried again.

'We're very worried. Kim has not arrived home. She was here last night. All we're asking is that you check with the Carters that she left here safely and at what time.'

'There's no point my checking. All the guests are gone.'

'You're a cunt,' Owen said.

The guard gave them both an insolent smile and made a finger gesture. He turned and went back to his stool and his newspaper. Owen looked murderous as Rob led him back to the taxi.

'Back to Oak Ridge?' the driver asked.

He had his windows down and had heard the exchange with the guard.

'Not yet. There must be someone else we can ask,' Rob said looking around.

'My cousin works in the big house,' the driver said.

Owen looked up.

'Is there another way in?'

'There's the staff entrance round the back. I'll take you there.'

He reversed up the drive and parked around the corner, out of sight of the guard at the front gates. Then he used his phone to call someone. He spoke rapidly and then turned to them.

'My cousin will come and speak to you.'

He pointed to the path that led down by the side of the garden wall.

'There's a door there.'

Rob and Owen walked down the path towards the door.

The driver followed a few steps behind them. After some minutes the garden door in the wall opened and a tired looking woman came out looking around nervously. The driver said something to her in Spanish.

'She was working at the party last night,' he said.

Owen spoke urgently to the woman.

'Did you see my wife? Kimberly Adams. Small, blonde curly hair.' He stopped and thought. 'Wearing a white dress.'

The woman nodded.

'I see her.'

'Did she stay here last night?'

'I think so. At the top of the house.'

'And she's still here?'

'No, she was gone when I come this morning.'

'What time was that?' Owen asked.

'About seven-thirty.'

Owen exhaled and leaned against the wall as if he needed it to support him.

'You're sure she's gone?' Rob said.

The woman nodded slowly.

'She's gone.'

Owen had gone very white and his legs had buckled.

'They killed my Kimmie,' he said.

Rob took him by the arm and led him back to the car. The driver touched Rob's arm and jerked his head in the direction of his cousin.

'She's a widow and she's got three children to feed.'

'Of course,' Rob said.

He helped Owen into the car and then walked back and gave the woman a twenty-dollar bill.

*

It was a slow journey back on the bus and Anna felt deeply shaken by what she had read. It had shifted a lot of things in her mind. So his father in his great distress had found God who *would gather them all to his bosom*. Owen hated religion. But it must hold some fascination for him or why else would he have suggested they go watch the baptism on the beach? She understood now how Kimberly had been trying to protect Owen for years. She was a loving and loyal person; there could be no doubting that. But she wondered if Kimberly's way of dealing with it, keeping it all a deep dark secret, was the right way. She had learned through her work that buried trauma created misery and sickness. Owen suffered from acute insomnia. He had been self-harming for years. Those scars on his chest and stomach, which he hid from everyone, must be daily reminders of what he had witnessed. She found herself anxious and aware of how dangerous last night had been. Owen was an unexploded bomb.

And poor Jim Adams, his tormented father, he too was a victim. He had witnessed a horror which he could not forget or escape. He had said *'I'm saving you'* as he stabbed his wife and daughter to death. Was it possible that Jim Adams thought that killing his family was an act of love? As she got off the bus at Oak Ridge she noticed two policemen with a huddle of people standing around them. The people were asking questions, talking in Spanish so she couldn't understand what it was about, but everyone looked grim. As she moved past the crowd she had an even stronger feeling than she'd had the day before that they should not have moved to the cabins. There was something about Oak Ridge that unnerved her. It was partly the smell of the place. There was the reek of rotting fish on the air. But it was also as if some equilibrium between the four of them had been disturbed when they left the boat.

She climbed the hill and when she got to the top she saw Kimberly sitting on the doorstep of their cabin. She looked dishevelled and was wearing her white party dress which was stained. She hurried over but Kimberly did not stand up; just sat there looking up at her with a weary expression on her face.

'Here you are, we've all been worried about you. Are you OK?'

Kim shook her head.

'I'm locked out. I've been sitting here for hours.'

'Rob and Owen are out looking for you.'

'It's a long story. But first I need a shower and can you lend me some clean clothes.'

'Of course.'

Anna unlocked their cabin.

Kim stood in the shower. Her nipples were very sore now and the jets of water were painful against them. She turned her back to the water and cried for a few minutes. She still didn't feel clean and she didn't feel ready to face Anna's clear-eyed questions. After Teyo had dropped her down by the harbour she had felt him watching her as she walked away. So she'd headed along the beach as if she was going to the boat. She kept walking until she was sure he had driven away. She saw a lounger left under a tree and sat down on it. Something precious between her and Owen was lost for ever. She lay down and cried herself to sleep. What woke her several hours later was the voice of a man demanding payment for the lounger. She'd had to explain that she had no money and he'd got nasty with her. When she'd got back to the cabins they were both locked up. She got out of the shower and dried and dressed herself in the panties and T-shirt Anna had given her. Anna was taller than her and she was glad the T-shirt was long enough to cover the beginnings of thumb sized bruises at the top of her thighs; those tell-tale bruises. She had the strongest impulse to throw her white satin dress away. She could not imagine ever wanting to wear it again. She bundled it up and joined Anna in the kitchen.

'I'm making tea. Do you want a coffee?'

'Yeah, thanks.'

She sat at the kitchen table and watched Anna put the kettle on.

'So what happened?'

'I had to stay over at the Carters' because of the storm. It was only when I was walking back this morning that I found my money and keys had been taken. I had to walk back all the way and I tripped and grazed myself.'

She showed Anna her grazed arms. Anna put a mug of coffee down in front of her.

'But where've you been all day?'

'It was a long walk back and when I got to Oak Ridge I lay down on a lounger and fell asleep. I drank too much Anna and I've been paying for it today.'

Anna was going through the ritual of pouring boiling water onto the tea bag and then the stirring and the fishing out. Kim thought tea was a disgusting drink. She wondered if Anna believed her story.

'Last night Owen had the highest temperature and was very sick,' she said as she sat down opposite her.

'He was OK when I left,' Kim said.

'He got worse and worse and then he started to cut himself.'

Kim put her mug down.

'My knife?'

'Yes. On his chest...'

For some reason Anna made the gesture of cutting with her hand.

'He was bleeding badly and when I got him to calm down he told me... he told me about what happened... when he was fourteen.'

The two women looked at each other for a long moment. Kim was devastated that it should be Anna of all people who was the first person Owen had ever told his secret to. It meant something she had suspected for a while was happening. Anna was getting very close to Owen.

'Please don't talk about that to anyone.'

Her voice was quite sharp, sharper than she had intended.

'I'm sorry, I already told Rob.'

'Don't say *anything* to anyone else. It's not known on the island and we want it to keep it that way.'

'It's nothing to be ashamed of. Owen was an innocent victim.'

'The last thing he needs is people going all compassionate on him.'

'I think it might help him if he could talk about it.'

'You don't know what you're dealing with here.'

'I do work with people who've gone through bad stuff you know,' Anna said.

'He doesn't want to be treated like a cripple.'

Kim's voice was even sharper and Anna looked dismayed. At that exact moment they both heard the men's steps outside the cabin and rose to their feet. Anna opened the door and they saw Rob supporting Owen as they came towards them. Owen's T-shirt had a great dark stain at the front and he looked dreadful. He saw Kim and made a kind of moan and she ran to him and embraced him and he flinched as her head touched his chest.

'I need the keys darlin',' she said.

She unlocked their cabin and helped him in.

Back in their cabin Rob was strung out. He sank into a chair in the kitchen and told Anna that a woman's body had been found at the fish plant and how Owen had reacted to the news.

'He thought it was Kim. He was convinced it was her. It was awful. Then we went up to Port Royal to look for her.'

'He looks very ill.'

'His cuts keep bleeding. It's been a really tough day.'

She put her hand over his and stroked it. She wanted to tell him all the stuff she had found out about Owen but somehow they had seen enough darkness for one day. All their holiday light-heartedness was long gone.

'Do they know who the dead woman is?' Anna asked.

'No, not yet. Or if they do they're not saying.'

She remembered the two prostitutes she had seen down by the harbour, not far from the fish plant, and she shuddered at the thought that one of them might be the victim.

Owen stayed in bed all day, which was something Kim could not remember his doing in all their years of marriage. It was strange for her to watch him resting like this. It was as if he was catching up on years of missed sleep. She didn't want to leave him for long so she headed along the path by the cabins to the poor dwellings beyond where a local woman sold chickens, eggs and vegetables from her back yard. The old woman had laid down a potato sack and there were five decapitated chickens lying on it and a pile of earthy onions. The chickens were all scrawny and had been plucked inexpertly. Kim pointed to one and scooped up some onions.

She walked back to their cabin. The night before she'd told Owen her story about staying at the villa because of the storm and then finding her keys and money stolen; how she'd walked back, then fallen asleep on the beach. She was so sorry she'd worried him. He'd accepted it all without question; he had no suspicions at all. He was feeling faint from the loss of blood and had needed to lie down. She had helped him out of his clothes and unwound the bloody bandages around his torso, had cleaned his wounds and re-bandaged his chest. In the kitchen she found the bloody towel and T-shirt soaking in the pail. This was what happened when she left him alone. As she approached their cabin she could hear raised voices coming from Rob and Anna's cabin. She stood on the path and strained her ears but couldn't make out what they were saying.

Anna had made them coffee and Rob was drinking it in the sitting room while she was walking up and down restlessly, repeating the details from the articles she had read the day before. She couldn't seem to stop talking about Owen and his father and the killings and the suicide note and it was making Rob feel uncomfortable. He didn't know what to say and he had no idea how to stem her impassioned outpouring. This was exactly why Kim had been cagey about Owen's family, to stop this kind of poring over his terrible ordeal and to give him some privacy.

'Something so traumatic and what does Kimberly do? She hides what happened; she's made it into a great big taboo.'

'But I think she's probably right.'

'Why do you say that?'

'She's protecting his privacy. She doesn't want people to discuss him and pity him; like we're doing right now.'

'Can't you see it's not helping him? He's been cutting himself for years.'

He wanted her to stop obsessing about Owen.

'He gets by,' he said.

'He needs help.'

She had said it fervently and a crushing realisation was dawning on him. He stood up.

'You're in love with him,' he said in a shocked voice.

'No!'

She stopped in her tracks and he moved in front of her and looked at her intently.

'You're in love with Owen.'

She drew back from him a step.

'I'm not. But my heart aches for him.'

'Oh my God, you think you can save him, don't you?'

'I want to help him yes.'

'That's bullshit. You want to be with him.'

'What about you and Kimberly? You're always going on about how she's so gutsy, so brave, so resourceful. I'm sick of hearing it.'

'Well she is.'

'You fancy her.'

'You can't see her goodness can you?'

'And you of course can, nothing to do with the fact she's an attractive blonde.'

They looked at each other appalled at the pent-up anger and revelations which were coming out. It felt as if this had been building for a while.

'I can't deal with this,' he said.

He flung himself out of the cabin and charged down the hill propelled by the ferocity of his rage against Anna. It felt as devastating as the moment when his mum had abandoned him for Elliot.

Kim was in the kitchen planning to make fried chicken and her special salsa. But she couldn't find her knife. She crept into the bedroom and looked around the room and under the bed as Owen slept on. She felt in the pockets of his shorts. She searched the bathroom and the sitting room. It was gone. She picked up one of the cabin knives from the kitchen drawer and it was hopelessly blunt and made hard work of severing the chicken into pieces. As she reached in the cupboard for a can of tomatoes she found her knife case, tucked behind the cans. She opened the case and there was her knife. Anna must have hidden it there. She remembered with a pang that if she hadn't left her knife lying around Owen would not have cut himself and Anna would not now know his secret.

Owen woke up but he felt so drowsy from his deep and dreamless sleep. He could not remember the last time he had slept like that. He lay in the bed and noticed the smell of chicken frying. He sat up slowly still feeling a bit faint and dizzy from the effects of the loss of blood. He swung his legs out and slowly dressed himself and joined Kim in the kitchen.

'That smells good.'

'You feeling better darlin'?'

'A bit, but like I did ten rounds with Tyson.'

'I made you your favourite,' she said.

They sat in the kitchen and she served up the fried chicken and her salsa.

'I'm thinking we should go back to the boat Kimbo,' Owen said.

'But we haven't even started the varnishing yet.'

'I know. I'm sorry but I wanna get out of this cabin. I don't wanna owe Money Joe any favours. I bumped into him here and he was acting weird.'

'I'm with you there. He's a lowlife. But maybe one more night here?'

He shook his head.

'This place is getting to me.'

'What happened? When Anna was here?'

'I was cutting myself.'

'You were cutting yourself in front of her?'

'I think so. It's all a blur. I know she bandaged me up so she must have seen my scars.'

'What did you tell her?'

'The truth Kimbo. Everything.'

'I wish you hadn't.'

'It's OK. Anna's not the kind to spread it around.'

He sounded so sure of that and it angered her.

'Have you got feelings for her?' she blurted it out.

He put his fork down and looked at her with surprise.

'Not the kind of feelings you're suspecting.'

'What kind of feelings then?'

He shook his head at Kim's interrogation.

'I said, what kind of feelings Owen,' she repeated.

He sighed.

'I think she tries to be a good person. I think she wants to help people.'

Kim was shaken by the intensity of her jealous feelings at these few apparently innocent words. She crashed the plates together as she cleared them from the table and threw the cutlery into the sink. There was a tap on the cabin door and she pulled it open and Olivier was standing there, white, breathless, swaying in his agony.

'Olivier, sweetheart, what is it…?'

'They killed *maman*,' he said.

Rob found a dark bar near the fish plant which suited his mood and he bought himself a beer. They had had fights before but never anything like this, never something that so rocked his belief in the rightness of their being together. He felt bitter towards Owen. He thought he was his friend, and to think he'd been glad when Anna seemed to be growing closer to him. He finished his beer and bought himself another one. He had fallen deeply in love with Anna so quickly. The miracle was that she had loved him back. She had understood the destructive eruption of Elliot into his life. He had been a happy little boy, secure in the love of his beautiful enchanting mother. And then Elliot had arrived like an ugly demanding toad, had seduced his mum and taken her away from him. Meeting Anna on the tube had begun a healing process. For the first time in years she had made him feel good about himself.

Two men came in and sat down at the table next to him. They sat hunched and silent over their beers for a few minutes.

'*Viviana, ¡qué guapa era*,' one man said finally.

The other man shook his head mournfully.

'*No puede ser.*'

'*Un acto sucio.*'

Rob had started listening when he heard Vivienne's name. He had a little Spanish and he tried to understand what the two men were saying. He thought one man had said the words 'a dirty deed' and it gradually became clear to him that they were saying it was Vivienne who was the dead woman; it was her body that had been found at the fish plant.

He needed air. He got out of the bar and walked along by the sea, away from the town and the fish plant. To think of Vivienne lying there, in that rotten stink and mess. He reached the western end of the harbour and there was a small bridge you crossed to the narrow point facing the ocean. There was no beach here, only exposed rocky coral. There was a decaying wooden church on the point but no-one was around. He headed to the end of the point and sat on the rocks and looked out at the sea, the eternal restless sea.

There was a gentle tap on their door and they heard Anna's voice calling tentative greetings.

'I can't see her,' Kim said.

Owen opened the door, came out quickly and closed it behind him. Before Anna could say a word he said:

'Best you don't come in. Kimmie is distraught.'

'Why? What's happened?'

He looked over his shoulder and then led her away from the

cabin. They walked a little way down the hill. This was the first time she had seen him alone since she had read the articles and knew all the details of what he had endured as a boy. She glanced at the side of his face and he looked pale and drawn and his jaw was working as if he was trying to keep something in.

'You don't look well Owen. Do you need to sit down? Come back to our cabin.'

He stopped walking and turned to face her but said nothing.

'What is it? You look so strange.'

'We just found out it was Vivienne who was murdered; stabbed.'

Her hands went up to her mouth and she stared at him, her eyes huge. Vivienne, who was such a warm and vibrant human being, murdered.

'Horrible, horrible, horrible,' she said in a whisper.

'Olivier is in the cabin with Kimmie now. They're inconsolable.'

'Stabbed?'

'That's what Olivier said.'

'She was such a good person,' she said.

'She was.'

'Who would want to hurt her?'

He shook his head helplessly.

'I need to get back Anna. We're gonna take Olivier back to his mom's place and stay the night with him. He can't be left on his own.'

'Of course, of course...'

He saw that her eyes were filling with tears and she looked so bereft that he felt bad about leaving her. He felt moved to reach out and touch her shoulders and squeeze them.

'I'd hug you if I could but my chest is too sore. I don't

remember much about the other night but I know you looked after me, so thanks for that.'

Kim put Olivier to bed, like a child.

'She seemed so happy. I thought she was in love,' he said as Kim cradled him in her arms and they sobbed together.

Finally he had fallen asleep. He had taken one of his mother's scarves to bed with him. It carried her smell, the Jicky perfume she always wore. Kim joined Owen in the sitting room and sat down on Vivienne's purple sofa. Everywhere there were signs of the wonderful warm woman Vivienne had been. She told Owen that Olivier had been advised to stay on the island during the investigation into his mother's murder. His three friends were packing up the villa at West End and were moving in with him the next day. She picked up one of the cushions and buried her face in it.

'My friend, oh my friend...'

She started to cry again. Owen moved over next to her and stroked her back.

'They killed my friend. I can't stay here any longer Owen. I can't do this life any longer. I *have* to go home.'

'We can't just leave the boat.'

'I don't care. I'm going back to Florida.'

She was getting frantic and her voice was rising. Owen got up and closed the door worried she would wake Olivier.

'You need to give me some time.'

'You could sell it like that if you wanted to,' she snapped her fingers aggressively.

'There's that Dutchman. But you won't call him, I know you won't. You stay here Owen and keep the boat. I'm going home.'

Anna lay awake in the flimsy cabin she now hated and was sick at heart and itchy. She had had a miserable day and had gone to bed early when it was clear that Rob was staying out for the evening. She hadn't secured the mosquito net properly and mosquitoes had been feasting on her when she fell into a troubled sleep. She could feel the little bumps on her arms. She sat up in bed. How could Rob have left her alone tonight? It was scary to feel so alienated from Rob. What was even scarier was a thought that had been troubling her all evening. At first it had been a tiny flicker, but lying alone in the cabin it had grown. In her training to be a speech therapist she had learned something about Post-Traumatic Stress Disorder. She knew that people who survived atrocities alternated between feeling numb and reliving the event. On the night of his fever Owen had been hallucinating. He had left the cabin and gone down into Oak Ridge and he had Kimberly's knife with him. When he came back there was so much blood on him, the towel had been wet with it. It had seemed excessive to her at the time. She remembered soaking the towel in a pail and watching the water turn red.

She got up and went into the bathroom to find the cream that would take the itch out of her bites. The tube was nearly empty. She squeezed at it in frustration and applied a tiny amount to the itchy red bumps. There was a touch of death about Owen. His mother, father and sister were dead and now their great friend Vivienne was gone; her life cut off prematurely. She heard someone trying to unlock the cabin door and she was afraid.

'Is that you Rob?' she called out.

His voice came through the door, tired and angry.

'Who else would it be?'

He came in and went straight into the kitchen and got a large bottle of water out of the fridge. She followed him in there.

'You heard about Vivienne?' she said.

He nodded and sat down at the kitchen table, poured himself a large glass of water and drank it slowly not looking at her.

'I want to leave here. It's a horrible place, beautiful on the outside and rotten underneath,' she said.

'I want to go too but we have to stay until our flight,' he said.

A bleak silence followed as they contemplated having to stay in the cabin for another two days with such a toxic atmosphere between them. She couldn't bring herself to share her suspicions about Owen with Rob. She needed longer to think about them.

DAY TWENTY

Olivier's three friends had arrived from West End. The bar was closed indefinitely and they had been given guest rooms. Kim was making a large pot of coffee for them. Olivier had asked her to stay over another night and she'd agreed. She watched how his three friends gathered around him protectively, held him in their affection and concern. They seemed to be kind boys and she hoped their presence would help him get through the dark days ahead. She took the coffee pot out to Owen who was sitting on the verandah and poured him a cup.

'I said we'd stay another night,' she said.

'Fine by me.'

She looked up and to her horror she saw Gary and Gail walking along the street and they were coming towards Vivienne's Bar. They stopped and Owen waved to them and they came up the steps of the verandah and approached the table. As Gail spotted Kim she pulled herself up and lifted her chin. Kim was frozen to the spot. She tightened her grip on the coffee pot while she tried to think of something, anything to say. Gary spoke first.

'We're devastated, just devastated. We came to pay our respects.'

'We stayed here last night, to be with Olivier,' Kim said, looking down at the ground.

'That poor boy. What a burden to carry for the rest of his life,' Gail said with feeling looking over at Owen.

'Yeah,' Owen said.

An awkward silence followed and Kim felt it must be obvious to the men that she hadn't been able to look Gail in the face.

'I'll go get Olivier,' Owen said standing up.

'No, no, it's OK, don't disturb him. I'm glad you're with him. Could you tell him we came by,' Gary said.

Kim stood there silent and paralysed with awkwardness and shame.

'Well can we get you a coffee at least,' Owen said.

'Oh yeah, please do sit down and I'll go make some fresh,' Kim said.

She hurried back into the building, glad to get away from them. Gail wasn't going to make any reference to the party or to Gideon Carter but she wasn't going to make it easy for her either. She had been so friendly before and Kim felt the judgement of her silence.

'You know I think we'd best be off. We just wanted Olivier to know that we're thinking of him,' Gail said.

'Everyone on the island is,' Gary said.

They shook hands with Owen and walked away arm in arm.

Kim returned five minutes later with a fresh pot of coffee and two mugs.

'They decided to go. What's up with you?' Owen asked turning to her.

She sat down and pushed the pot and the mugs away from her and put her head in her hands not looking at him.

'I'm so sad.'

He stroked the back of her neck under her hair but she didn't respond, she kept her face in her hands.

'I'm gonna go out to the boat now and check a few things. Do you wanna come with me?' he said.

She looked up then.

'No. I'll stay here with the boys. But I meant what I said last night Owen. I'm going home.'

Owen rowed out to his boat and walked around the deck. He knew every plank, every hollow, every last angle of it. He stroked the mast and leaned his forehead against it remembering all the sailings he had done on his beloved boat. Then, with a sad shrug, he went down into the saloon and searched through the lockers to find the papers and bill of sale for the *El Tiempo Pasa*. He put these into his rucksack and rowed back to the shore. He secured the dinghy and headed round the harbour towards the bus stop when he saw Anna sitting on a wall by the fishing boats. She was on her own and was reading.

'Anna...'

She looked up.

'Hello Owen.'

Her voice was strained, he thought, as she closed her book and got off the wall.

'How are you today?'

She asked this as she was putting her book away in her bag and she had not looked at him properly. He could feel the change in her manner towards him. The last time he'd seen her she was affectionate, emotional and acting as if she didn't want him to leave her side. Now she seemed awkward towards him.

'I'm a lot better, thanks.'

'And how is Olivier doing?' she asked.

'He's a strong boy. He'll get through it somehow. Where's Rob?'

'I don't know. We agreed to spend the day apart.'

She lifted her bag onto her shoulder as if she was planning to walk away.

'I hate it here. I want to go home,' she said.

So she was spooked as well.

'We're all badly shaken up,' he said.

She took a deep breath and looked him straight in the face for the first time.

'Who would want to kill Vivienne?'

He looked back at her.

'You think I know?'

She lowered her eyes and blushed.

'What's going on Anna? You're being weird.'

'Where did you go?'

'What do you mean?'

'The night of your fever; you left the cabin.'

'What the fuck!'

'I'm just asking where you went.'

'Well you can fuck right off with your questions.'

He walked away from her fast. She had made him very angry with her suspicions and she could go to hell.

Anna watched his retreating figure. All their relationships seemed to be breaking down in the most nightmarish way. She wanted this disastrous holiday to be over and to go home so badly. The prospect of another day on her own in Oak Ridge was bleak. Perhaps she would take that wildlife tour of the mangrove swamps that Kimberly had mentioned; anything to stop her mind replaying that night with Owen again and again.

Owen found a bar and made the call to Sander Haak, the Dutchman who seemed to know a lot about his boat. He arranged to meet him in Coxen Hole in two hours' time. He boarded the bus and slumped into a corner seat at the back. Anna was like a speck of grit in your eye or a pebble in your shoe. He couldn't get comfortable with himself. That she could even for a moment think him capable of that. Vivienne was loved by Kimmie and liked by nearly everyone. She had been a force for good on the island and whoever had killed her was evil. Evil.

By the time the bus reached Coxen Hole Owen's anger was dissipating and changing into something gentler and sadder; a profound sense of loss. He had virtually no recollection of the night of his fever. He made himself try to recall what had happened but it was as if there was a kind of silence and blindness about the events of that night which he could not penetrate no matter how hard he tried; all he could call up was the image of his father plunging the hunting knife into his mother's neck.

Rob had taken the bus to French Harbour. He wanted to see Kim but did not want to meet Owen, so he was relieved when he saw her on her own. She was sweeping the dead bougainvillea blooms from the verandah of Vivienne's Bar. The pink blooms were shrivelled and brown and Kim looked devastated.

'Oh Rob, it's good to see you.'

She put the broom against the wall and they hugged each other. He noticed that her eyelids were red and swollen from weeping.

'Where's Anna?' she said.

'We're barely speaking.'

'What did you fight about?'

'I'm sorry Kim but I think she's become obsessed with Owen.'

'Yeah, I think she's got a thing about him. I'm so sorry.'

'She thinks she can save him,' he said bitterly.

'I reckon she does.'

'She can be so fucking high-minded sometimes. She drives me nuts.'

'But you're still in love with her; otherwise you wouldn't be so angry and hurt.'

He nodded.

'Owen's gone down to the boat. We're hardly speaking either. Come on up and I'll get you a drink,' she said.

They sat at Vivienne's kitchen table as her grandmother's clock on the dresser chimed twelve.

'One of the last things Vivienne said to me was about that clock. She said it had the sweetest chimes and it does.'

Her eyes filled with tears.

'She got it mended you see. Viv liked things to be real nice around her.'

Her voice broke.

'I'm sorry to see you so sad. I know she was your dear friend. But you mustn't worry about Owen. He would never cheat on you. You two are the strongest couple I've ever met,' Rob said.

She shook her head at his words and more tears started to run down her cheeks. He reached for her hand and stroked it and she cried harder. She gulped.

'I feel so guilty.'

'Why?'

There was a long moment as if she was debating with herself what to say to him. Then she lifted her eyes and whispered:

'I cheated on Owen. With Gideon Carter. I feel so cheap.'

'Bloody hell,' he said.

He withdrew his hand from hers involuntarily and then

put it back on top of hers seeing how upset she looked at his gesture.

'I drank too much. I was angry with Owen and it was a stupid, ugly thing to do. I never did that before. All these years and all these men coming onto me and I never once considered it.'

Rob was feeling a strange prickling sensation all over his body, like he'd fallen into a bed of nettles. Yes he probably did fancy Kim a bit, as Anna had accused him. He had certainly grown fond of her and felt there was an understanding between them. But he'd never once thought to act on his feelings. She and Owen were so much part of each other it was like they were welded together. Yes, that was how he had seen them, like they were a functioning piece of machinery, each one entirely dependent on the other. And now this confession. It was a jolt.

'And he must *never* know,' she said.

'I won't say anything.'

She moved her hands from under his and blew her nose on a piece of kitchen roll.

'Don't think badly of me, please.'

'We all make mistakes sometimes,' he said.

But he was so disappointed that she had cheated on Owen.

Gideon Carter ran his property rental business from a large office in the centre of Coxen Hole. Owen had arranged to meet Sander Haak outside the office which was on a junction with large windows on two sides of the road. There were photos of villas to rent on display in the windows. He stood and looked at the photographs. He recognised some of the villas and they'd been made to look better than they were by clever photography. While he waited he saw Gideon Carter through the window. He had come out from the back and was talking to a hard-faced blonde who sat at the reception desk. Owen saw at once that Gideon was a changed man from the figure he had seen circulating at Gary's hog roast only a week ago. It was as if some small element of his face had caved in and this had changed his look completely. He looked shattered.

'Owen Adams?'

A tall sandy-haired man with a broad face was approaching him on the sidewalk.

'Guilty as charged,' Owen said.

Owen and Sander Haak sat in a bar and over several beers they talked prices and finally agreed a figure for the *El Tiempo Pasa* that satisfied both men. He asked Sander Haak to pay the cash into his account and they left the bar to go to the Banco Atlántida together. On their way there Owen caught sight of Teyo on the steps of the post office. He was standing with his legs planted wide and his arms crossed over his chest. The two men exchanged hostile glances but no words and as Owen walked past him he could sense Teyo's eyes on his back. Money Joe had probably told him how Owen had avoided him that day. He felt a flush of humiliation at the way he had crouched in the water under Money Joe's house. Well they would leave the island as soon as Sander Haak's money had cleared and he'd never need to worry about that lowlife again.

His boat was sold and he was bereft. He took the bus back to Oak Ridge and when he got there he couldn't stop himself even though he knew it would cause him pain. He walked down to the scrubby beach and sat on the shingle. He couldn't bring himself to set foot on his boat again. He corrected himself: his former boat. He would leave his books and his charts and Kim's battered kitchen utensils. Let Sander Haak dispose of them all. He sat and looked at his oat until the sun set behind its mast. He had always loved he shape of his boat. His eyes refused to stay dry and he linked the tears away.

It was time to pack up the cabin. He headed up the hill nd packed the few belongings they had brought with them. Ie left a fifty dollar note on the kitchen table for the electricity costs. He wasn't going to owe Money Joe anything. 'hen he went next door to say goodbye to Rob and Anna ven though he was mad as hell at Anna. But the cabin was ark and all was silent and he assumed they were out or sleep. He went back into his cabin, found a flyer and wrote message on the back and wrapped some dollars in the ote. He pushed this under their door. The moon was high n the sky as he walked down the hill to Oak Ridge for the ast time.

When he got back to Vivienne's place Kim flew at him.

'Where've you been all this time? Why are you punishing ne like this?'

'Punishing you? I've been to Coxen Hole and I sold my oat.'

She looked at him in stunned disbelief.

'You sold her?'

'Yeah and we're gonna get out of here. Catch the boat to a Ceiba first thing tomorrow.'

'Tomorrow?'

'First thing. And we're going for good,' he said.

'You sold her.'

'Yeah, because of Vivienne and because of what you said.'

She felt a surge of forgiving love filling her up. He had istened to her at last.

'Thank you darlin'. I know what a big thing that was for ou.'

He rested his face on her head and smelled her hair. He was grateful that he still had Kimmie to hold on to.

They got everything ready for their early start the next morning and lay down next to each other. He knew he wouldn't be able to sleep tonight. That sighting of Teyo in Coxen Hole had shaken him. The way he had looked at him with open hatred made his mind jump around. He kept playing back the words he had heard Money Joe and Teyo exchange that day. He had the strongest feeling that Teyo was coming after him. He felt for his baseball bat by the side of the bed, then got up and checked that the doors and the windows of Vivienne's house were all locked. He never felt as safe in a house as he did on a boat. On a boat you could hear an intruder approach. When he got back into bed he was hyper alert to the sounds outside. Kimmie was sleeping fitfully beside him and his last night on Roatán was a long one.

DAY TWENTY-ONE

Owen and Kim were up at sunrise. The night before she had told Olivier they were leaving the island for good and that he must stay in touch; his wonderful mom would have wanted that. He said he would. He wanted to give her something of Vivienne's to take with her. She had chosen a framed photograph of Vivienne standing outside her bar on the day it opened. Vivienne looked so proud and happy in the photograph and they had cried together as they looked at it.

'I'll never forget her,' she said.

The motor vessel *Galaxy Wave* left from the dock near the airport at 7 a.m. It was a ninety minute crossing to La Ceiba on the Honduran mainland. They planned to get the first direct flight to Florida and they were the first in the queue on the dock. Behind them a line of local people with tired children and shabby luggage gradually grew in length. There were a few backpackers too. Owen kept looking over his shoulder, scanning the people behind them.

'Is something up?' Kim said.

'I wanna get off the island as soon as we can.'

'Me too. And you've got the money for the boat?'

'Every last dollar,' he said.

'I'm sorry I couldn't say goodbye to Rob and Anna and I'm glad you left that note.'

She took his right hand and kissed his palm and he smiled at the gesture and stroked her cheek, but he still looked on edge she thought. They were on their way home at last. He'd said they'd never come back to Roatán so there was no chance of them bumping into Gideon Carter, no chance of Gail letting out what had happened the night of the party. She had been spared. They had the money to buy her café and most important of all they were united again.

When Rob got up he found a piece of folded paper that had been pushed under the cabin door. He opened the paper. Inside was a wad of dollars and a note from Owen:

Kim and I had to go and I'm sorry we had to leave without saying goodbye. I've sold my boat and by the time you read this we'll be gone. We cut your charter short so I'm leaving some dollars in case you want to leave early. We couldn't stay on the island a moment longer after what had happened to Vivienne. I'm sorry. Owen

He was stunned. He read the note three times and counted the dollars. There were five hundred. He went into the bedroom and Anna was sitting up in her single bed with her book open but not reading. She looked strained, as she had for the last three days. He sat down on the edge of her bed and spread the dollars out and handed her Owen's note. She looked at the money in puzzlement and read the note, turned it over and read it again.

'They've gone,' she said.

'Yes, and left us five hundred dollars.'

She pushed the dollars away from her with a violent gesture.

'Blood money!'

'What do you mean?'

'I think he stabbed Vivienne.'

'That's ridiculous.'

'Is it? You weren't here that night. He was hallucinating. And then he left the cabin with Kimberly's knife. He came back covered in blood.'

They stared at each other. He shook his head emphatically.

'I don't believe it.'

'Why have they gone so fast then?'

'I don't know.'

'And left us money? He feels he owes us something.'

She looked so angry and disgusted.

'They just cut and run,' she said.

'I saw Kim yesterday. I don't think she had any idea they were leaving today,' he said.

'Well he wouldn't tell her he killed Vivienne would he?'

'No, you've got that all wrong.'

'I don't want to wait for our flight tomorrow. I don't want to spend another minute in this horrible place.'

'Nor do I.'

She jumped out of bed and he scooped up the dollars.

They showered and dressed quickly. Now they had decided to leave they both seemed anxious to waste no time. He put the dollars in the bag around his neck and pulled on a shirt. They packed their rucksacks and jumped every time they heard a cabin door bang in the wind.

'I feel scared,' Anna said as she pushed her notebook into the top of her rucksack.

'We'll walk down to town and get a taxi to the airport and get the first flight out of here,' he said.

'Yes.'

'But he didn't kill her Anna. I'm sure of that.'

They left the cabin where they had both been unhappy.

Rob locked the door and slid the keys under the gap at the bottom. They walked down the hill to the town. Teyo was standing in Owen's cabin and watched them leave. He had heard about the boat sale and had smashed his way into Owen's cabin ten minutes earlier. He had seen that Owen and Kim were gone. He noticed that the two *Ingles* were carrying full rucksacks. They were on their way off the island.

At last a steward in a neon jerkin came down the steps of the ferry and moved towards the queue where Owen and Kim waited. He waved the passengers on board. They stood on deck and watched as the motor vessel moved away from Roatán. The weather was turning bad and a wind was whistling around the upper deck so they found seats in the large saloon below. Kim went to get them a coffee and Owen became aware of a man who was watching him. The man looked Garifuna and was dressed in working clothes, his blue jacket stained with oil. He had a large sad face and thick greying hair in tight curls and he was definitely looking at Owen. When Kim came back with the coffees he suggested they move to the other side of the saloon. They did this. A few minutes later he noticed that the man in the blue jacket had moved position too, was near them again and was looking at Kim now. Owen suspected he was one of Money Joe's henchmen. He had a network of people on the island that he drew on to do his dirty work. He said quietly but insistently that Kim must give him her knife case.

'Why are you asking?'

'I won't use it unless I have to but a man has been watching us since we got on the boat.'

'Which man?'

'Don't look now. Blue jacket. I don't like the way he's been watching us.'

'Why would he do that?'

'Give me the knife, Kimmie.'

She heard the authority in his voice and unzipped her money belt and handed over her case. Owen opened it and took out the small sharp knife and held it up so that the blade caught the saloon's overhead light. He looked over at the man who had been watching them and he held up the knife so that he could not fail to see it. If that man came near them and attacked them he would protect Kimmie and he felt an adrenaline surge making him feel powerful and almost complete. Kim looked over in the same direction and said:

'Elroy?'

The man in the blue jacket nodded his large mournful shaggy head.

'I know him,' Kim said.

She got up and walked over and sat down next to him. They talked for a few minutes. To Owen's astonishment he saw the man start to weep. Tears rolled down his creased cheeks as Kim patted his hand. Owen put the knife away in its case, feeling foolish. He got up and joined them.

'Owen this is Elroy. He worked for Vivienne, looked after her buildings and her garden.'

Owen sat down next to Elroy.

'Sorry buddy. I mistook you for someone else.'

'It's OK.'

Elroy brushed his sleeve across his eyes.

'She was a very good woman. She helped me and my family very much,' he said.

'Elroy saw Olivier last night.'

Elroy nodded.

'Poor broken boy,' he said and his voice was rough.

'He loved his mom so much,' Kim said.

'He need justice,' Elroy said and he looked at Owen and then around the boat uneasily and then back at Owen.

'Let's go on deck,' Owen said.

The three of them stood in a close knot on the deck. The wind was still fresh and there were few other people around.

'What is it Elroy?' Owen said.

Elroy held onto the guard rail and looked out at the sea. It was an age before he spoke.

'Miss Vivienne, she got too close to Mr Carter,' he said.

'No...' Kim whispered.

She seemed to shrink into herself as if in horror.

'Why do you say that?' Owen asked.

'I saw them, once, at night, down by the harbour.'

'Tell us.'

'I see a couple kissing in an alcove. The man was holding the woman so tightly like he didn't want to let her go.'

'You're sure it was them?'

'I'm sure. Couldn't mistake Miss Vivienne.'

'When was this?'

'Earlier this year.'

Kim's head drooped.

'And you never told anyone?' Owen said.

'No-one. You tell a secret like that and it makes big trouble But I think Mrs Carter knew.'

Barbara Carter. Owen remembered someone telling him don't underestimate Barbara Carter; said she was the smar and ruthless one in that marriage. And the words he'd heard at Money Joe's house when he'd stood in the water frightened and ridiculous under the duckboards made perfect sense now

'So she noticed his wandering eye?'

280

'Yeah, finally...'

'She'll pay for that.'

What lengths would Barbara Carter go to, to hang onto her husband? Gideon must have fallen for Vivienne very hard indeed. He had looked shattered that last time he saw him. This was the work of a woman in the grip of insane jealousy. Did Barbara Carter think she could get away with it? Maybe she did. And maybe she could on the island. Elroy crossed himself.

'God bless Vivienne. May she rest in peace,' he said fervently.

Not much chance of that thought Owen. He tried not to think about what Vivienne's last minutes had been like. If Teyo had been hired to kill her he could imagine how he was the kind of man to take pleasure in a woman's fear and pain. He closed his eyes to stop the tears that were pricking at the corners. He had never been a man to cry before but he'd been getting all leaky, ever since the night of his fever when he told Anna about his family and had cried in her arms. You let the pain rise to the surface and the tears came. Maybe it was better after all to feel the pain than to keep pushing it down. He put his arm around Kim who looked deeply shocked. She was trembling violently but had said nothing.

'I'll make sure someone knows; someone in authority. But don't you repeat this to anyone else, ever. OK? You need to think of your family,' Owen said.

Elroy nodded.

'Get justice for her boy,' he said.

Anna tried to keep up with Rob's rapid pace down the hill. Why had Owen decided to leave the island so suddenly? It

281

magnified all her suspicions. She wanted to believe Rob that Owen wasn't capable of hurting Vivienne, but he had been hallucinating that night and reliving his mother and sister's terrible murder. If Anna hadn't been so preoccupied she might have been more aware of her surroundings. If she had looked over her shoulder she would have seen Teyo following them at a distance but close enough to keep them in his sights. They reached the outskirts of the town and they both slowed down as they walked past the fish processing plant. It was open again and men were working in the yard. One workman was sweeping debris into a pile. Teyo moved into the shadow of a doorway as they stopped. Rob and Anna peered through the gates and both were thinking about Vivienne's last hours.

'Come on,' Rob said. 'Let's get the hell out of here.'

He charged on through the streets towards the taxi place he knew. He was angry that Owen and Kim had gone like that. But most of all he felt a growing sense of unease about being in Oak Ridge.

'I know a taxi firm near here,' he called out.

They passed islanders going about their business. Rob headed for the alley next to the little church.

'Down here Anna,' he called.

She had a stitch in her side from trying to keep up with him. She slowed down to a walk and rubbed her side. Teyo drew closer. In his pocket he was holding his switchblade ready. She could hear a hymn being sung and the voices were coming from the little white wooden church that bordered the alley. Vivienne would be buried here on Roatán she thought and neither Kimberly or Owen or either of them would be here to pay their respects. It seemed wrong somehow; a betrayal of that lovely woman. Rob had already urned into the alley and as Anna turned to enter the dark passage Teyo sprinted up, silent on his toes, and grabbed her from behind. She felt a sharp tug on her ponytail and gasped in terror as he pushed her into the alley and wrapped his arm around her neck. He clapped his hand over her mouth as she made a strangled cry. In his other hand he held a knife with an open blade. Rob heard her gasping cry. He spun round and saw Teyo holding a knife to Anna's throat and her terrified eyes above it.

'Tell me where Owen went. Now or she gets it!'

There was a moment of intense stillness, like a freeze frame where the moving picture holds on an instant of action. Everything was in the sharpest focus: Anna standing near the mouth of the alley with this black-haired man grasping her tightly and a knife blade right up against her throat. And then Rob came to life. He felt no fear. He didn't think of anything as adrenaline pumped through his veins. It was a pure and instinctual act of love as he leaped at Teyo with a roar. Rob swung a fist at him and Teyo let go of Anna. She slid down the wall onto the ground of the alley coughing and gasping for breath as she saw Rob and Teyo's bodies come together with a thud. The two men wrestled violently in the confined space of the alley. There were grunts and scuffles and then Teyo pulled away and she saw blood on the blade of his knife, right up to the shaft. She let out a heart-stopping scream. Teyo turned and looked at her as she continued to scream wildly. He hesitated one moment then ran down the alley away from them.

Teyo's knife had gone in beneath Rob's ribs. The blade had cut through skin, fat and muscle and gone deep into Rob's gut. Rob fell back and slid down the wall and put his hands over his stomach. Blood was seeping through his fingers. Unknown to him the contents of his gut were spilling out into his abdominal cavity. He felt little pain. Anna staggered forward and fell to her knees by his side. A man was running out of the church and two other men were following him. They ran into the alley. Anna was bending over Rob trying to staunch the flow of blood with her hands on top of his bloodied fingers. One of the men pushed his way to the front. It was the pastor from the church. He kneeled down next to Anna.

'Let me. I'm trained,' he said.

She rocked back on her heels as the man bent over Rob. She recognised him as the man from the baptism on the beach. He opened Rob's shirt and undid the top of his trousers and looked at the wound. Anna saw that the bag around Rob's neck, the bag in which he carried his money, was already soaked with his blood.

'You must save him. I can't lose him!'

'Get me a clean cloth now, a clean altar cloth,' John Morgan said to a man in a blue shirt standing close behind Anna. A third man was using his mobile to call for help.

'We can't wait,' John Morgan said. 'We need to get him to Oaks straightaway. We'll use my car.'

'What's Oaks?' she said frantically.

'It's the only hospital on the island.'

The third man helped Anna to her feet and led her out of the alley. She was trembling and she leaned on him.

'You have to save him, please, please save him,' she said.

'I reckon we can,' he said trying to soothe her, although he thought that the cut looked deep.

'And you're not cut anywhere?' He scanned her face and neck and torso. She had blood on her hands and on the front of her T-shirt but it was Rob's blood. She shook her head.

'He held a knife to my throat. Rob jumped him and he stabbed him.'

'Who did this?'

'Teyo. Oh God he must have been following us.'

The second man had come back holding some pristine altar cloths. He handed these to John Morgan. The pastor folded one and held it against Rob's stomach, putting pressure against the stab wound. Rob was still conscious but his body had gone into shock, his face was grey and sweaty and he could say nothing.

'We're gonna take you to the hospital now,' John Morgan said.

They helped Rob to his feet and they half-carried half-dragged him out of the alley and towards the car. Morgan threw his car keys to the man in the blue shirt.

'You drive. I'll sit in the back with him.'

'Where's the hospital?' Anna asked.

'Coxen Hole,' the driver said starting the engine.

Rob was lying on the back seat of the car with his head on John Morgan's lap. Anna was sitting up front. She was leaning forward and watching intently as the driver tried to overtake a lorry and then a bus on the road out of Oak Ridge. They were making slow progress.

'How long will it take us?'

'It's about eighteen miles to Coxen Hole.'

She remembered how long it had taken on the bus; those wretched winding roads.

'And it's a proper hospital?'

'There's intensive care there. They'll be able to help him,' he said.

In the back of the car John Morgan picked up a second white altar cloth. The first one was already soaked with Rob's blood. He folded the new cloth and kept the pressure on the wound.

'Did someone ring ahead to say we're on our way?' Morgan asked.

'Yep, Tam called and they'll be waiting for us.'

'You hang in there buddy,' Morgan said.

There was no sound from Rob. A quiet moan escaped from Anna. In her mind she kept remembering the account she had read of John Lennon's shooting. Rob idolised John Lennon, the man, his music and his ideas. He had given her a book about Lennon last Christmas. She had read the book to please him but the description of Lennon's death had been deeply upsetting. The deranged fan Chapman had fired five bullets into John Lennon's back as he walked towards the entrance of the Dakota building where he lived. Four of the bullets went into his body. They were the kind of bullets that expanded when they entered the body. What a truly evil invention that was, bullets that expanded to cause maximum damage to tender human tissue. The first policemen at the scene had carried John and laid him on the back seat of their squad car as they couldn't wait for an ambulance. John Lennon had no chance. Someone said that if the shooting had taken place in an operating theatre with surgeons standing around they could not have saved him. He lost 80 per cent of his blood. Dead before he reached the hospital. She must not think about this, she really must not. When would they get to the hospital? She started to wring her hands.

It took them forty desperate minutes to get to Coxen Hole and another five before they pulled up in front of Oak Hospital, a faded 1970s two storey building. A doctor, two orderlies and a nurse were waiting for them with a trolley.

They approached the car and lifted Rob from the back seat onto the trolley. He was semi-conscious now. The doctor lifted the blood-soaked altar cloth from his stomach and looked at the wound.

'Straight to theatre,' he said.

They wheeled the trolley up the ramp and into the hospital and John Morgan led Anna into the waiting area on the ground floor.

They sat together on hard hospital chairs under fluorescent strip lights. He could see that Anna was shivering from deep shock. He got a blanket from a nurse and put it around her shoulders. Then he walked over to the drinks machine and got them both coffees, putting sugar into Anna's. She cradled the cup in her hands and kept saying that it was Teyo who had stabbed Rob. She described how he'd grabbed her from behind and how Rob had leaped to save her. She was reliving that moment again and again. John Morgan sat with her and listened and nodded. He had heard stories about this Teyo from his congregation, but he had not got to the alley in time to see the man who had attacked Anna and Rob. He believed her though. He knew that some of his flock were afraid of Teyo, saying he was not an islander; he was a bad one from the mainland. Morgan had put a call into the police an hour ago but so far no-one had turned up at the hospital. It was a long and grim wait.

Inside the operating theatre Rob had been put under anaesthetic and the surgeon had repaired the cuts in his gut. The knife had gone in deep and then been twisted. There was extensive damage to his intestines and he had lost a lot of blood and needed a transfusion. The surgeon had sewn up the wound. His fear was that an infection might take hold because the contents of Rob's gut had spilled into a sterile area. They would have to keep him in and be alert to any signs of septi caemia or peritonitis. For now the immediate danger was over and the surgeon was satisfied that he had stopped the internal bleeding.

It was an hour later when a lone policeman walked into Oaks Hospital and asked for John Morgan. An orderly came over and Anna and Morgan were shown into a small room which the hospital kept for family members who were going to be told bad news. Anna's first thought was why was there only one policeman? That couldn't be right could it? There should be two policemen, so that they could corroborate what was said. Straightaway her suspicions were alerted. The policeman took out a pad and started to ask questions. His English was not good. Anna described in a faltering voice what had happened. She said twice that it was Teyo who had stabbed Rob. The policeman looked at her with an impassive face and wrote something down. He turned to John Morgan and asked him if he had seen Teyo with his own eyes. Morgan responded that no, when he reached the alley there were only Rob and Anna there. But there was no reason to doubt Anna's account was there? She had been up close and personal. The policeman stood up and put his pad away.

'Thank you for the information,' he said.

'What happens now?' Anna asked.

'I report these details back at base.'

He made for the door.

'That's it? But we need protection,' Anna said.

The policeman stopped at the door and looked at her.

'That man stabbed my boyfriend. He's out there somewhere and he may come back to finish off the job. Can't you see we're in danger?'

'He would be very foolish to come here,' the policeman said.

With these words he turned and left them. John Morgan took her hand and squeezed it.

'How could he go like that?' she said.

'I sometimes think this island is a moral quagmire,' he said.

John Morgan led Anna over to the reception desk and the nurse told them that Rob was out of the theatre and she could go up now. Rob had been taken to a room on the second floor and a nurse would take her there. Morgan said he had to go as there was an evening service to conduct but he'd be back in the morning to see how they were doing. She went to shake his hand but he embraced her. She thanked him fervently.

'You probably saved both our lives,' she said.

He shushed her and then he was gone. She had a sick feeling that by naming Teyo to that policeman she had put herself and Rob into even greater danger.

The nurse took her up to the second floor. Rob had been put into one of the private rooms with an en-suite bathroom. He was lying unconscious on the hospital bed and was hooked up to two drips. A doctor was standing by him.

'Come now, please sit here,' the doctor said.

She sat down on the chair by the bed and the nurse left the room and closed the door.

'He's unconscious,' she said and her voice was shaky.

'It was a deep cut and he lost a lot of blood. We have sedated him.'

The doctor was speaking to her in a grave tone of voice and it scared her.

'But he's going to be all right?'

'We stopped the internal bleeding. There is a risk of infection.'

'But he will get better?'

'We need to keep a close watch on him for the next few days.'

'Can I touch him?' she asked.

She followed the direction of the doctor's eyes and saw that there was dried blood all over her T-shirt. It was Rob's blood. And there was blood under her fingernails too. She remembered she had her clothes with her, in her rucksack.

'If I shower and change can I hold his hand, please?'

'Yes of course.'

The nurse had come back into the room.

'Please let me stay here with him,' Anna said.

'You'd be more comfortable at a hotel. There's one very close and—'

'No, I can't leave him. I must stay here. I must...' Her voice was getting frantic.

'Please calm yourself and wait here,' the doctor said.

The doctor and the nurse left the room and she could hear them talking in the corridor outside the door. When they came back the doctor agreed that she could stay the night in Rob's room. They brought a daybed for her to sleep on and an orderly set this up for her. The doctor left saying he'd be back later to check up on Rob. Anna turned to the nurse.

'I'm going to shower now but I'm afraid to leave him on his own. Will you stay while I take a quick shower?'

The nurse nodded and sat by Rob's bed while Anna went into the bathroom. There was a basin and a shower and two white towels on the rail. She left the bathroom door open so that she could see into the room and see over to Rob's bed.

She stood under the hot water and soaped herself thoroughly and quickly, scrubbing at her hands to get out the blood from under her fingernails. She stepped out and dried herself. There was a small white stool in the bathroom with chrome legs and she sat on this as she dried her legs and her feet. Then she changed into a complete set of clean clothes.

Back in the room she thanked the nurse and at last she was alone with Rob. She sat down by his bed, held his right hand and stroked it gently along the vein that ran from his wrist. The pulse in that vein seemed weak. She was pierced by a powerful stab of remorse as she looked at his pale face. After that came deep shame. She had become obsessed with Owen over the last few days and that must have caused Rob so much pain. She had thought that she might be in love with Owen. She remembered someone once saying that you fell in love when you were anxious. Well she had certainly been anxious for this whole holiday, from the moment they set foot on the boat. And Owen had grown bigger and bigger in her consciousness as the days had passed. It had started on the night of that storm when she was on watch with him and was scared they would drown. Anxious or not it was no excuse. She had behaved horribly, had hurt Rob deeply and had alienated Kimberly.

'It was all a delusion darling,' she said aloud knowing that Rob couldn't hear her but hoping that he might.

Yes, it had all been a phantom that had fled the second she saw Rob lying and bleeding in the alley. He had leaped to save her from Teyo's knife with no thought for his own safety. She had taken Rob's love for granted. She sat and gazed at his dear face for a long time and stroked his hand.

'Get well my darling and I'll make it up to you, I promise I will.'

She got up and walked over to the window which over-looked the car park at the front of the hospital. It was up to her now to keep him safe from any further harm. Somehow she was going to have to stay awake all night. She opened the door onto the corridor and looked out. There was a nurse's station further up the corridor and she could hear someone talking on the phone.

For the first few hours Anna felt comparatively safe. There were two nurses and the doctor on duty. One of the nurses would come in and check on Rob's drips and vital signs every hour or so. At one point Rob gained consciousness briefly. His eyelids fluttered and opened. He said nothing, gazed up at Anna for a moment and then slid back into a kind of drugged sleep. She stood up and stretched and she noticed the closet by the door. She went over and pulled it open. Rob's clothes had been folded and left in a plastic bag on the top shelf. His shoes were on the lower shelf. She picked up one of his shoes and saw there was blood on it and the blood had turned brown. She reached for the plastic bag on the upper shelf and opened that. His blood stained shirt was wrapped around his small fabric bag where he kept his dollars. She pulled the dollars out and they too were soaked with his blood. She pushed the dollars back into the bag and bundled up his shirt again and went and washed her hands thoroughly.

There was no phone in the room and the feeling was growing in her that she must tell her father what had happened. Someone from beyond the island needed to know that she and Rob were at risk. A nurse came in to check Rob again and Anna asked her where she could make a call. She was directed to a public phone under a hood at the end of the corridor. When the nurse had gone Anna found her wallet and left the room, locking it behind her. It was late now and there were few staff on duty and it didn't feel safe to leave the door unlocked. She walked past the nurses' station and reached the phone. To her relief she saw that it took credit cards. This might be a long and expensive call. It was late in England and the phone rang and rang before she heard her father's sleepy but irritable voice on the end of the line.

'Who is this?'

'It's Anna. I'm so scared Daddy.'

It was years since she'd called him that. Not since the Ricky episode.

'What's wrong?' he sounded confused.

'Rob's been stabbed.'

'Stabbed...?'

'Yes, in the stomach. I'm calling from the hospital.'

'Where are you? Are you in Mexico?'

'No, we're in Roatán; it's this island off Honduras.'

'What happened?'

Her father sounded more awake now. She could imagine him sitting up in bed and reaching for his glasses.

'This man stabbed Rob in the stomach.'

'But why would anyone—'

'This man Teyo. He was following us because he thinks we know where this other man has gone, Owen Adams, the guy from the boat. He stabbed Rob and I'm so scared he's going to come back here and finish the job off.'

She was talking fast and getting breathless and as she voiced her fears they were becoming ever more palpable and she understood what great danger she and Rob were in.

'You need to calm down Annaboo. If you're in the hospital, you're quite safe.'

He hadn't called her Annaboo for years either. It meant he was on her side but also that he thought she was exaggerating.

'We're not safe. You don't know what it's like here. It's a weird kind of frontier place and there was a murder two days ago, a lovely woman we knew. He must think we know something about it. I've been sitting in Rob's room all evening and fearing every person coming down the corridor and I'm freaked out Daddy, really scared. I need to go back to Rob's room now. I'm scared to leave him any longer.'

'Anna wait, I have an idea. I'm going to track down the British Consul out there and tell him there are two British nationals at risk. What's the name of the hospital?'

She told him and she could tell he was writing it down.

'I'm going to do this right now, OK. You must call me again in an hour, OK?'

'Yes I will, in an hour.'

She put the phone down. At least her father had believed her and he was trying to help. She walked back to Rob's room feeling a little less alone. She locked the door behind her and stretched out on the daybed close to Rob. He was still sleeping and his breathing sounded regular, thank God.

An hour later she left the room and locked the door behind her again. She called her father from the public phone and his voice sounded weary.

'It's not good news I'm afraid. I can't raise anyone. I've looked on the website and the consular services are run out of Guatemala City.'

'That's no help at all.'

'I know. I'm going to contact them again first thing in the morning. Report what you told me and insist that they make contact with you. Now darling I'm sure you'll be safe in the hospital tonight.'

She knew that her father had thought about it over the last hour and decided that it was her over-active imagination at work. She did not have the time to persuade him otherwise.

'Daddy listen, will you call Rob's mum now. I haven't called her yet and she needs to know. I'm scared to leave Rob alone in that room any longer.'

As she passed the nurses' station she saw that it was deserted. Surely there would be some staff on night duty? Maybe the nurse was checking up on another patient. Rob looked so vulnerable lying on the bed all rigged up with tubes and drips and still sedated. He was as helpless as a baby. She knew it was no good looking for protection from outside and it was up to her now.

She stood at the window and looked out at the car park. It was nearly three in the morning and there was no activity below. She stood in a kind of trance for many minutes watching the cold light of the moon reflected on the bonnets and roofs of the few cars parked there. Those must belong to the staff she thought. She had got a sense that there were not many patients staying overnight in the hospital. Some small mammal was walking around the perimeter of the car park. Was it a cat? She tried to get a better look but the animal, cat or rat, had gone under one of the cars and was lost to sight. Then her eyes caught the glimmer of the lights of a car driving along the outer road of the town. The car was driving with just its sidelights on and these flashed as it rounded a corner. She saw it was heading in the direction of the hospital. The car slowed as it drew up outside the gates of Oaks Hospital and she saw that it had prominent fins. It came to a stop and did not drive into the car park and she watched as the lights of the car were turned off. She had a very bad feeling about that car. Who would be driving here at this time of night? She strained her eyes to see if anyone had got out but she could see no further activity. She suddenly wondered whether or not she had locked the door of the room when she came back from making her second phone call? No she hadn't. She crossed quickly and peered out into the corridor. All was silent; no voices came from the nurses' station, there was no sign of anyone at all. She locked the door and returned to the window to keep watch of the car park and the street beyond.

It was about ten minutes later when she heard something. It was a faint footfall in the corridor outside the room. She waited for the nurse to tap and say she was coming in to do a check on Rob. But no tap came. No voice came. With a feeling of profound dread she moved away from the window and silently made her way over to the door. As she walked over she saw that the door handle was being moved, was being lifted up and down. The person on the other side of the door had established that it was locked. Anna put her ear to the door. And then she heard a click, click, clicking as a knife was brought to bear on the lock of the door. She knew it was Teyo and she knew he had come to kill her and Rob. He was unpicking the lock with his knife. She had a moment of total paralysis and her mind went blank.

Then she remembered the stool in the bathroom. She crept in there and took hold of the stool by its round cushioned seat and walked back to the door, making no noise. She needed him to believe that she was asleep. She positioned herself so that she would be hidden when the door opened. An element of surprise was the only advantage she had. She held the stool firmly with the three chrome legs pointing outwards. Click, click, click – Teyo's knife was feeling into the lock and pressing against the resistance of the catch. It was dim in the room. There was only a night light by Rob's bed, and the light from the corridor under the door. She watched the handle with horror as Teyo tried it again. Still the lock held. She heard him pull the knife out and then jam it back into the lock with greater force. How had he known to come to this room? Who had told him? And then the lock gave and the door started to open. She lifted the stool above her head and as Teyo moved into the room she brought the legs of the stool down onto his right arm with all her strength. She never understood where she got the strength from but she felt the impact of her blow shudder through the leg of the stool as she smashed it onto his right arm. He grunted with pain at the blow but he held onto the knife and continued to push into the room. With a wail like a banshee coming unbidden from her lips Anna swung the stool up and at his face. This time one of the metal legs made contact with his jaw. She heard the sound of metal hitting bone. He grunted and staggered back, struggling to say on his feet. As he tried to regain his balance, still clutching his knife, she drew her right leg back and then kicked up hitting him right between his legs with her last ounce of energy. The knife fell from his fingers and skidded across the floor. He rolled on the floor clasping his balls and groaning.

The screaming and the crashing had woken Rob from his drugged sleep. He watched in amazement as Anna lifted the stool again and crashed one of the legs against the back of Teyo's right shoulder. She grabbed the knife from the floor and pointed it at him and, because it had worked before, Anna started to scream for help at the top of her voice. Teyo was lying sprawled out on the floor but she never took her eyes off him. She was ready to attack him with his knife if he should move. She screamed and screamed for help and then she heard footsteps running along the corridor and the night nurse ran in, followed closely behind by the orderly.

'Such courage,' Rob managed to say as he looked up at Anna.

TEN DAYS LATER

London

Anna was on her way to Rob's family house in Crouch End. It had been an exhausting ten days; a roller coaster of hope and despair. The British Embassy had got involved and had sent an Honorary Consul to check up on Anna and Rob. Teyo had been arrested on the night he was found in Rob's room and was facing two charges of attempted murder. He was locked up in the local prison and Anna had slept a little easier lying on the daybed by Rob's side.

After his early signs of improvement Rob had started to run a very high temperature which indicated that an infection was taking hold inside him. The doctors had pumped him full of antibiotics and had sedated him heavily but he was clearly getting worse. Anna was in daily contact with Rob's mother Robin giving her bulletins on his condition. When Robin heard that Rob was sinking she cut short her honeymoon and flew into Roatán. The moment she saw her son she was a woman possessed. She had arranged for Rob to be flown back to London under medical supervision and installed in a London hospital.

And still Rob was in a critical condition. Anna hadn't left his side for days. Robin joined her at the hospital each morning and the two women went down to the cafeteria. They sat opposite each other nursing their coffees.

'I need you to do something for Rob,' Anna said.

Robin looked tired as she raised her beautiful sad eyes to Anna's face. 'What is it, my dear?'

'You must believe Rob about the drug bust and you must tell him that you believe him.'

Robin looked faintly outraged.

'I don't understand why you're raising this now, Anna. My boy is fighting for his life.'

'That's exactly why I'm raising it now. It hurt him so much that you didn't believe it was Elliot who reported the commune and he needs you to believe him.'

Robin sighed.

'Robbie hated Elliot the moment he set eyes on him.'

'You sure that wasn't a two-way thing? Rob says Elliot was always calling him a loser, out of your earshot of course.'

Robin shook her head wearily.

'You weren't there and can't possibly understand. There is always conflict between a child and a step-parent. A child's hostility is a very powerful thing and Robbie nearly broke us up.'

'But he didn't break you up. You're still together and you're married. Tell him that you believe him. *Please.*'

There had been a long drawn out and awkward silence after that.

The next day had been the turning point. Anna was sitting by Rob's bed and she thought he looked slightly better. He was still attached to two drips but had spent a calm night and his temperature was coming down at last. The doctor came in and examined him. Now he said to her:

'He scared us there for a bit but the antibiotics are working and he's improving now.'

She cried with relief and joy and wanted to hug the doctor. Instead she called Robin and told her the good news.

'Oh joy,' his mother said.

Yesterday Rob had been well enough to be taken home to his mum's house to convalesce. He was lying on a reclining chair looking at his mother's garden. His mum had planted lavender and fuschia and polyanthus and the bees were droning around the pink and purple blooms. His mum came out of the French doors and joined him.

'How's my best boy doing today?'

She sat down beside him.

'Getting better and feeling stronger. Mum, there's something I've been thinking about for ages and I need to talk to you about it.'

'I know darling.'

'You know?' he looked puzzled.

'I know you want me to believe that Elliot reported the commune to the police.'

He looked surprised at her words.

'Well yes, I *would* like you to believe that. And he did Mum. I know he did. But, that wasn't it.'

'So what is it darling?'

Rob took hold of his mother's hand and squeezed it gently.

'I *need to know* who my dad is.'

'Oh darling—'

'Listen, please. It's not just because I nearly died. I've been feeling this way for months. I need to track him down. I need to make contact with him.'

Anna got off the bus and headed up the road to the Edwardian house where his family lived. She rang the doorbell and Robin opened the door to her. She thought his mum looked a bit shaken, but she hugged Anna and said in a warm voice:

'He's resting in the garden.'

Anna hugged her back.

'Well I better go find his lordship then.'

Anna was pouring Rob a glass of water. She held the glass to his lips as he drank.

'Thanks. I'm glad my Mum came to Roatán,' he said.

'She had to cut short her honeymoon to get there.'

'I know and I'm getting a lot of satisfaction from that thought,' he smiled weakly.

'That means you're definitely getting better. She loves you so much Rob.'

'I told her that I need to track down my dad. And she finally agreed to help me.'

'Oh Rob, I'm so pleased.'

'It matters you see. You need to know where you come from. Even if it's bad news, even if it turns out he's a drunk or a wife beater.'

Later, inevitably, they returned to the subject of Owen and Kim who still loomed so large in both their minds.

'Do you think we'll ever hear from them again?' Rob said.

'No chance. Owen doesn't want anyone to know where they've gone. He sold his boat and he ran away.'

'That's a harsh thing to say Anna. He's had so much trouble in his life.'

'Harsh maybe, but his running away nearly got you killed. And I'm not ready to forgive him for that yet.'

She stroked the hair away from his forehead and kissed his eyelids with their long dark lashes that gave him that immensely endearing look.

'But I was wrong about Kim. She is a good person, so loyal and faithful to Owen. It can't be an easy life for her and I wish we'd parted on better terms,' she said.

Rob thought about Kim's confession of her infidelity on

that nightmare day when all their relationships seemed to be in meltdown. It struck him that Anna did not always get things right. She had her convictions, always so clear and always so strong, but not always right. She was as flawed as the rest of them. But she had shown courage when it was needed and he loved her.

'You've forgiven her the stolen magazines then?' he said with a mischievous smile.

'Yes, of course.'

'And you finally got round to calling her Kim,' he said.

TEN DAYS LATER

Clearwater, Florida

It was late afternoon and Owen had come to the cemetery to visit his mom and sister's grave. The afternoon sun slanted low rays through the branches of the tree-lined cemetery. It was a leafy peaceful oasis and the place seemed empty of others as he walked along the paths.

Since they got back to Florida he and Kim had stayed at a motel on the outskirts of Clearwater. They had booked into the motel because he didn't want to stay under the same roof as Jared and there wasn't enough room at his aunt Cally's flat. Today Kim was spending the day with her parents and he had wanted to come here on his own. He walked along the path until he found their grave. His mom and little sister shared a last resting place and a simple headstone. It was carved with their names, the dates of their lives and the three words Rest In Peace. He stood looking down at the stone.

'Sorry I couldn't help you, Mom,' he said aloud.

He felt tears gathering at the corners of his eyes and this time he let them roll down his cheeks. He had started to cry more over the last few weeks and he put that down to Anna. She had helped him see that it was OK to cry for your dead mom and your dead kid sister.

He was still strung out from their flight from Roatán. He

had felt shadowed by a threat the whole time they were travelling back to Florida and even now he felt the need to keep on moving. When they had reached the airport at La Ceiba he had found a public phone and put in a call to an American news outfit based in Honduras. He got through to the newsroom and he reported his suspicions about Teyo murdering Vivienne. He said he believed that Teyo had been hired by Barbara Carter of Roatán to do the killing. The journalist had heard of the Carters and was interested at once; Owen could tell that from the rising excitement in his voice as he asked him more questions. Owen gave him as many details as he could, including dates, the method of the killing and the location of Vivienne's body. He said the motive for the killing was the love affair between Gideon and Vivienne. The journalist asked him for his name. He refused to give it in spite of the journalist pressing him several times and saying that he would be quite safe, they always protected their sources.

'Look just follow this up. It's a huge story and I've given it to you exclusively,' Owen said and hung up.

From Miami they had flown to Tampa. Kim had had an emotional reunion with her parents and his aunt Cally had been very happy to see him. Tomorrow they were setting off again. He had told Kim he couldn't stay in Clearwater and the plan was to drive along to the east coast of Florida and then head up North along the coast until they found a place that appealed to them both, maybe someplace in North Carolina or Virginia. He had bought a second-hand pick-up truck for their journey and was itching to be on the move again. They had enough money and they could take their time in finding the right place to settle. It would be somewhere on the coast, that was his only condition.

He heard something to the right of him that sounded like muffled footsteps. He looked around and there was no-one there that he could see. He looked back at the headstone and bent to brush some dead leaves away from its base. There it was again, the sound of furtive movements in the grass between some gravestones up ahead. It sounded like someone who did not want to be seen but who was approaching him stealthily through the grasses. Owen stood up straight, pulled his shoulders back and started to walk in the direction of the rustling sound. He stopped in his tracks when he saw a large dog half crawling, half limping between the gravestones ahead. The dog was in bad shape. He was skin and bone and had been in a fight that had hurt him. There was matted bloodied fur on one of his haunches. Owen walked slowly towards the dog and kneeled down. He held out his hand showing an open palm.

'You been in the wars, old boy,' he said in a gentle voice.

The dog made an attempt at a bark but it came out as a whimper. Owen drew nearer and reached out his arm and touched the dog's head. The dog let him stroke him.

'You look hungry.'

He looked like some kind of Border Collie cross. He was black and had a white throat. The matted fur was covering a wound to his back leg. He stroked the dog's body and felt his ribs. This dog had not eaten for a while. Owen felt in his pockets. Nothing. He tried to remember if he had seen any shops near the cemetery. No shops but he recalled seeing a café near the entrance. He patted the dog's head again.

'You wait here old boy. I'm gonna get you some food and water.'

The dog made a whimper as Owen walked away.

He hurried back towards the gates at the top of the

cemetery and his heart was beating fast because he didn't like leaving the dog behind in that condition. He found the café and bought three burgers, a ham sandwich and a large bottle of water and asked the café owner for a paper cup. When he got back to the cemetery the sun was sliding down the sky and the shadows of the gravestones had lengthened. He retraced his steps to his mom's grave and then walked on to where he had seen the dog before.

'Where are you, old boy?' he called out.

He heard a feeble bark and he followed it to find the dog lying stretched out beneath a bench with his head on the ground as if he was completely spent and was lying down there to die. Owen sat on the ground at the dog's head and first he gave him water to drink, pouring it into the paper cup several times and letting the dog lap it up. Then he broke off pieces of the burger meat and laid them on the ground and the dog wolfed these down, all three of the burgers went in no time. He gave him the ham sandwich and the dog's tail began to move a little from side to side.

'Feeling better?'

He stroked his head and his neck. There was no collar. He had a fine shaped head and hazel brown eyes. He guessed the dog had been abandoned and had been fending for itself until he got into the fight that had weakened him. He wondered what had attacked him as he was a big dog. The food and water had revived him and the dog lifted his head and rested his jaw on Owen's knee and gazed at the man who had fed him. Owen scratched behind the dog's ears. More foolish tears filled his eyes. What was happening to him?

'You wanna take your chances with me, old boy?' he said.

There would be room for him in their truck and his big-hearted Kimmie would be OK about it. He would get a taxi now and take the dog to a vet to get that nasty wound looked at.

Owen got to his feet and walked back once more to his mom and sister's grave.

'Always missed,' he said.

He headed slowly towards the gates so that Old Boy could keep up with him. Near the gates he glanced over to the space in the left hand corner where he knew his father's unmarked grave lay. Then he walked with a firmer step out through the gates with Old Boy, his new life companion, limping along at his side.

The poem Rob remembered when he was diving:

'The Kraken'

Below the thunders of the upper deep,
Far, far beneath in the abysmal sea,
His ancient, dreamless, uninvaded sleep
The Kraken sleepeth: faintest sunlights flee
About his shadowy sides; above him swell
Huge sponges of millennial growth and height;
And far away into the sickly light,
From many a wondrous grot and secret cell
Unnumber'd and enormous polypi
Winnow with giant arms the slumbering green.
There hath he lain for ages, and will lie
Battening upon huge sea-worms in his sleep,
Until the latter fire shall heat the deep;
Then once by man and angels to be seen,
In roaring he shall rise and on the surface die.

ALFRED TENNYSON

ACKNOWLEDGEMENTS

Heartfelt thanks to Laura Palmer, my editor, who made some brilliant suggestions which brought out what I was trying to achieve in this novel. Thanks also to the tremendous team at Head of Zeus and to Becci Sharpe for her support.

Gaia Banks, my agent at Sheil Land, has been a true champion throughout. Thank you.

There are many other people to thank for their expert knowledge which they shared so generously: Steve Marsh and Strat Mastoris on sailing; Amelia Trevette for information on the fashion industry; Chris Maddison on fishing; Chris Briscoe for information about Roatán; Bob Merrilees for the Spanish translations, and Lynne Thomson for medical details.

Roomana Mahmud and Jan Thompson read an early draft of *After the Storm* and gave invaluable feedback on my characters. And thank you Heather and George Walter for the use of your house when I needed a quiet place to go to complete a final edit.

I am delighted with the cover designed by Jessie Price and thank you Victoria Pepe for your meticulous copy-editing.

Most of all my special thanks to Barry Purchese for his loving encouragement and support throughout.

Twitter: @janelythell
Facebook: Jane Lythell Author

QUESTIONS FOR YOUR BOOK CLUB

• Anna hates secrets and is annoyed when Rob keeps things from her. Do you agree with her that secrets are better brought out into the open?

• Rob has a Robinson Crusoe fantasy and dreams of finding his own 'paradise island'. Is this a dream you can identify with? To what extent does it make him overlook Anna's wishes for their holiday?

• Anna and Kim are very different women. Do you think this is why there is awkwardness between them, or is there some other cause?

• Do you think there is sexual attraction between the two couples?

• Why do you think Kim behaved as she did at the Carter's big party?

• Anna is scared of many things: flying, cockroaches, being on her own in a dark cabin; but, when faced with Owen's breakdown, she is emotionally brave. Is this a contradiction? Which type of courage do you value more?

• Do you think Owen is a threat to other people or only to himself?

• How do the settings – first the cramped boat, then the seeming paradise of Roatán – contribute to the tension in the book?

• Do you think that the four characters have changed by the end of the book? Who has undergone the biggest change?

A letter from the publisher

We hope you enjoyed this book. We are an independent
publisher dedicated to discovering brilliant books,
new authors and great storytelling. Please join us at
www.headofzeus.com and become part of our
community of book-lovers.

We will keep you up to date with our latest books, author
blogs, special previews, tempting offers, chances to win
signed editions and much more.

If you have any questions, feedback or just want to say hi,
please drop us a line on hello@headofzeus.com

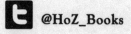 @HoZ_Books

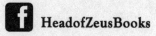 HeadofZeusBooks

www.headofzeus.com

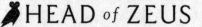 HEAD *of* ZEUS

The story starts here